UNFIXABLE

A Buck Lawson Mystery

THE BLOOD RIVER SERIES BOOK #1

By Donna Ball

ALSO BY DONNA BALL

The Raine Stockton Dog Mystery Series:
SMOKY MOUNTAIN TRACKS RAPID FIRE
GUN SHY
BONE YARD
SILENT NIGHT
THE DEAD SEASON
ALL THAT GLITTERS
HIGH IN TRIAL
DOUBLE DOG DARE
HOME OF THE BRAVE
DOG DAYS
LAND OF THE FREE
DEADFALL
THE DEVIL'S DEAL
MURDER CREEK

Dogleg Island Mystery Series:
FLASH
THE SOUND OF RUNNING HORSES
FLASH OF BRILLIANCE
PIECES OF EIGHT
FLASH IN THE DARK

Copyright 2021 by Donna Ball, Inc.
All rights reserved
No part of this book may be reprinted without the permission of the author www.donnaball.net

Published by Blue Merle Publishing

Drawer H

Mountain City Georgia 30562

www.bluemerlepublishers.com

ISBN: 978-1-7351271-2-5

First Printing September 2021

Cover Art by mysticsartdesign

This is a work of fiction. All characters, events, organizations and places in this book are either a product of the author's imagination or used fictitiously and no effort should be made to construe them as real. Any resemblance to any actual people, events or locations is purely coincidental.

AUTHOR'S NOTE

Readers who try to book a stay at one of the historic B&Bs in Mercy, Georgia, or take a cruise down the Blood River will be disappointed, as neither the city nor the river exists. Likewise, many of the Georgia roads and highways mentioned in this book will not be found on any map outside the author's imagination.

Many thanks to LuLu Johnson, who not only inspired the title, but was quick to point out that "unfixable" is not even a word. Maybe not, but it's good enough to be the basis for a whole series of books!

Likewise, thanks to Eileen Goudge, who will recognize many of the scenes herein that were inspired by conversations on my porch over two years ago. No one writes alone!

PROLOGUE

The Blood River winds its way through southern Georgia for a mere fifty-two miles, which falls short of qualifying it as a major waterway. It's a slow, wide blackwater tributary of the Suwanee that gives birth to a maze of wetland marshes, estuaries, and the kind of dark, slithering swamps that have fired the imaginations of horror-film makers for generations. Sunset turns the mirror-black water into the rich red color that gives the river its name—or so the board of tourism would have you believe. Those who live there know that more than one body has disappeared beneath those waters; more than one life has been swallowed by the swamp. Blood River has earned its name.

If you follow the river west from its headwaters about thirty miles, you'll come to the little town of Mercy and its once-famous sulfur springs. Five miles outside of town, at the end of a flat dirt road lined with cottonwood trees and black-berry brambles, sits a farmhouse that has been in the same family for 112 years. Not many people can say that out here on the marsh. The heat, the wet, the living, writhing, ever-encroaching jungle of nature swallows up men and most of man's accomplishments in no time at all.

Homer lives alone in the farmhouse and has done so since his kid went and joined the army three years ago June. Homer doesn't miss him. The kid was a strange one, moody and quiet. Watching, always watching. Maybe the army will teach him how to behave, but probably not. Some things just can't be fixed. Meanwhile Homer is glad to have his peace and quiet back. That's what he likes most about the marsh: the quiet. It lets him concentrate on his work.

It's so quiet that he can hear the sound of the tires heading toward the house the minute the car turns off the paved road. That gives him time to clean up a little, to put his tools away, strip off his rubber apron, and wash his hands. He doesn't have time to put on his shoes. He doesn't get much company out this way; it stands to reason he's not exactly prepared to entertain.

He watches his visitor through the window over the kitchen sink as he gets out of the big Chevy Impala with the loop antenna and the five-pointed star painted on it in gold. The driver lets the door thud closed behind him, standing for a moment with his gaze roaming over the dirt yard, the house, the outbuildings. He walks over to the cinder-block garage, which had been a commercial enterprise with two lifts and an oil pit before Homer retired. Now it's closed up tight, the bay doors rusted and padlocked, the windows sealed up with concrete blocks. The visitor does not walk behind the house, where a fish-cleaning station stands weathered and stained beneath a spreading oak. He therefore doesn't see the trinkets hanging from the low limbs like Christmas ornaments, catching an occasional breeze or glint of sunlight, that Homer has collected over the years. Perhaps the encounter would have ended more quickly if he had.

Homer comes out onto the porch in his bare feet and lets the screen door slam behind him, calling out a greeting. His visitor raises a hand in reply and ambles across the yard toward him.

"What brings you out of the house on such a miserable hot day?" Homer inquires pleasantly.

"Just thought I would ride out and check on you," the sheriff replies as he approaches, "you being out here all by yourself."

"That's mighty Christian of you."

"Thought I'd sit with you a spell, if you've got the time."

He comes up the steps and right there, third one from the top, bright as a new penny against the weathered wood of the tread, is a spot of fresh blood. Maybe he won't notice.

Maybe he will.

"Sit yourself down there on the swing," Homer invites. "How about a Coke?"

The other man takes out a handkerchief and mops his brow. "Best offer I've had today."

Homer goes inside to get a couple of bottles of Coke from the refrigerator, and when he comes back out, he has a .45 tucked into the back waistband of his sagging jeans, just in case.

They sit on the porch and sip their Cokes, talking about the weather and the construction on the highway and how bad the gnats are this year. The sheriff asks what Homer hears from his boy, which isn't much, and shares some of the news from around town. He's a friendly fellow, the sheriff. Talkative. Then he says, "I see you blocked up the windows on your garage."

"Had to. Damn rattlesnakes started nesting in there, couldn't keep up with 'em. Figured the only way to keep them out for good was to shore up the cracks with concrete."

The other man nods. The swing creaks in a desultory fashion as he moves it lazily back and forth with his feet. "You know Laine Potter? Lives down the road a piece. Said she heard some kind of disturbance coming from out this way late last night. She said it sounded like a woman screaming. You didn't hear anything like that, did you?"

Homer replies thoughtfully, "Can't say I did. Of course, I sleep pretty sound. Could've been a loon. You know what an awful racket them things can make. Enough to wake the dead."

"Yeah, you're probably right. Most likely, that's exactly what it was." But his eyes are moving, always moving. Who knows what he's seeing?

Finally the sheriff stands, holding up his empty bottle. "Thank you kindly for the Coke. I'll just put this in the trash."

Homer takes the bottle from him. "I'll take care of it."

"Mind if I use your facilities before I hit the road? That Coke went right through me."

Homer steps forward to block the door. "Sorry. Water's out. Need a new fitting for the well pump."

The other man nods thoughtfully. "Sorry to hear that." But his gaze is on the floor just inside the screen door, where Homer has left his boots. They're covered in blood. There's even a bloody footprint on the threshold.

He looks back at Homer. His eyes are steady now, and sad. "I hoped I was wrong, Homer. I hoped it wasn't you. But there's a smear of fresh blood on the wall of your garage, outside the door there, and more blood on the steps, and on your boots. So I reckon you'd better come with me."

Homer is silent for a long time, just looking at him. Then he inclines his head. "Just let me get some shoes on."

"I'll come with you."

The sheriff opens the screen door to let the other man go in first. But when he takes a step back to let the door swing toward him, Homer moves suddenly. Before the sheriff can react, Homer takes out his gun and shoots him dead.

CHAPTER ONE

The dashboard clock read 4:51 when Buck's headlights flashed on the road sign announcing, *Mercy 7 Miles.* The first time he'd seen that sign it had struck him as ironic, like somebody making a promise he couldn't possibly keep. It had made him smile. Now he couldn't think of anybody who needed mercy more than he did, and he didn't smile.

He had left Hanover County, North Carolina, a little before 11:00 p.m. the previous night, counting on a seven-hour drive that would get him into Mercy, Georgia, around 6:00 a.m., plenty of time to have breakfast and maybe even get checked into his motel before his 8:00 a.m. meeting with the mayor. He hadn't counted on how much faster it would be driving at night, nor how much time would be cut off the trip by taking 1-75 all the way, rather than the more scenic highway. Not that it mattered. By the time he'd packed up everything he owned that was worth taking and secured it beneath a tarp in the back of his pickup truck, he'd just wanted to leave. No reason to wait until sunrise, nothing to say goodbye to. Now he was seven miles from town three hours earlier than he was expected and he thought he probably should have planned a little better. Because he was also almost out of gas.

The radio was playing the Charlie Daniel's Band. *Devil Went Down to Georgia,* wouldn't you know it? Buck clicked the radio off.

Buck liked driving at night. What he did not like was stopping for gas in the middle of nowhere in the pitch dark. The middle of nowhere was exactly where he'd been ever since leaving the freeway an hour ago, and the only gas pumps he'd passed since then had been standing in front of a dark mom-and-pop store that advertised *Fresh Bait* and *Diesel* on handwritten signs. He should make a note of that for next time. If there was a next time.

The only thing he hated worse than stopping for gas in the middle of nowhere was stopping for anything at a convenience store at night, which was why he hadn't gassed up when he got off the freeway exit. Ever since what had happened last spring, the mere sight of one of those places made his gut clench. It was stupid, he knew. Lightning didn't strike twice. But here he was, the fuel light on his dashboard blinking madly, and the lights from the Mercy Stop & Go shining like a damn mirage in the desert two hundred feet ahead. He grit his teeth and swung into the parking lot.

At least this one wasn't deserted. There was a red Acura at the first pump in a bank of three, doors closed, windows dark. Apparently the driver was inside the store. A mud-spattered gray Jeep was parked at a sloppy angle at the side of the building, and farther away, close to the dumpster, a battered Ford that probably belonged to the night clerk. It seemed like a good bit of activity this time of night for a little store in the middle of nowhere, but maybe the coffee was good.

The humid night air hit Buck in the face like a wet dishrag when he got out of the truck. Welcome to south Georgia in May. His leg throbbed when he first put weight on it, which wasn't surprising after so many hours of sitting. So he stood there for a minute, leaning against the door and taking in his surroundings, while the circulation returned. The red car had a Mercer University parking sticker on it, and a miniature pink teddy bear swinging from a ribbon over the rearview mirror. The gray Jeep had mud smeared over its tag. Insects buzzed and snapped in the sickly yellow overhead lights. The air smelled like sulfur and diesel fumes; the landscape surrounding him was flat, featureless, and alien. *I don't belong here*, he thought. Nothing about this place had anything to do with him.

Nonetheless, he unscrewed the filler cap and swiped his credit card. A message flashed: *See clerk inside.* He tried again. Same thing.

"Damn it," he muttered. This must be one of those places that didn't allow self-pay after midnight. He twisted around, trying to see if he could get the clerk's attention inside. He couldn't see anybody at the counter. He pocketed the card and made his way across the parking lot to the door.

Every instinct in his body went electric the minute he pushed open the door: heart slamming, breath stopping, fingers tingling. A flash of white-hot wrongness, like that moment just before you step on a copperhead and you think, *Shit!* And every nerve in your body slams into overdrive. If you're lucky, you take a big step back and watch the critter slither into the undergrowth. If you're too late... well, you're too late.

There was an instant, just half a second, when he thought

it was just a flashback to the spring, but then he saw the girl's eyes.

At the same time, he knew what was wrong. The door hadn't chimed when he opened it. No bell had jangled. The lights to his right were out, and the security camera over the counter was just a blank screen. Inside the store was as quiet as death. And the girl, pressed up against the cooler at the back of the store, her hands raised to the level of her shoulders, streaks of blond hair caught in the perspiration on her face, blue eyes filled with abject terror. This all swept over him in the next half a second.

He glanced at the polished chrome dome over the counter, the one that gave a somewhat distorted 360-view of the entire store. He saw the gunman standing a few feet away from her, a red bandanna pulled over his face. Beside him was an open door that looked as though it might lead to a storeroom. The gunman kept cutting his eyes tensely between the storeroom and the girl in a way that let Buck know the three of them were not alone.

And all of that was in the next half a second. Or at least that was how it seemed to Buck. He hadn't even stepped through the door, just opened it half a foot. Now he eased it closed again, thinking, *Crap! Crap! Crap!* with every slam of his heart.

He pressed himself against the brick wall outside the store and fumbled out his phone, punching in the numbers. He could hear the hiss of his breath like a freight train in his ears. When the operator answered, he whispered hoarsely, "Robbery in progress at the Stop & Go on County Road 215, seven miles north of Mercy. At least one armed gunman, holding a female at gunpoint."

The voice replied briskly, "Help is on the way. Please stay on the line. Are you safe? Sir?"

Buck disconnected and dropped the phone back into his pocket. He slipped his Glock out of the holster on his hip and eased back into the store. *Crap, crap, crap.* But what was he supposed to do? Leave the girl alone in there? Who knew how long it would take the police to respond in a place like this?

The girl saw him, her eyes panicked. He lay a finger aside his lips for silence. Her eyes shot back to the gunman.

Buck ducked silently into an aisle lined with Cheetos on one side and baby formula on the other. There was a shout. "Now! Hurry up!" An odd accent. A very nervous-sounding voice. He could no longer see the reflecting dome, which was good. If he could see them, chances were they could see him.

He crouched down at the end of the aisle, with motor oil on one side and breakfast cereal on the other. He tried to breathe through his nose, quietly, evenly. He wasn't having much luck. His heart was like a jackhammer. He could see feet, nothing else. The gunman in battered sneakers and rumpled jeans. The girl in sandals and shorts. A can of Red Bull had rolled under the freezer, apparently when she'd dropped it. She was shaking so hard he could see her ankles trembling. Jesus, how scared did you have to be that your ankles trembled? But that didn't worry him nearly as much as how scared the gunman was.

"Now!" the masked man shouted. The edge in his voice was close to panic. "Hurry!"

Buck saw another pair of feet emerge from the open door of the storeroom, and he took a chance on straightening from his crouch to peer around the corner of the aisle. A smaller man, Middle Eastern or Indian, came through the door with two bulging bank bags and thrust them urgently into the gunman's hand. "Here it is! This is everything. Go now!"

The gunman clutched the bags to his chest with one arm, still holding the gun, somewhat less steadily now, on the girl. "The register—"

"No!" cried the other man. "It is enough!" He said something in a language Buck didn't understand, making a pushing motion with his hands. The other man shouted something back in the same language and took a step backward.

Buck stepped out from the aisle and pressed the barrel of his gun into the back of the thief's neck. "Get on your knees," he said. "Put your gun on the floor."

The man hesitated, stiffening, and for a minute Buck thought he might bolt. For the first time Buck noticed a metal door not ten feet from where they were standing with a lighted exit sign over it. Reading the other man's thoughts, Buck pushed the barrel harder into his neck. "Bad idea," he said.

The two bank bags tumbled to the floor as the gunman raised both hands and sank to his knees. He carefully placed the gun on the floor beside him and Buck scooped it up. The girl sobbed. The other man, the one Buck assumed to be the night clerk, raised his hands too, looking as though he didn't know whether to be terrified or relieved.

In the distance Buck heard sirens. *Thank you, Jesus*, he thought.

"Okay," he breathed. "Everybody just stay calm. Miss, sir..." He didn't dare takes his eyes off the thief long enough to look at them. "Are you okay?"

The girl wrapped her arms around herself and pressed herself against the door of the cooler, still crying. "Y-y-yes. I... I..." Nothing else was intelligible. The clerk just stood there with his hands up, staring at the bank bags on the floor.

Blue lights flashed on the front windows, strobed through the store. Buck kept his eyes on the gunman. "Now would be a really bad time to move," he told him. He risked a quick glance toward the front, saw two officers cautiously approaching the store, one from the east and one from the west.

The girl saw them, too, and cried out, lurching away from the cooler. The clerk shouted, "Help us! Help us please!"

When Buck saw the door open, he called out, "In the back! By the coolers!"

In return there was a shout of, "Police! Stay where you are!"

There was the sound of thundering feet, something crashed, more shouts: "Police! Freeze! Drop your weapons!"

The girl screamed and covered her head, dropping to her knees. The store clerk lunged forward, crying, "Help! Help, we're here!"

Buck shouted to the clerk, "No, stay there!"

From behind him somebody shouted, "I said drop the goddamn gun!"

Buck half turned his head, and as he did the thief in front of him scrambled to his feet, sweeping up the two bank bags and sprinting for the exit door like a linebacker with two seconds left to play. Out of the corner of his eye Buck saw a blue-uniformed officer in shooter's stance with his weapon leveled straight at Buck. Another officer came from the aisle to Buck's right, gun drawn. An alarm started to shriek as the thief plowed through the emergency exit. Buck thought, *Shit!*

Buck put up his hands, a gun in each one. "Law enforcement!" he shouted.

The next thing he knew he landed hard on the floor, his

cheek pressed into the sticky tiles, the weight of somebody's booted foot squarely between his shoulder blades. He made himself go limp. The girl was screaming. The alarm was shrieking. Everybody was shouting.

Somebody jerked his arms behind his back, roughly enough to make him wince, and snapped on a pair of metal cuffs. "Your suspect is getting away!" Buck raised his voice over the sound of the alarm. "Red bandanna, white running shoes, blue jeans! Through the back door!"

"Shut up, asshole!" was the reply. The boot ground harder between his shoulder blades.

The alarm abruptly stopped. Buck made an effort to lift his head, but someone grabbed his hair and pushed his face back down, hard, against the floor. Buck said tightly, "Back right pocket. You'll find my wallet and ID. My name is Buck Lawson."

"Oh yeah?" The voice had a jeer to it, along with the slightly breathless remnants of an adrenaline rush. "That make you something special?"

"No," replied Buck levelly, his face still pressed against the floor. "It makes me the new chief of police."

CHAPTER TWO

It was probably less than five minutes before the tall, shaved-head man in a Mercy police uniform strode through the door, heading straight to the back where Buck, now propped up in a sitting position against the wall, was guarded by the two officers who'd tackled him. Five minutes wasn't much, unless you were sitting in handcuffs with your back to the wall, and it was more time than Buck needed to study his assailants' faces, memorize their badge numbers, and take their measure. He knew without a doubt that, had his skin been a different color, he'd be dead by now.

The younger one, Torrance, looked nervous and unsure, and he kept darting his eyes toward his partner, Baker. Baker was a tall, fit-looking Black man with a strong forehead and hard eyes, probably in his early forties, probably ex-military. He stood with his feet apart and his hands resting on his gun belt, his stare uncompromising and fixed on Buck. He'd been the one with his boot on Buck's back, Buck was sure of it. The other thing Buck was sure of was that behind that hard-as-stone glare there was a flicker of fear. Not fear of Buck, nor even of the consequences for what he had done. Just fear.

The newcomer had a name tag that read Sullivan. He took Buck's wallet and ID from Baker and glanced at them briefly. He knelt beside Buck, and Buck twisted around, presenting his cuffed wrists while the other man took out his key. When the cuffs were removed, Buck got to his feet, hoping nobody noticed how he staggered a little when his weight hit his left leg.

Sullivan handed him his wallet and said, "I'm real sorry about that, sir." He looked sharply over his shoulder and snapped, "Give the man back his damn weapon."

Torrance, the younger one, looked uncertain. "Um, it's in the evidence safe in the unit."

Sully barked, "Well, go and get it!"

Torrance took a step forward and hesitated. "I, uh, there were two guns and…"

"The Glock is mine," Buck said, shortly. "The .22 belongs to the suspect."

Torrance darted a glance toward Baker, who did not even look at him, then said quickly, "Yes, sir."

Sullivan extended his hand. "My name is Don Sullivan. People call me Sully. You probably don't remember, but we met a few months back, when you were down here before. I'm your second in command. That is…" His expression grew rueful. "If I still have a job after this. Like I said, I'm real sorry. We weren't expecting you until later today. Did you drive straight through?"

Buck hesitated only a moment, and then shook the man's hand. As a matter of fact, he did remember meeting Sully before, when he'd first toured the town and talked to Chief Aikens about the job. Aikens had spoken highly of him, and Buck hadn't seen anything there to dislike.

Buck said briefly, "Yeah. I've got a meeting with the mayor this morning. And there's nothing to apologize for." He kept his gaze on Baker when he said that, who still stood there, hands on his belt, unflinching. "Your boys were just doing their jobs." He had a few things to say about *how* they had done them, but that was for later. If there was a later. "But while they were busy disarming me, your suspect ran out the back. My guess is he ran straight for a beat-up looking gray Jeep, 2005 or 2006, looks like it just finished a mud derby."

Sully nodded thoughtfully. "Yeah, I think I passed it on the way in."

Torrance returned with Buck's weapon. Buck checked the magazine and returned it to its holster as Sully added, "Chief Lawson, these two jackasses are Jim Torrance and Leon Baker." He scowled as he turned to the two men and said harshly, "This here is the man who can have your jobs before end of shift. You got anything to say for yourselves?"

Torrance stammered, "I... yes, sir, I..."

Baker spoke over him firmly, "Pleased to meet you, sir."

Under other circumstances, Buck might have smiled at that. There was absolutely no humor in Baker's expression. Buck turned back to Sully.

"The door chime didn't work when I came in, and neither did the security camera," he said. "The suspect talked to the clerk in a language he understood. I'm guessing Hindi or something. He might have been Indian."

Sully looked unhappy. "Got it." He jerked his head at Baker. "You and Torrance, back on the road," he said. "Chief, excuse me for a minute."

Buck opened his mouth to tell him not to call him "Chief,"

but then changed his mind. He watched Sully walk to the front of the store, where two officers were guarding the front entrance and another was interviewing the store clerk, then crossed a couple of aisles to the coffee machine. The girl was standing there next to the machine, sipping a bottle of water, nervously fingering a silver necklace with one of those half-heart symbols suspended by a chain. Her half was engraved with the word "Best." Another officer was standing nearby, blocking the aisle between her and the door.

Buck managed a companionable smile as he approached. "You okay?"

She nodded stiffly, her eyes darting to the door and back. "Are you really a cop?"

"I am," Buck admitted.

She took a quick gulp of the water and screwed the cap back on, dancing her eyes around the room, and then briefly back to him. "Are you… you're not the one I talked to. Before, I mean. You're not him."

Buck returned a sympathetic look, recognizing her nerves. "Do you mean the one who took your statement? No, I'm not. I just wanted to check on you."

Her restless, frightened gaze focused on him for a moment, narrowing a little. "I'm Peyton. I was supposed to meet somebody here."

Buck glanced around but saw no one aside from the sea of uniforms and the clerk, who was now sweating bullets as he gave his statement to one of the officers. He said, "A friend of yours?"

She gave a single shake of her head. "Look, I need to go." Her voice was tight, still trembling a bit around the edges. "This place is screwed up. I can't hang around here waiting any longer. This is crazy. I need to go. Can't I go?"

Buck glanced around again. "Did one of the officers question you?"

She snapped back. "What's to question? I told you, I was supposed to meet somebody. I had to get gas anyway, and there was nobody at the counter, so I went to the cooler to pick up a Red Bull and when I turned around there was this…" She gulped. "This guy with a gun and a bandanna over his face. Pointing the gun right at me. You saw it. You were here."

He nodded sympathetically. "Your name is Peyton?"

She swallowed nervously. "Peyton McGilroy."

He smiled again. "That's a pretty name, Peyton. I'm Buck. Do you live around here?"

She shook her head, seeming to relax a fraction. "I'm a student at Mercer. I have a 10:00 class. I need to go."

Buck said, "Mercer University? That's in Macon, isn't it?" He remembered passing the exit sign on 1-75. "What were you doing down this way?"

Her eyes shifted to the left and quickly back again, looking for someone. "I already told you that! My friend... God, you people are impossible! Look, my dad's an attorney and I know my rights. You can't keep me here after I've already given my witness statement."

Buck was far, far too exhausted to argue with the half-informed logic of a college student with a lawyer for a dad. He said, "Do you want me to call him for you? You look pretty shook up."

"No." Her reply was a little too fast, a little too adamant, and it might have held just a hint of alarm. "God no, my folks would totally freak. They didn't want me to come in the first place. They were right. This place is crazy."

Buck nodded, as much in agreement as sympathy. "Okay."

He glanced around the store. "Well, I don't see any reason to keep you hanging around here. You've got a long drive and I don't want you speeding to make that class."

Her shoulders sagged visibly with relief. "Thank you."

"Just let me have a look at your driver's license and student ID, and we'll get you on your way."

She bristled. "Why? I didn't do anything wrong. I'm not even in a car. You can't ask for my license."

"Actually," Buck replied with just the faintest trace of apology in his voice, "I can. You're a witness to a crime and I can detain you until I have all the information I need—including your ID."

Her lips tightened and her nostrils flared, but she snapped open her purse and dug around inside until she came up with a collection of cards. One was a hotel key card. Buck recognized it because it was from the same Comfort Inn on the outskirts of town at which he had made a reservation. She sorted through the cards—library card, insurance cards, two Mastercards, and a debit card—until she came up with her driver's license and student ID. Buck took them with another polite smile of acknowledgement.

"I gave that officer my contact info," she protested. "My cell and my address at school. I don't see why you need these."

Buck checked the driver's license. Peyton McGilroy, age twenty-one, Savannah address. He glanced up at her. "This your folks' address?"

A sudden pleading came into her eyes. "Don't call them, okay?"

He looked at her for another long moment, but he could see he'd gotten all was he going to get out of her before she broke down into tears. And he'd had more than enough drama for one morning.

Buck reached toward his pocket for a notebook to take down her information, then realized his tee shirt held neither a pocket nor his notebook. He took out his phone instead, snapped a picture of both cards, and returned them to her. "Don't forget to pay for your gas," he told her. "And be careful on the road."

She fumbled the cards back into her purse, shaking her head. "I've got half a tank. I can make it to the expressway."

He didn't blame her. He would have left this place behind, too, if he could have.

"Hey," he said as she hurried toward the door.

She looked back anxiously.

He took out his wallet and found an old business card. The title was out of date—Chief Investigator, Hanover County Prosecutor's Office—but the name and phone number were still good. He handed it to her.

"This is my cell number," he said. "Call me if you think of anything that might help us find this guy, okay?"

She looked a little puzzled but was too impatient to be out of there to question. She mumbled, "Yeah, sure."

She stuffed the card into her purse behind her driver's license and left quickly. Buck was surprised to hear the door chime when she pushed it open.

Sully came toward him, giving a jerk of his head over his shoulder. "The circuit breaker was flipped," he explained. "Took out the camera and the door chime, along with a bank of lights over there. According to the time stamp on the camera, it happened a few minutes before the break-in."

"Convenient," Buck observed. "How much did he get?"

"About eight thousand in cash, a roll of lotto tickets."

Buck lifted an eyebrow. "Not bad, for a little place like this. You'd think most of their sales would be on a credit card."

Sully nodded. "Weekends, a lot of beer and lottery ticket sales are in cash. Then when you turn off the card reader at the pump so people have to come inside, they usually buy something besides gas."

Buck said, "You put a BOLO out on the Jeep?"

"Oh, sure. I also sent a couple of cars out to Daksh's house. We'll have the perp in custody within the hour."

Buck was starting to put it together. He looked at the night clerk, the Indian man who was being interviewed by one of the officers. He answered the questions with big, enthusiastic gestures and kept mopping his perspiring face with a paper napkin while darting his eyes about the store as though looking for inspiration.

"Daksh," he conjectured, "is the clerk?"

"Owner," Sully corrected. "He claims the perpetrator was a two-hundred-pound black man. That, and the fact that he's tried this before, leads me to believe this was an inside job. He lives with a whole bunch of uncles and cousins and whatnot in a doublewide outside of town. I'm betting we'll find that gray Jeep parked in front if we don't run it down first."

Buck grunted. "Why'd a man want to rob his own store, do you reckon?"

"Insurance, for one thing. And the franchise fee is based on profit on these places. You can't do anything about the credit card sales, but keeping the cash is like a paying yourself a bonus. Anyhow, we've known what he was up to for a while, just couldn't catch him at it. Good thing you came along when you did."

"Looks that way."

Sully's eyes did one more sweep of the room. So did Buck's.

Sully said, "Tell you what. Looks like the guys have got it

from here. How about letting me buy you some breakfast? Seems like the least I can do. The Huddle House up the road makes a mean short stack, and they always save a booth for cops."

Buck hesitated, but only for a second. He had more than a few questions, and breakfast seemed like as good a time as any to start getting answers. "I've got to gas up," he said. "I'll meet you there."

They walked toward the register, and Buck couldn't quite disguise his limp. Being thrown to the floor that way hadn't done his leg any favors, and neither had sitting on the floor with his hands behind his back while he waited to be released. Sully gave him a quick, concerned look. "Are you okay, man? You need to get checked out?"

"Old war injury," Buck replied. And because he could tell Sully wasn't the kind to let it go, he explained, "I took a bullet in the leg last year, outside a convenience store a lot like this."

Sully shook his head sympathetically. "Damn," he said. "Did you ever consider maybe…"

"Staying out of convenience stores?" Buck supplied. "Yeah, I thought about it."

They reached the register and Sully pointed to Buck's truck, visible through the window. "Is that yours?"

"That's right."

"Hey, Daksh," Sully said. He waved his arm and the nervous-looking clerk hurried behind the counter. "Turn on pump three and put it on the city's tab," Sully told him.

Buck began, "That's not—"

"And this." Sully took a six-pack of Miller from the endcap display at his shoulder and placed it on the counter.

Daksh's fingers flew over the cash register while he continually shifted his anxious gaze between Sully and the officer who'd interviewed him. Buck looked at Sully skeptically. "What's this for?"

Sully grinned. "Your cooler. You're meeting with Miss Corrinne this morning, am I right?"

"Corrinne Watts? The mayor? Yeah, I'm supposed to see her at 8:00."

"Trust me," said Sully, "by 10:00 you'll be needing one of these."

Sully picked up the six-pack and they walked out together. The fetid, sulfuric air hit Buck in the face again, and he couldn't help grimacing. "What *is* that smell?"

Sully replied, "Oh, that's just the river. Some days it's worse than others, the summer in particular. You get used to it."

Buck doubted that. "It smells like shit, if you don't mind me saying."

Sully chuckled and clapped Buck companionably on the shoulder. "Welcome to Mercy, boss. Before long, it's going to start smelling just like home."

CHAPTER THREE

According to Wikipedia, which Buck had to check after his first conversation with Chief Aikens, Mercy, Georgia—known back then as Medicineville—was established on the banks of the blackwater Blood River in 1843 as a resort destination whose primary attraction was the supposed healing properties of its sulfur springs. It had been spared the ravages of the Civil War by a Union general who had found balm for his palsy in its waters, and who had established a hospital for wounded soldiers in one of its grand hotels. In gratitude, the town had changed its name to Mercy.

The 2020 census reported that the current population of Mercy was 5,166 souls over a total area of 4.2 square miles. The composition was 38.2 percent Black, 48.7 percent Caucasian, 10.1 percent Hispanic, and 3 percent other. The Chamber of Commerce went on to describe the historic downtown area, which was characterized by stately, white-columned homes set along the banks of the river, charming shops and restaurants, and the still-operational sulfur springs which had been turned into a twenty-five-acre park on the south side of town. There were four hotels, numerous bed-and-breakfasts, five churches, and three schools. The primary industry was agriculture; the largest employer the Danvers meat packing plant at the edge of town. The median annual income hovered at around $36,000. Violent crime, according to the FBI's crime statistics, was less than 0.05 percent.

Buck recalled thinking at the time that a person could do worse. Now he wasn't so sure.

He washed the grime of the convenience store's floor off his face and hands in the bathroom of the Huddle House and popped a couple of Motrin for his leg. The cold water on his face cleared away a little of the fog of the all-night drive and most of the adrenaline of the incident in the convenience store. By the time he returned to the booth where Sully was waiting, he felt almost human again. The sight of the big mug of coffee at his place took him the rest of the way.

As soon as he sat down, the waitress put a plate of pancakes, eggs, and bacon in front of him, and another in front of Sully. Sully, who had been checking his phone, put it away and acknowledged her with a smile and a "Thank you, darlin'." To Buck he said, "I hope over-easy is okay. I went ahead and ordered for you, seeing as how I figured you'd want to be at the station for change of shift."

"It's fine." Buck unwrapped his paper napkin and silverware, nodding toward the pocket where Sully had just stashed his phone. "Anything on our suspect?"

Sully sliced a triangle out of his stack of pancakes and speared it with his fork. "Yeah, they're bringing him in now. Still had the bank bags stuffed with cash in his car. Farhan Singh, twenty-five, two outstanding warrants for possession.

He claims his uncle Daksh set the whole thing up, just like I figured."

Buck dug into his bacon and eggs. "From possession to armed robbery, that's a big step up. Especially for a scam."

"Yeah well, I figure he didn't plan on getting caught."

"What about the uncle?"

"We'll bring him in for questioning. I doubt we'll get anything."

"Do you process them here, or over at county?"

"We've got a holding cell here, but if they don't bond out in an hour or two we send them over to county detention with their paperwork."

Buck asked a few more innocuous questions that he already knew the answers to while they finished their breakfasts, just to get the feel of the man. He signaled for a refill on his coffee and sat back with the cup. He said, "So are you working nights, or did they get you out of bed for this?"

Sully grinned and took a toothpick from his pocket, chewing on it. "Nah, each shift rotates through one weekend of nights every six weeks. Last night just happened to be my turn. I would've gotten out of bed to welcome you to town though. I just didn't expect it to be like this. So, listen." He leaned forward a little. Buck caught a whiff of cinnamon and realized it was from the toothpick. "What're you thinking about doing with Torrance and Baker? Torrance is young and a little eager, so I can just about give him a pass. I don't know what the hell Baker's problem is, but he's a good man. Little bit of an attitude, but a solid cop. Been on the payroll almost four years. I'd hate to lose either one of them over this."

Instead of answering, Buck said, "I notice y'all don't wear body cameras."

Sully leaned back, picked up his coffee cup. "It's a small

town, big ticket item. I guess the chief never saw the need for them."

Buck sipped his coffee without comment. "How long have you been with the department?"

"Ten years come February."

Buck asked the obvious question. "How come you weren't tapped for the job when Chief Aikens decided to retire?"

Sully replied with a short shake of his head and a grunt of amusement. "Man, you couldn't pay me enough. I've got a good job, good benefits, and when I go home at night I throw the ball around with the kids, turn on the TV, and forget all about work. I don't need the hassle, and that's the truth."

Buck said, "So you and me, we don't have a problem, right?"

Sully looked surprised. "What, because they went outside the department to hire you? No way. Like I said, I've got no interest in your job. We're good."

"Glad to hear it. I'll probably be counting on you a lot until I get to know my way around."

"Anything you need."

Sully brought his coffee cup to his mouth so that Buck couldn't entirely read his expression, but there was something about his body language that suggested relief. Of course, anybody would be relieved to be in the good graces of his new boss, especially after what had happened this morning.

A misty morning light was filtering through the restaurant's windows, and more headlights flashed by as traffic picked up on the highway. Buck checked the clock on the opposite wall. It was 6:45. "We'd better get the check," he said, "if we're going to make it to the station by 7:00."

"Don't worry about the bill," Sully said, and put down his

coffee cup with a wink. "One of the benefits." He left a $5.00 tip and waved to the waitress as they walked to the door.

Buck said, "I should have said something sooner, but with all the excitement I didn't get a chance. I was real sorry to hear about Chief Aikens."

Sully shook his head sadly. "It was a blow, all right. The man works all his life and then, a month before retirement, something like that happens. It sure makes you think." Again he shook his head. "The whole town turned out for the funeral. And I've got to tell you, some of the guys on the force still aren't over it."

Buck said, "Understandable." He paused a respectful moment before adding, "I didn't get any of the details. What was it? His heart?"

Sully paused with his hand on the door, staring at him. "Nobody told you?"

Buck had a really, really bad feeling as he replied, "All Mayor Watts said was that the chief had passed unexpectedly and they needed me to start early. I've been up in the woods camping the past week, and I just got the message to call her yesterday."

Sully said softly, "Damn."

He looked at Buck for another minute, then opened the door. They stepped out into the sultry air again. Steam was rising from the pavement in the murky light, and clouds of gnats were already starting to swarm. Sully said, "Man, the chief didn't just die. It was on the news. We pulled him out of the river with a bullet hole in his head."

CHAPTER FOUR

Buck had first come down to Mercy in February, when everything in his hometown was crusted with a skin of dirty snow, where the skeletal fingers of things that once were living reached for the sky with a kind of bleak desperation. The days were gray there, the nights bitter. But here in Mercy, thirty-five miles from the Florida line, spring had come. Buck couldn't stop looking at the hedges of brilliant pink and white and magenta azaleas, the weeping cherries, the beds of pansies and tulips that people had planted in their front yards, and the shades of green that went on and on. If you were trying to get a fellow to leave everything he'd ever known and move south, you couldn't do much better than to walk him through the streets of Mercy in February.

He'd already been taken on the grand tour—the springs, the schools, the hospital, the big box stores and supermarkets along the highway, the meat packing plant, the ball field, the civic center—all accompanied by a running narrative from the chief of police. He'd seen more white-columned, antebellum homes than he even knew existed outside of New Orleans and had some of the best barbecue he'd ever eaten sitting on the screen porch of a cedar shack called Joe's Place, looking out over the moss-draped banks of the Blood River. Billy Aikens was clearly proud of his town and felt a protective responsibility toward making sure that whoever took over its stewardship was suited for the job. Buck liked that about him.

"Now in the summertime," Billy explained to him as they walked the brick-paved sidewalks of the four-block downtown area, "you're going to see a good bit more traffic. Folks on their way to Florida, stopping in to visit the springs or the fish camps. The City of Mercy provides police protection to two of the big motels on the highway, the county takes the other two. They run about 85 percent capacity most of the year; on holidays you can't find a room. On account of the big fireworks shows on the river, you know."

Buck didn't know, but he nodded as though he did. He wasn't seriously considering the job then, but Aikens had called twice, and after looking it up on the map Buck had noticed Mercy was less than two hours from the beach. He had vacation time coming. So did she. They'd decided to take a long weekend and meet at the beach. It was therefore understandable that, as he walked through the admittedly charming historic district with the police chief, his mind was on things a lot more compelling than municipal government.

"You've got thirty-two sworn officers," Aikens went on, "eight civilian employees. A good Number Two, Don Sullivan. I'll introduce you before you leave. You'll find most folks are pretty law-abiding. We've got our share of drug problems, juvenile offenders, that kind of thing. We're too far from the interstate to get the kind of situations some of the bigger towns do. The state patrol helps out a good bit with traffic on the highways, and so does the sheriff's office. All in all, it's a sweet little town. Good place to raise a family."

Buck agreed, "It sure is pretty, all right."

"You a family man, Buck?"

Of course, the chief already knew his marital status, from his employment application. He was just being conversational—or, more likely, trying to ascertain his character. "Not at the moment," Buck admitted.

"Well, you take my advice. You find yourself a good woman, and hold on to her as tight as you can. I treasure every minute I had with my sweet Gracie, God rest her soul. The only thing in this world that makes a man's life worth living is the love of a fine wife."

Buck smiled. "Yes, sir, I guess that's right."

There was a little park in the center of town where the four main streets came together. There were a couple of picnic tables and park benches, more showy azaleas and flower beds, and in the center a splashing fountain presided over by a soldier on a rearing horse. They crossed the street against the light, and Aikens gestured to one of the green park benches facing the fountain. "I'm real sorry you didn't get to meet Mayor Watts," Aikens said as they sat down. "Family wedding over in Dothan." He gave a small, amused shake of his head. "She is a character, all right. But folks love her. She's been in office almost as long as I have. She does the hiring and firing of city employees, her and the town council, of course, so she'd be your boss if it comes down to brass tacks. Truth is, she mostly lets each department run itself, which is how it should be. Easy working relationship. We'll make sure to get you together with her next time."

Buck cleared his throat. "Well, sir, the truth is…"

Chief Aikens, with one arm stretched comfortably along the back of the bench, gave a dismissive lift of his hand. "Yeah, I know, you're just exploring your options. And no need for that 'sir' stuff. Call me Billy. Everybody does."

Buck smiled. "Good enough. So Billy…" He nodded toward the statue. "Who's the dude on the horse?"

The police chief grinned at him. "That there," he replied, "is my great-great uncle Seth Aikens, or so they tell me. His daddy was one of the founders of the town."

"War hero?"

Billy chuckled. "Hell, son, as far as know he wasn't even *in* the war. But way back in the twenties somebody decided we needed a statue in town, and that statue needed to be of a Confederate hero, so there you go. As far as I'm concerned, the thing is an eyesore, but you'd start another Civil War around here if you tried to take it down."

Billy Aikens was a big man with a thick mane of white hair, a neat beard, and an easy manner about him that Buck liked. He'd told Buck he'd had a heart scare a year ago and needed a stint put in, which had caused him to start thinking seriously about the time he had left and how he wanted to spend it. He was a fisherman, and he planned to spend his retirement between his cabin on Lake Seminole and traveling around the country in his RV, visiting his eight grandchildren. He'd made it clear that he would always be available to his successor, and that while he was looking forward to a well-deserved retirement, his heart would always be in this town. Knowing that his connection to the place went back to its very founders only underscored his devotion to it. Buck had to admire that.

Billy said, "So, Buck. You've been with the sheriff's office up there in Carolina what? Twelve, fifteen years?"

"Something like that."

"I know the man that used to be sheriff up there. Ro Bleckley. As fine a fellow as you'd ever want to meet."

"Yes, sir. He speaks well of you, too."

Ro Bleckley had been in law enforcement longer than Buck had been alive, and there wasn't much he didn't know about keeping the peace in the south, or the officers who were charged with doing it. What he'd said about Billy was that he seemed like a good man who treated people right, which was bottom-line criteria for a peace officer in Ro's book. He'd then hesitated and added that the town had had a few problems over the years, but Billy had handled them quickly and efficiently, which was proof of a good relationship with his community. Buck had thought about researching what kind of problems he'd been talking about, but never got around to it.

Billy said, "You went from road deputy to chief deputy to sheriff and then to chief investigator. Bet you've seen a lot along the way."

"Some," Buck agreed.

Billy looked at him. "Tell me something. In all that time, all the things you had to deal with, did you ever do anything you regretted?"

"Sure, I guess. Who hasn't? Things I wish I hadn't had to do. Things that needed doing. It's part of the job."

Billy nodded thoughtfully, gazing out over the park. A woman with a baby in a stroller stopped beside the fountain, cooing to the child as it squealed and kicked its chubby little legs in delight. Billy waved to her and she smiled and waved back. But when she returned her attention to the baby, Billy's smile faded. He said somberly, "I had to shoot a man a few years back. You might've heard about it. Killed him. I hated it, but I didn't have a choice. He was holed up in his house out on the swamp holding his girlfriend and his two little boys hostage, threatening to kill them one by one and set the house on fire. I got him to come out on the porch, while a couple of my boys circled around back to try to get the kids out. I thought I'd about talked him into giving himself up, but then he took a shot at one of my officers." He shook his head sadly. "I had to shoot him. He died right there on the porch in front of his kids. It was rough."

It was the kind of story that didn't demand a comment, so Buck gave none. He just sat there in respectful silence until a decent amount of time had passed, and then he said, "What happened to the kids?"

Billy gave him a measured look that told him he liked the question. He replied, "Well, the mother was kind of a mess to start with. Went to live with her folks, ended up swallowing a bottleful of pills a year or two later. The youngest boy, sad to say, didn't live past fourteen. Hanged himself. Sometimes when things are that messed up at home, the kids don't stand a chance. It's like it gets passed down through the generations, you know, like blue eyes or something. But the oldest boy, now he turned out okay. Grew up to be a cop."

Buck nodded. "Yeah, I've seen that happen myself. Two brothers raised by a drunk—one will grow up to be a drunk, the other a preacher. Depends on how hard you're willing to work I guess."

"Exactly what I think." Then Billy said, "You were in a shoot-out up there in Hanover County a couple of years back, weren't you?"

Buck tensed at the reminder. It was not a day he liked to think about. "Yeah. We were assisting the Feds on a raid."

"I liked the way you handled yourself in front of the cameras afterwards."

He said, a little stiffly, "Just doing my job."

A long silence followed, and Buck got the impression Billy was waiting for him to go on. He had no intention of doing so until, in fact, he heard the words coming out of his mouth. "There's probably something you should know about that day."

Billy waited.

Buck said, without looking at him, "My wife at the time was a deputy under my command. She was pregnant. She shouldn't have been anywhere near the scene. It all went south and she took fire. We lost our baby, a little girl. A few months later, we lost the marriage. You'll notice a gap or two on my employment history. That's why. The whole thing left me pretty shook up."

Billy said, "Did you get counseling?"

"Yeah," Buck admitted. He was surprised by how relieved he felt to share the story with Billy. Very few people knew what he had been through during that time. "It helped some."

Billy nodded slowly. "They say time heals all wounds, but it doesn't. You get used to the pain, you live with the way it changes you. And you do better. Or at least you try."

Buck said quietly, "Yeah."

They listened to the sound of the splashing fountain, the voices from the sidewalk, the intermittent traffic. The sun was warm on their shoulders, and the light breeze held just enough of the memory of winter to be pleasant.

Billy said, after a time, "Used to be that a peace officer in a town the size of mine or a county the size of yours could go his whole career without ever firing his service weapon. But those are not the times we live in anymore."

Buck agreed unhappily, "I guess not."

Then Billy said, "So, let me ask you. In all your time on the force, did you ever think about bending the rules a little? Maybe even more than think about it. Maybe crossed the line?"

Buck was no stranger to job interviews, both giving and taking them. He knew the trick questions, like "What's your biggest weakness?" and "If you could change one thing about your boss, what would it be?" But this one caught him off guard, not because he wasn't sure how to answer it, but because he wasn't sure why it was asked.

He said, "Yeah. I've thought about it. Maybe put a toe over the line now and then." He met Billy's gaze without shame. "Last year our K-9 team pulled over a car with a broken taillight and ended up making a drug arrest. The suspect was later charged with multiple homicides, attempted homicide, fraud, racketeering, and a half-dozen narcotics counts."

Billy inquired mildly, "Did you plant the drugs?"

"No. But that taillight might not have been broken when he parked his car. Sometimes there's a difference between what's right and what the law allows."

Billy smiled and nodded. "Well, there you go. There's not a man alive who's been on the job as long as you that hasn't blurred that line at least once, and if you'd denied it, I would've known you were lying. I can abide a lot of things, but not a liar." And before Buck could even react to this, Billy added, "You work many homicides?"

"A few."

"Probably," prompted Billy, "it's a lot like it is here, where you come from. You pretty much know the perpetrator the minute you see the victim."

"Most of the time," Buck agreed. "Domestic violence,

somebody follows somebody else home after a bar fight and finishes the job, a jealous ex… It's a rural county. Not a lot of stranger-on-stranger crime."

"But some." Billy looked at him shrewdly. "And your solve rate is just about one hundred percent. I couldn't help but notice."

Buck had never thought about that before. He'd just considered solving crimes part of the job description.

"So here's what I'm thinking, Buck," Billy said in that relaxed, companionable way of his. "I already let Miss Corinne and the council know my last day would be July the sixth, get us through Independence Day weekend and all that. I figure my replacement could sign on the first week of June, kind of get the feel of the place, let me walk him through things, ease him into the job. You probably already figured out this little town means a lot to me, so I wanted to give myself plenty of time to find the right man. Well, sir, as far as I'm concerned, you're the right man. Most of your credits will transfer from North Carolina, but you'll have to take a few hours of POST training and pass Georgia certification—all at our expense, of course. What I'm saying is the job is yours, if you want it."

Buck was a little taken aback by the offer. He hadn't expected it to come today, and he honestly hadn't thought much past the interview. Finally he managed, "Look, Billy… it's a nice town, and your offer is more than generous…"

"You won't find a better one in the state for a town this size," Billy pointed out.

"But it's a big change, and I've got some personal stuff to sort out…"

Billy nodded in easy confidence. "Well, you've got some time to think about it." He changed the subject. "So, heading down to the beach, are you? Planning to do a little deep-sea fishing?"

Buck's plans really hadn't gone that far. "Maybe, if the weather holds."

Billy smiled, his eyes crinkling in fond reminiscence. "I remember the first time I went out. Me and a bunch of guys chartered a boat, caught our limit of grouper in the morning, and were just about to head back when I swear to God, I hooked a blue marlin. Had to be four, five hundred pounds. That thing jumped and damn near swamped the boat. Scared my buddy so bad he almost fell overboard."

Buck grinned, knowing a good fish tale when he heard it.

Billy grinned back. "Well, I strapped in, fought it for a while, but that son of a bitch wasn't about to be caught. The captain let me have my fun, but we'd only paid for the morning, and he was ready to turn back. Said the boat wasn't outfitted for marlin, best to cut the line and try again next time. 'You don't go after the big one your first time out, son,' he said, and I reckon he was right. But you know where that big old fish is today, Buck?"

"On your wall?" Buck guessed.

"You're damn right." Billy gave a pleased nod of his head. "I forked over all the cash I had to keep that boat in the water, and so did my buddies, and I held on to that sucker till sundown. Used grappling hooks and marine line to haul him onboard. I couldn't move my arms for three days after that, but I learned an important lesson that day."

"Always listen to the captain?" Buck suggested, amused.

Billy's eyes twinkled. "Is that what you do?"

"Hardly ever," Buck admitted.

"Didn't think so." Then he grew thoughtful. "The thing that came to me when I finally saw that monster stretched out on the deck at the end of the day was that you don't always have to outsmart them, or out-fight them, or out-maneuver them. Sometimes you just have to outlast them." He looked at Buck and smiled. "Something to keep in mind, if you ever find yourself in a similar situation."

Then he said, "Well, I'm keeping you from your good time. I appreciate you coming down and talking to me like this. How about I give you 'til the first of April to make up your mind? Meantime, we'll be in touch. And I want you to know I won't be talking to anybody else."

He stood and extended his hand, indicating the interview was over. Buck shook the man's hand, looked into his eyes. Months later, he would still be trying to understand what he saw there.

Then Billy turned and gestured the way across the street, where Buck was parked. "Now you do like I say and take 319 the rest of the way. It'll cut half an hour off your trip. You can drive to the beach any Sunday from here and be back for work the next day. Something to think about, huh?"

Buck admitted it was.

"And listen, once you get yourself settled in, maybe I'll take you out on the water, see what we can hook. But you've got to make me a promise, first."

"What's that?"

Billy winked at him. "If you get a chance to go after the big one," he said, "do it."

Buck chuckled. "Yes, sir, you've got yourself a promise."

But as it turned out, Buck hadn't gone deep-sea fishing that weekend, or any other since, and he hadn't gotten a chance to keep that promise. Now it didn't look like he ever would. Billy was dead.

Not just dead, but murdered.

CHAPTER FIVE

The police station was a stately, two-story, pink brick building that dominated the corner of North Main and Dominion, facing the park with its cascading fountain and Confederate statue. It had an arched nine-foot-tall glass-inset door with the words "Mercy Police Station" stenciled in black on the fanned brick facing, and "Protect and Serve" lettered in gold on the glass. On the right side of the door at eye level was a small brass plaque that read, "Est. 1923." This did not indicate, as the plaque implied, that Mercy had not had police service until 1923. As Billy had explained to Buck, the building, built in 1923, had once been a Sears and Roebuck. The city had purchased and remodeled it for a police station in 1961, and even though the fire department and City Hall had long since moved to more modern structures, the town elders thought the look of their police station set the tone for the character of the town and decided to keep it where it was. Postcards were printed with the park and statue in the foreground, and the police station in back.

Buck pushed through the door and found Sully already

there waiting for him. Hardly surprising, since Buck had wasted time going around to the employee parking lot behind the building, only to realize he didn't have his parking pass yet and couldn't get past the automatic gate. He was mad enough by then to plow right through it, but thought better of it and drove around to park on the street.

Standing outside the Huddle House, all Buck had said was, "Did you get the killer?"

To which Sully replied, "Yeah."

Buck had wanted to know more, of course, but not there, standing in a parking lot with the sound of traffic and the smell of grease and swamp in the air. So he said, "We'll talk at the station." He got in his truck and spent the five-minute drive to town getting madder and madder. He felt like he'd walked into an ambush. He should have been told. This was not what he had signed up for. None of it was.

Inside the building the charm of the exterior gave way to a functioning modern police station. There was a reception desk on a dais near the front, manned by an efficient-looking woman wearing half-glasses on a chain, typing on a computer keyboard. She looked up curiously when he entered. A couple of uniforms were leaning against the desk, talking with Sully. By the way they straightened up and tried to look busy when Buck walked in, it was clear they had been talking about him. Sully stepped forward and looked as though he was about to introduce the men, but Buck ignored the gesture. "Let's go," he said shortly.

Straight ahead behind the desk there was a metal detector with a sign over it that read, "Visitors MUST enter here." To the left was a wooden staircase that led to the training room, conference rooms, break room, and lockers. To the right was a metal door that led to the administrative offices, including,

Buck recalled, that of the chief of police. Buck instinctively started to walk straight ahead because that would have been the way to reach his office if he had been at home, then caught himself, once again feeling that strange disorientation. *I don't belong here.*

Sully gestured toward the stairs. "I texted both shifts to assemble in the call room," he said.

Buck felt his leg catch when he turned toward the stairs, and Sully must have noticed because he said, "There's an elevator."

Buck barely stopped himself from snapping back that he knew that, and instead walked silently to the small elevator set behind the stairs. The night was catching up with him. His eyelids felt like sandpaper and there was a pressure at the back of his skull that signaled a headache to come. He needed a shower and a shave and a change of clothes. He needed some answers.

As soon as the elevator door closed, he said, "Talk."

"The chief didn't report in for work on Monday, May 10," Sully said. He was a man who was used to giving reports and knew how to keep it concise. "He wasn't at home, didn't answer his phone, nobody'd seen him since Sunday morning church. We initiated a drone search and spotted the chief's personal vehicle about six hours later in the Lost Creek Wildlife preserve. His body was located by boat about half a mile downstream, caught in the undergrowth near the bank. The murder weapon, a Glock 9 millimeter, was located in the weeds not far from the car, along with a pair of blood-stained work gloves. The ME estimated the time of death to be 2:00 p.m. on Sunday. We traced the fingerprints on the gun to Carl Tucker, a crazy old drunk that manages a run-down trailer park outside town about ten miles. We've been trying to get him on meth charges for a while now but never could. The chief went out there on a domestic complaint the Thursday before he died and I guess they got into it. We hauled Carl in but he was out twenty-four hours later. We've got witnesses that heard Carl say he was going to track the chief down and put an end to him, and it looks like he did just that. We arrested Carl for murder on Wednesday."

Billy's words echoed in Buck's mind like a ping-pong ball bouncing off a wall: *You work many homicides?*

Damn it. Why did that have to be the thing he remembered?

The elevator bounced to a stop and Sully added, "I knew you'd been off the grid the past week, but I thought you'd been told by now. There's no excuse for that."

"Not your fault," Buck replied briefly. The door slid open and they stepped out. "I want to see the report."

"I'll make sure Lydia has it on your desk before you get down there."

"Who's Lydia?"

A corner of Sully's lips turned down in briefly wry amusement. "Your AA—administrative assistant. She pretty much runs things around here. Best to keep on her good side." He gestured Buck down a short hallway to the left. "I thought I'd just introduce you, let the men know about the change of command. You might want to say a few words."

Buck's ex-wife, Raine—the one he'd married twice—once said he made a good politician. She hadn't meant it as a compliment, and he hadn't taken it as such, but he knew it was true. Most folks liked Buck. He had a natural charm about him; he always knew what to say. It wasn't something he cultivated, but he wasn't unaware of its value, either. So even though he was tired and disoriented and still feeling a little like he'd stepped off the edge of a cliff—or been pushed—when he walked into that room full of blue uniforms, he knew a simple nod and a "How y'all doing?" wasn't going to be enough.

There were about fifteen men and three women in the rows of folding chairs that were set up in front of the whiteboard, most of them nursing cups of coffee. Some looked tired, some looked impatient, some looked suspicious. A few looked completely disinterested. But when Sully introduced Buck as the new chief of police, the expressions on all their faces were alert.

Buck stepped forward. He made eye contact with as many as he could. He said, "I'll keep this short. I know you've all got things to do."

He took a breath, settled his nerves. This was crazy. He wasn't even sure he wanted the job anymore. Maybe he wouldn't even stay.

But if he did stay, these were his people, and he'd never get a chance to change what they thought of him this morning. So he said, "I'm sorry we had to meet this way. I know you're grieving. I didn't know Billy as well as most of you, but what I did know, I liked. I was looking forward to working with him, learning the ropes from him. We even planned a fishing trip together."

That made him think of their conversation in the park, the part that wasn't about homicide. But he had to focus. He pulled his thoughts together.

"This is not what any of us expected," he said. "I get that. I want you to know I'm not coming in here trying to take Billy's place. He was one of a kind, and I don't think I could if I wanted to. What I will do is try to make this transition as easy as I can for you, and I'd appreciate it if you did the same for me. I'm going to be meeting with each one of you privately in the next day or two and I hope we all can give each other a chance, over the coming weeks, to get to know each other. In the meantime…" For some reason, at that moment, his gaze landed on Baker, who happened to be the only Black man in the room. "If you have any concerns, my door is always open." Another breath. "All right, then. Let's get back to work."

He hesitated, looking around the room, and said, "Who's the watch commander for this shift?"

A hand went up. Buck gestured him forward.

He didn't even bother to read the man's name tag. "Carry on," he said quietly, as the others filed out of the room, "just like you've been doing. I haven't even been sworn in yet."

———

Buck shaved and changed his shirt in the men's room, then walked across the park to City Hall. He arrived at the mayor's office with two minutes to spare.

He followed the signs down a hallway to a frosted glass door that read "Mayor's Office." Inside was a room as featureless as any other in the building, with tile floors, beige walls, and the usual office equipment. There were a couple of metal desks with a female employee behind each one, and on one wall was a closed wooden door with a brass nameplate that read, "Corinne Watts, Mayor." An elected official had to be pretty confident in herself to have her name engraved in brass on the door.

The two women at the desks were chatting when he came in, one of them sorting through file folders and another scrolling through her computer screen. Both women looked up when Buck came in. The one nearest the door smiled and said, "Can I help you?"

He replied, "I'm Buck Lawson."

"Of course!" She sprang from her seat, her smile broadening. "I'll tell Miss Corinne you're here."

But before she could do that the mayor's private door opened and a large young man with slumped shoulders and an angry red face stalked out, tossing over his shoulder, "Forget it, Mama! Just forget it!"

A woman replied in a weary tone, "Oh, for heaven's sake, Roland, don't pout."

Her answer was the slamming of the outer door as Roland strode through.

The receptionist gave Buck a quick apologetic look and poked her head into the mayor's office. The woman at the other desk said, "Can I get you a cup of coffee, Mr. Lawson?"

The truth was, he probably could have used a cup, but he wasn't sure he'd be there long enough to drink it. At any rate, it didn't matter because just then the receptionist stepped back, holding the mayor's door open for him, and gestured him inside. The door snicked closed behind him.

The room in which he found himself was a striking contrast to the one he had just left. The moss green carpet was plush, the draperies brocade, the furniture a deep wine leather. The window overlooked the park and the cascading fountain. Behind the elegant Queen Anne desk was a mirrored bar stocked with crystal decanters and a variety of barware, along with a silver coffee service on a tray. A woman who Buck could only assume was the mayor stood at the bar with her back to him, pouring coffee from the silver pot into a travel mug. But by far the most striking feature of the room was the six-foot-by-six-foot oil painting of a marsh at sunset that hung above the sofa. Its colors were so rich and moody, the subject matter so intense, that the viewer was drawn in with the first glance. Buck couldn't help staring.

"'How still the plains of waters be,'" a musing, sugary voice quoted softly from behind him. "'The tide is in his ecstasy. The tide is at his highest height: and it is night.' The Marshes of Glynn by Sidney Lanier."

Corrine Watts came around to the front of the desk, gazing at the painting with him. "It was my daddy's favorite poem. He made all us kids memorize the whole damn thing."

Buck turned to look at her. He had never met Corrine Watts and wasn't sure what to expect. What he saw was a tall, slender woman somewhere past sixty with cheekbones sharp enough to slice tin foil and ice blue eyes. Her short platinum hair was pushed behind her ears and her lipstick was bright red. She wore a white pantsuit and spike-heeled shoes the same color of her lipstick, and she leaned against her desk with arms and ankles crossed, smiling at him in an appraising fashion as she turned her attention from the painting to him.

"Well, Buck Lawson," she said, her smile deepening, "just look at you. Aren't you something to write home to Mama about?"

Her accent was as thick as sorghum syrup and just as sweet, reminding Buck of beauty pageants and rose-scented dusting powder. It was the kind of accent you either had to work hard to keep, or you were too confident to care that it was half a century out of style. Buck suspected the latter.

She crossed the room with her hand extended, and when he shook it she held onto his fingers, looking him up and down appreciatively. "Oh, my word, yes, you're bound to have the girls shimmying out of their panties faster than their daddies can get a rope around them, that's for sure. I'll tell you the truth, if I were twenty years younger I wouldn't mind taking a run at you myself, but, Lord God, when you get to be my age sex is just too damn much trouble, you know what I mean? Well, of course you don't, sugar, but you take my word for it. You'll see."

She gave his forearm an affectionate pat and moved back to her desk, waving him to the leather sofa on the adjacent wall. "Have a seat, sweetheart. Lord, did you drive straight through? You must be exhausted. And I hear you had quite a welcome when you got to town."

Buck found his voice. "Word gets around, I see."

"Oh, honey, you'll find there's nothing that goes on around here I don't know about as soon as it happens." She picked up a tall red UGA travel mug with the picture of a bulldog face on it and sat down behind the desk, regarding him benevolently. "Now, sit down. Did those girls offer you some coffee? How about a cinnamon bun?"

Buck remained standing. "I don't want any coffee, ma'am," he said levelly. "What I want to know is why you didn't tell me what I was walking into when you said you needed me down here right away."

She lifted her eyebrows in a pretty expression of confusion. "And what, exactly, did you walk into? You're surely not talking about that little contretemps at the convenience store this morning."

"You know exactly what I'm talking about. Homicide." He didn't bother to hide the harsh edge to his voice. "You neglected to mention that little detail when you told me Billy was dead."

The plastic straw in her travel mug made a scraping sound against the side of the lid as she moved it up and down, still regarding him with big eyes and a gentle half smile. "Well, it hardly seemed appropriate to go into specifics over the phone. And if you hadn't been out of reach the past week…"

"I wasn't due to start this job for a month," Buck reminded her. "What I did in the meantime was my business. When I got back into a cell service area the only message I had from you was the one telling me to call, and it was less than twenty-four hours old. You could have texted. You could have called the sheriff's office or the forest service if you needed to find me. You could have told me the damn truth when we talked on the phone yesterday."

She sipped from the straw. "I could have," she admitted.

"But you thought I might not take the job if I knew my predecessor had been murdered."

"Oh, please." She gave a dismissing wave of her hand. "We have a contract."

He gave her one more hard look, his patience at an end. "Sue me," he said shortly. "You'll get a two-bedroom farmhouse in North Carolina and a pickup truck with twenty-four payments left on it." He turned toward the door.

His hand was on the doorknob when she said, "Carl has an alibi."

He turned, his gaze sharpening.

"The man they arrested for Billy's killing," she explained. "His wife claims he was home all day, passed out in front of the television set."

He took his hand from doorknob somewhat reluctantly. "Sully said they had fingerprint evidence. The wife could be lying."

"Yes, she could," agreed Corinne mildly, holding him with those pale, steady blue eyes. "Or they could have the wrong man."

Buck came cautiously back into the room. "Why did you wait a week after Billy died to call me?"

She said, "They made an arrest."

"And now you think they made a mistake."

"I always thought they made a mistake."

He sat down in one of the red leather wing chairs in front of the desk, folded his hands across his abdomen, and waited.

She sipped again from her travel mug, the stern confidence in her eyes fading into something resembling annoyance as his silence went on. "The Aikenses have run this town for a hundred fifty years," she said. "Billy was a beloved figure. The boys wanted to get his killer and they wanted to get him fast. I don't blame them for that. And if Carl did it, I hope he gets the chair. But if he didn't…" Her expression hardened. "I want the person who did."

Buck said, "Do you have any particular person in mind?"

She shook her head slowly, fingering a pen on her desk. It was one of those expensive ones, with a walnut body and silver nib, and she tapped the tip against a memo pad in a slow, steady rhythm. She never broke his gaze as she said, "No. I don't."

Buck said, "If you've got a problem with the way this investigation was handled, you need to call the GBI. That's what they're for."

"You're the chief of police."

"Which is not the same as a private detective."

She sat back in her chair. "If you knew Billy at all, you know how much he loved this town. You're the one he chose to turn it over to. I think he knew exactly what he was doing when he made that decision. So you tell me. Did he make a mistake?"

Buck refused to flinch from her gaze. "I guess we'll see, won't we?"

"Good enough." She gave a satisfied smile and stood. "Now, then, we have a lovely installation ceremony planned for Sunday afternoon at 4:00 right here in the main auditorium—flowers, a choir, inspirational readings, lots of photo ops. Make sure your dress uniform is ready by then. But let's go ahead and get you officially sworn in so you can start to work, shall we?"

He didn't move for another long moment, and he was gratified to see just the smallest flicker of unease cross her eyes. She knew he could still walk out. So did he.

When he thought the moment had gone on long enough, he stood up. "We use a Bible where I come from," he said. "How do you do it in Mercy?"

CHAPTER SIX

The Bible was located, the two ladies from the outer office stood as witnesses, and for the third time in his life Buck placed his hand on the Bible and swore the Oath of Honor. *I do solemnly swear I will support and defend the Constitution of the United States of America; I will support and defend the Constitution of the State of Georgia; I will support and defend the Charter and Ordinances of the City of Mercy...*

And even as he spoke them Buck could not help being aware how odd the words sounded: *State of Georgia. City of Mercy.* He had spent all his life serving Hanover County, North Carolina. This was not his place. Would he ever feel like it was?

The oath was signed, the ladies dismissed, and the Bible returned to the shelf where it had been found. Corrinne walked over to the bar and filled two shot glasses with whiskey. She held out one to him, and he thought for a moment she was joking. It was eight thirty in the morning.

"Welcome aboard, Buck Lawson," she said, and he took the glass reluctantly. "To a long and successful partnership." She raised her glass to him in salute and downed the contents without flinching.

Buck discreetly placed his glass on the corner of the bar, a gesture she noticed with amusement. "Too early for you, sugar? Well, you'll get over that soon enough." She went over to her desk and retrieved her travel mug, pouring the contents of Buck's glass into it. "Did you ever hear about the fishing town with a little drinking problem? Well, Mercy is the drinking town with a little fishing problem." She topped off her mug with more coffee from the silver pot and replaced the lid. "Myself, I'm a functioning alcoholic. Highly functioning, I might add. My doctor gives me seven years before I'll need a new liver, so I'm enjoying every one of them. Did you know you can't drink for a year after receiving a liver transplant? Ridiculous."

She sipped from the cup, regarding him with a contented expression. "Well, then. I imagine you'll want to unpack and get settled. Take the rest of the day off and catch up on your sleep. Tomorrow's soon enough to get started."

But Buck did not move. "Let me ask you one more time," he said.

She rested one perfectly manicured hand lightly on the desktop and gave an inquiring tilt of her head.

"If you were so anxious to have Billy's murder investigated by an outsider, why did you wait until the day before you needed me to start before you called me?"

"But Buck, honey," she replied with just the faintest hint of reproach in her voice, "you're not an outsider. You're one of us now." She added practically, "And the town charter specifies that when the police chief vacates his office, voluntarily or involuntarily, a new chief must be sworn in within ten days. Today is day eight."

That felt like the closest thing to a straight answer Buck had gotten all day.

She opened her desk drawer and took out a set of keys and a pair of sunglasses. The keys she dropped into her pocket, the sunglasses she pushed up into her hair. "You don't mind walking, do you? They haven't let me have a driver's license since 2010. My boy Roland generally drives me everywhere I need to go, but it's just a couple of blocks and the heat's not too bad this time of day. That was him you saw storming out of here when you came in. He's in charge of the city's motor pool, by the way, paid way more than he's worth, but it's never enough for him. Always asking for more. But that's what kids do, isn't it? They suck you dry, it's their job." She picked up her mug and gestured him toward the door. "You'll find out soon enough, though. Enjoy them while they're young, then send them to military school, that's my advice."

Buck opened the door for her. "Where are we going?"

"I'm just going to show you to your place, then I'll leave you be." She paused by the receptionist's desk. "Wendy, honey, I'll be back in half an hour. Be sure to get that memo out to all departments about our new police chief. And the press release, too."

Wendy smiled at Buck. "Yes, Miss Corinne. Welcome to Mercy, Chief Lawson."

Buck smiled back and thanked her, still not entirely comfortable with his new title. Corinne had already opened the outer door and was waiting for him.

"I appreciate it," Buck told her as they walked down the hall, "but there's no need for you to go to any trouble. I already have a motel reservation."

She laughed. "Oh, honey, I don't think so. You cancel that

reservation, and if they give you any trouble, just mention my name."

They stepped out into the soupy morning sun, and Corinne lowered her sunglasses, taking his arm as she gestured him across the street with the hand that held the travel mug. "You heard the story of old Colonel Aikens, I imagine," she said, indicating the statue. "The scoundrel. Word is he actually turned over the town to Sherman during the war. Gave him the location of one of our battalions and let all those poor boys be slaughtered in exchange for sparing Mercy, *then* invited him to make himself right at home here, set up a hospital, whatever he needed."

"Sherman, huh?" replied Buck. "I heard it was just some general with the palsy or something. And all he did was offer the town for humanitarian purposes."

She grinned and sipped from her cup. "Well, there you go, hon. History depends on who's telling it, doesn't it? But the point is, the Aikenses are not to be trusted. They'll do anything for this town."

He said, "Do you mind me asking, ma'am, what your name was before you married?"

Though her eyes were obscured by the dark glasses, Buck could not mistake the shrewd upturn of her lips as she glanced at him. "My mama was an Aikens," she admitted. "Billy was my second cousin."

"I had a feeling," he said.

"And, sugar?" She took another sip from her cup. "You can call me Mayor, or Miz Watts, or Miss Corinne, or sweetheart if you want. But you call me ma'am again and I'm gonna have to slap you, okay?"

He tried not to smile. "Yes, ma'am, Miss Corinne. Who do you think killed Billy if Carl didn't?"

"I don't know. He was chief of police for a long time. He had to have pissed a few people off. Somebody he put away, or didn't put away…" She shook her head. "I don't know."

Before Buck could press her further, or even decide whether he wanted to, she raised her cup to a woman who was just unlocking one of the storefronts and called, "Morning, Shelby! Have you met our new police chief?"

By the time they reached the end of the block he had made the acquaintance of three more shop owners and one councilman, all of whom had issues they wanted to talk to him about, from street parking to noise violations. He listened politely and promised to look into each complaint, after which he was warmly welcomed to town and they all moved on.

They passed the big brick Aikens Hardware and Sundries building, established 1892, which took up half of one block and most of another, and turned right onto Magnolia Street. Immediately they were suffused in the quiet charm of an old-fashioned southern neighborhood, with wide lawns and colorful flower beds, big old houses with wraparound porches set far apart, weeping willows and decorative koi ponds. The street was lined with live oaks and lush, waxy-leafed magnolia trees studded with saucer-sized white blossoms. The marshy smell of the river combined with the sickly sweet aroma of the magnolias to form something that was almost pleasant. It even seemed cooler here.

"The beginning of our historic district," Corinne explained. "Lovely, isn't it?"

Buck remembered driving through it with Billy, but he hadn't paid that much attention at the time. Seeing it on foot did add a whole new dimension; one he would have enjoyed had he been in the company of someone else.

They walked past a neat gravel driveway and Corinne

turned toward a set of three stone steps set between a hedge of white roses. "Here we are," she said.

At the top of the steps there was a discreet iron sign of the kind that are used to mark historic places. It read "Aikens House 1853." A walkway led to a brick house with a deep, white-columned porch decorated with the requisite white wicker rockers and fern stands. Boxwoods lined the foundation, and a tall oak tree dappled the lawn with shade. Paddle fans turned lazily overhead on the porch. Had he been in a better mood, Buck would have smiled at the sheer southern charm of it all. Raine's aunt Mart—who was practically his aunt, too, out of affection if not relationship—would have swooned over this place.

"I appreciate you going to the trouble," he said, "but I'm not really a B'n'B kind of guy. I think I'd better keep my motel room and look for something more permanent after a week or two."

Corinne chuckled as she turned the key in a dark wood door inset with leaded glass panels. "Sweetie, this isn't a bed and breakfast. It's your house." She opened the door wide and held out the key to him. "If you want it, of course."

She stepped inside and held the door for him, but he remained where he was, staring at her. "Billy deeded the place over to the town about thirty years ago," she went on, "on the condition that it be used to house the chief of police after he died. I think he had in mind that his son would take over from him back then, but Bill Junior is in St. Louis now, building some kind of insurance empire. Never showed the slightest interest in law enforcement, which I'm sure was a disappointment. Parents always expect children to follow in their footsteps. Billy's daddy was chief here before he was, did you know that?"

Buck murmured, "He mentioned."

"At any rate," Corrine went on, "the house situation turned out to be a good deal for everybody—the city pays the taxes and upkeep, and Billy got to keep his ancestral home. Not to mention the town's vested interest in preserving our historical landmarks, which is getting harder and harder to do these days, and it doesn't cost us a penny. It all comes out of state grants. Of course, we have to charge a minimal rent—$100 a year, I think—for legal reasons, and you can't make any structural changes to the house while you're living here, but otherwise the place is yours. It's not as big a white elephant as it looks. Three bedrooms, three baths upstairs, new appliances in the kitchen, bathrooms remodeled in the nineties I think, air conditioner replaced last year. You're responsible for the utilities, of course. Remind Lydia to get everything changed over into your name. There's a pretty backyard overlooking the river, nice and quiet. Of course, the mosquitos can be a plague in the summer, but most evenings we get a cool breeze coming off the water. No penalty if you decide not to stay here, of course, but our feelings would be hurt." She smiled at him sweetly and dangled the set of keys between her fingers. "And I can promise you won't find a better deal."

Buck stepped inside and took the keys cautiously. "You know this is a little crazy, right?"

She shrugged. "Consider it a signing bonus." She crossed the shadowy foyer, her heels clicking on polished cypress floors, turning on lights as she went. "Billy's kids were here last weekend, packing up his personal things, and they took the furniture that they wanted, so you might find the place a little bare. The historical society took possession of the art, books, and other artifacts with historical significance as per

Billy's will, but he did ask that his study be left untouched. And he left you something."

Her narration was a tossed salad of words that he would try to sort out later, and the rooms they passed were just a background blur—fireplaces with carved mantles, faded squares on the walls where pictures had hung, orphaned chairs and end tables scattered across bare floors. But when she stopped and gestured him inside the latest room, Buck took notice.

"Left me something?" he repeated, following her through the door. "What?"

But then he stopped, staring, and he couldn't prevent the grin that tugged at one corner of his lips. "The fish?" he said.

She confirmed, "The fish."

The room was pleasantly furnished with a faded rug, comfortable-looking suede recliners and sofa, and a desk with a nail-head-trimmed leather swivel chair. There was a flat-screen television over the fireplace, and big windows on two walls looking out onto a shade-dappled backyard and a spreading magnolia tree. Dominating the wall opposite the desk was the biggest mounted marlin Buck had ever seen.

He shook his head slowly, touched by equal measures of rueful admiration and sentimental remembrance. "Now *that* belongs in a museum," he said.

"Maybe," she agreed, regarding the artifact with an expression that was somewhere between bewilderment and dismay. "Lord knows his wife did nothing but complain about it while she was alive. But he was very specific it should go to you. Put a codicil in his will and even left a note in with his important papers making sure nobody touched it but you."

Buck's smile started to fade. "When did he do that, do you know?"

"Honestly honey, I couldn't tell you. You'd have to check with his lawyer, Ken Jeffries. I imagine he'll be in touch with you, anyway, about the legal papers on the house. He's the best lawyer in town, by the way, if you need any work done. Also, the city attorney. Now, let me show you the kitchen."

She seemed in a hurry to move on, so he dragged his thoughtful gaze away from the marlin and followed her down another corridor and into one of those big, old-fashioned kitchens that builders used to locate at the back of the house so that the cooking odors and the servants would be out of way. An obvious effort had been made to modernize it somewhat, with tile floors and countertops, and the appliances were stainless steel. The walls were painted a cheerful buttery color with a built-in china hutch. There was a table big enough for family meals and a set of glass doors that opened onto a screened porch. Buck could see a couple of rocking chairs with faded cushions on the porch, and a green wicker side table that was beginning to unravel near the bottom.

"Now, Betsy was in to clean on Friday, so the beds upstairs are made with fresh linen," Corrine said, "and the church ladies were over here yesterday to leave some food." She opened up the refrigerator door to check and smiled. "Oh, look. Fried chicken and potato salad, and one of Marge Hensley's lemon meringue pies. You've got milk, bread, and eggs, too, coffee for the morning and a nice pitcher of sweet tea. That should get you by until you have a chance to buy groceries, but I wouldn't be a bit surprised if your doorstep didn't fill up with ladies bearing casseroles before then. There's nothing the women of this town hate more than a man trying to fend for himself."

Buck looked at her in bemusement. First, they knock him to the floor and cuff him, then they give him a free house and stock the refrigerator with fried chicken and lemon pie. "This is all really..." He searched briefly for a word other than "weird." He settled on, "Nice of everybody. Really."

She turned to him with a smile that was both proud and a little wistful. "This is not bad place, Buck," she said. "Good people live here. All we need you to do is make sure it stays that way."

He gave the only reply he possibly could. "I'll do my best."

She returned a brisk nod. "Well then, I'll leave you to get settled in. Wi-Fi password and emergency numbers are on the fridge. There's a garage at the end of that driveway we passed where you can park your truck, and a workshop next to it. The keys are on the ring. There's a fishing pier right on the river, but be careful of water moccasins." A wisp of nostalgia crossed her face as she added, "Billy used to have a department picnic here on the Fourth of July, Christmas parties every year... even a wedding reception for one of the officers once. But of course nobody would expect you to keep that up," she assured him with a quick smile. "Now, if you need anything, call my office. Or your own. Lydia probably has more answers than we do anyway. And Buck." She laid a hand on his forearm as she passed by and gave it a warm squeeze. "Welcome to Mercy."

Buck stood in the kitchen and listened to the sound of her heels clicking on the wood floors as she retreated. When the door closed behind her, he found himself thinking longingly of the six-pack Sully had placed in his truck cooler that morning. It wasn't even 9:30 a.m.

He opened the back door and walked out onto the screened porch, looking out over the wide expanse of perfectly mown lawn that sloped gently toward a bank lined with moss-draped trees. Buck had always found Spanish moss a little creepy, hanging like tangled strands of hair from a skeleton. You never knew what was hiding in there. To his right, he could see the roof of the building he assumed was the garage, half-hidden by a tall boxwood hedge. And, barely visible in the shadows of the trees, he could make out the wooden rail of the fishing pier Corrinne had spoken of. He wondered idly what even swam in those inky waters. He should have asked Billy.

He pushed open the screen door, half-thinking to walk down to the pier and have a look, but in the end he just stood on the steps, gazing out over the lawn. It was too easy to imagine a dog chasing a ball across that emerald grass, a boy spiking a football, the smell of charcoal, the sound of laughter. The imagery almost made him smile. Almost.

He drew in a deep breath and let it out. "Well, hell," he muttered out loud. "I guess there's worse things."

He sat down on the top step and took out his phone. He tapped the number. She answered immediately.

"So," she demanded, "how is it?"

The sound of that voice was so familiar, so much like home, that he could almost taste it. He had to close his eyes for a moment against a sudden wave of longing. "Baby," he said, "you were right." He rubbed his hand over his face and blew out a breath. "This place is messed up."

CHAPTER SEVEN

Hanover County, North Carolina
Twelve Months Earlier

He'd brought flowers for Jolene's mother and a toy police car for her son, Willis. He called it a housewarming present, but it was clearly another apology for another fool thing he'd done or said. That surprised her. Men like Buck Lawson didn't usually apologize easily, but it seemed to come naturally to him. He was a hard one to figure out.

Buck had first come into Jolene's Smith's orbit at a law enforcement conference where she was scheduled to be part of a panel presentation on the Homeland Security initiative to provide bomb-sniffing dogs and handlers to high-risk communities. Buck was doing a program on small-town policing, and she had sat down in the back row, mostly to finish the coffee and pastry that was her breakfast. He talked about how small-town policing was entirely community policing; how it was knowing your neighbor and treating him with respect, guilty or innocent. He told a story about making a traffic stop for an expired tag and a broken taillight that he knew the guy couldn't afford to replace. He'd made a point of walking around to the back, where the fellow's kids were cowering in the backseat. "Hey, you guys," he'd told them with a wink, "your dad's somebody special, you know that? You be good to him."

Jolene had thought at that moment, *That's the kind of cop I want to be. That's the place I want to work.*

When the assignment to Hanover County, North Carolina, came up she jumped on it, and it had been great at first. Then a stupid misunderstanding—stupid on his part, entirely innocent on hers—had caused a breach between them. She'd spent a long time being mad at him, and he'd spent a long time trying to make amends. They were now at that awkward stage where neither one of them knew who they were supposed to be.

Now they sat on her front steps and drank the beer he'd brought in something like an easy silence for a while after he'd said his piece. They weren't friends; not even colleagues anymore, not really. They were somewhere on the slippery edge of in-between, each of them wary about where to go next. It wasn't a comfortable place to be. But it wasn't an altogether bad one, either.

Inside, the boxes from moving day were still stacked against the wall, waiting to be unpacked. Her mother clattered around the kitchen, putting away the supper leftovers. The tinny sound of the Charlie Daniels band came through the windows and they just sat, listening.

He said, after a moment, "So what's with the Charlie Daniels Band?"

She shrugged. "I don't know. I like some of what they've got to say. Nothing wrong with a plain-talking country boy." She slid a glance toward him. "As long as you keep your eye on him, of course."

Buck smiled, and let it fade. The night crept in around them, dampening the warm light from the house. Far away, a dog barked, and stopped. A door slammed.

"Do you ever feel like you're living somebody else's life?" Buck said, gazing into the shadows. He glanced at her. "I mean, look at you. How the hell did you ever end up here, in a two-bit town in the middle of the Smoky Mountains, with a six-year-old kid and a mother to take care of? You could be making twice as much in Raleigh, and God knows how far you could've gone if you'd stayed with Homeland."

She was silent for a moment, turning the bottle around in her hands, watching it catch the light from the windows. Then she said, "When I asked Mama to move here, I told her she'd be the only other Black woman in town besides me, maybe in the whole county. Do you know what she said? She said, 'There's worse things.' I've been hearing that from her all my life, whenever I worried about something. There's worse things. Maybe this time, she's right." She took a sip of the beer. "At least here there's not much chance of being blown up by an IED."

"I guess."

Inside the house, the music ended. They could hear water running and a child's voice. Buck said, "I never thought it would turn out this way. I married my high school sweetheart. I thought I'd be married forever. I thought I'd come home from work every day and mow the grass and weed the garden and eat supper across the table from a familiar face, every night. Right now, today, we should be raising tomatoes and kids and golden retrievers. Somehow it all got away from me. This is not my life. And I think I'm blaming everybody for that but me. Which is why I keep going off on you. So, again, I'm sorry." He finished the beer and set the empty bottle down on the porch.

Jolene was silent for a while. She took another sip of her beer, and said, "If this is what one beer does to you, you ought never to drink."

"Good advice." He stood.

She looked down at the bottle in her hand. She said, "Willis's dad, Bobby, he liked the Charlie Daniels Band. He was a redneck, like you, and a Marine. He died in Afghanistan. Sometimes listening to the music makes me feel like he's still here."

Buck nodded silently in the dark. "See you at work, Jolene. And welcome to the neighborhood."

She did not reply as she watched him walk to his truck and get in.

After a minute or two, Jolene's mother came out, cushioning the creak of the screen door with her hand. When she glanced around, Jolene could see the flowers he'd brought arranged in a Mason jar on the occasional table by the door. "Seems like a nice young fellow," her mother observed benevolently.

Jolene shrugged and picked up the toy police car he'd brought for Willis, running its tires absently across the floorboard of the porch. "I guess."

"Pretty manners," her mother added. "Not bad to look at, either."

Again Jolene shrugged, focusing on the way the blue light

atop the toy car lit up when she got the tires to spinning. Willis was going to love that. "Hadn't noticed."

"You crushing on that white boy, Jojo?"

Jolene looked up and frowned at the teasing light in her mother's eyes. She stuffed the empty beer bottles back into the six-pack he'd brought and got to her feet, but probably not quickly enough to hide her expression. "Don't talk crazy, Mama. I hardly know the man. I'm not sure I even like him. I know he doesn't like me. He was just being nice. Good office relations, all that. Besides, he's still hung up on his ex."

Her mother folded her arms over her chest, looking amused. "That's a lot of explaining when a simple 'no' would do."

Jolene moved past her, jerking open the screen door. "I've got to help Willis with his bath before he floods the whole house."

Her mother called after her, "Well I'm glad you've made a nice friend for yourself."

"He's not my friend," Jolene returned and let the screen door slam.

But six hours later she was organizing a blood drive to save his life and obsessing over the bullet she was going to put between the eyes of the man who'd shot him, and she was starting think that might not be strictly true.

Six months later she had him pressed up against a wall, tearing at the buttons of his shirt in such a white-hot passion that she ripped off more buttons than she saved. So did he. It was the best sex of her life.

Six months after that, she was actually considering marrying the man.

Life was strange.

CHAPTER EIGHT

"A house?" Jo said when he'd finished the story. "He left you a *house*?"

"And a fish," Buck clarified.

"Why?"

Buck said, "I don't know."

"You're supposed to be a detective," she pointed out. Her tone was a little acerbic. "Don't you think that's something you should be curious about?"

"Absolutely." He rubbed his eyes, trying to clear away the fog. He added, "It's a nice house. Big yard out back. And a river. Do you know how much houses on the river cost?"

"No."

"A lot. More than you and I together could afford, that's for sure, even with what they're paying me here. Your mother would like it."

"My mother," she repeated in a careful tone. "My *mother* would like living in a plantation house? That would be the same mother who marched on Washington and made my dad drive five hours out of his way on a family vacation just to show me the church Dr. Martin Luther King, Jr. preached in?"

"In the first place," Buck replied patiently, "your mother was eight years old during the march on Washington and she never pretended otherwise. In the second place, it's not a plantation house. Just a big old antebellum house with creaky floors and lots of windows." He smothered a yawn. "And porches. She'd like it."

"What's the kitchen like?"

"Yellow."

She replied dryly, "I'll tell her." Then she added, "Do you want to know what I think?"

"I always want to know what you think."

"I think that woman, the mayor, knows more about what happened to the former chief than she's letting on. And I think she's spent the past week either trying to figure out how much to tell you or trying to cover up the truth."

He thought about that for a moment. "You know something? I'm so tired that almost makes sense." He hesitated, then added, "I was upset when I left. I said some things. I'm sorry."

"You should be." Then she conceded with obvious reluctance, "I guess I said some things too."

He smiled to himself. The only thing she hated worse than being wrong was admitting it. "And?"

"Oh, all right, I guess I'm sorry too," she returned impatiently. "Kind of."

That made him chuckle. "Music to my ears."

She added uncomfortably, "It's just that I have this thing about…"

"About people leaving you," Buck supplied gently. "I know. And I really am sorry it went down this way, Jo."

She said softly, "I know."

They were quiet for a moment, at ease with each other. Then he said, "How's my guy?"

"He was digging a fire pit in the backyard when I left for work, like you taught him." She sounded disgruntled. "You and your damn backwoods skills. He insisted on eating his eggs out of a tin cup this morning. Next thing I know he'll be eating grubs out of the dirt like that guy we saw on TV."

Buck couldn't prevent a grin. "For the record, I didn't tell anybody to dig a fire pit in the backyard. But don't make him cover it up, okay? He worked hard on it. Just hide the matches and tell him to text me a picture."

Now it was her turn to pause, and when she spoke her voice was sober. "He wants to know when you're coming home."

He sighed and rubbed hand over his eyes. "Tell him I'll call him tonight."

"I'm not going to do that. Soldiers and first responders don't make promises about things they can't control."

That was another thing of hers. There was no point in arguing. "I keep my promises," he said anyway.

"Buck Lawson two-point-oh?" He could almost see the dry downturn of her lips.

"That's right."

"Last I heard that version was still in beta."

"Yeah, but early results look promising."

"I'll tell Willis you called."

"Tell him I miss him," Buck said, "and that I'm proud of him."

"That I can do." Her voice softened a fraction as she added almost tenderly, "Get some sleep, before you get so punch drunk you do something stupid."

"Like what?"

"Like deciding to stay there."

He pushed a hand through his hair and sighed. "I'm the chief of police," he replied heavily. Until he spoke the words out loud, the weight of it hadn't really hit him. "I think that means I kind of *have* to stay here."

After a long time she said, sadly, "Yeah. Well."

To which he replied, "Love you."

And she answered, "You, too."

They disconnected, and Buck sat there alone for a long time, feeling the heat, and the silence, and the oppressive strangeness of the place that surrounded him. Then he gathered himself, locked up the house, and left.

―――

He took another couple of Motrin for the ache in his leg and walked back across the street to the police station. He had intended only to pick up his truck and drive to the Comfort Inn, where he'd take Jo's advice and try to catch a few hours' sleep. Instead, he found himself pushing open the door of the station and going inside.

The air-conditioning hit the film of sweat on his skin and gave him chills. The woman at the desk glanced up from her telephone conversation, murmured, "Hold just one moment," and smiled at him. "Good morning Chief Lawson," she said.

"Good morning…" He read her name tag. "Stephanie." He gestured toward the metal door that led to the administrative offices. "Do I need a pass?"

"No, sir, you're all set. Lydia has your paperwork waiting for you. I'll just let her know you're here."

She turned back to her telephone, and he said, "Thanks,

Stephanie." He even managed to give her a weary smile as he pushed through the metal door.

The sheriff's office in Hanover County was a much smaller, more utilitarian space than Mercy's police station, with fewer offices and far fewer employees. During the brief time that he'd held the office of sheriff, he'd never once picked up the phone to summon his AA; a shout was all it had ever took. But behind that metal door was a busy, brightly lit hub of ringing phones, whirring office machines, and purposeful-looking civilian employees. Private offices for the police chief, his administrative assistant, the assistant chief, and investigators were arranged on either side of a large open space that held several computer stations, a wall-mounted television set tuned to an all-news station with the volume muted, filing cabinets, copy machines, and a few nicely cared for potted plants.

A woman carrying a large manilla envelope and a notebook met him as soon as he came through the door. "Good morning, Chief Lawson," she said briskly. "I'm Lydia Browning, your administrative assistant. We met when you were here before."

He remembered being introduced to her in February; he just hadn't made the connection between this young, crisply attractive woman and the person everyone seemed to imply virtually ran the police department. She was probably younger than he was, with a short black bob and oversized glasses, a firm mouth, and a cool, no-nonsense demeanor. She wore one of those blouses with a floppy bow at the neck, and a dark pencil skirt that complemented her hourglass figure. She also wore a wedding ring. When he extended his hand, she shook it firmly. He liked that.

"Yes, of course," he said. "It's good to see you again. I look forward to working with you."

She replied, "The same here, sir. If you'll come with me, I'll introduce you to your staff. This is Darryl from IT; he'll help you get your computer set up. Marion is our file clerk, Helen, your officer liaison…"

He shook hands with a circle of faces whose names he knew he had very little chance of remembering and followed Lydia's clacking Cuban heels across the linoleum to the closed door of the office upon which was stenciled, Chief of Police. She held the door open for him.

"Mayor Watts sent word that you are of course to choose whatever furnishings suit you and invoice the city. I'll set up an appointment with the decorator from Aikens Furniture for later this week."

Buck followed her inside, looking around cautiously. "I'm really not that particular."

"Yes, sir." She marched over to the window and opened the blinds, revealing a room that was plainly but comfortably furnished with a big oak desk, two club chairs for visitors, and a plaid sofa that looked as though it had provided a fine nap or two over the years. A United States flag and a Georgia state flag stood beside the desk and, displayed behind glass on the adjacent wall, was the emblem of the City of Mercy police force. There was a big framed map and a bookcase with matching leather-bound volumes about government and law enforcement on one wall, and beside it a row of photographs of former police chiefs dating back to the beginning of the twentieth century. The last one was a much younger-looking Billy. It occurred to Buck that his photograph would be next in line. The most striking feature, and one Buck remembered from his previous visit to the office, was the head of an alligator, mouth open and teeth gleaming, that was mounted behind the desk. Buck remembered thinking at the time he didn't know how a man could work with that thing looking down on him.

In the center of the desk was a nameplate that read Buck Lawson. He wondered how they had gotten it here so quickly, but then he realized it must have been ordered weeks ago, when he'd first accepted the offer. Everyone, including Buck himself, had been preparing for this transition since March. They just hadn't expected it to come so soon. Or to come like this.

"You have a private bathroom," Lydia went on, opening the door to a bathroom that, while small, was big enough to contain a shower.

Buck lifted an eyebrow. "Sweet. Wish I'd known about that before I shaved in the upstairs men's room this morning."

She didn't smile. "Yes, sir." She crossed the room and opened another door. "This leads to my office. Feel free to ask for anything you need. You can also reach me by dialing 'one' on your desk phone. I work from 8:00 until 5:00 weekdays. Marion takes over my desk during my lunch hour, which is noon to 1:00. If you need me to stay late, I'm pleased to do so, but I'd appreciate at least an hour's notice."

He tried once again to get her to smile. "Husband waiting at home?"

"Wife," she corrected without expression.

"Right," he said, amusement fading. "Sorry."

"On your desk is the report you requested from Captain Sullivan this morning," she said, and placed the envelope she was carrying on his desk beside the tabbed folder. "In here you'll find your badge, your parking pass, and your department phone preprogrammed with all the numbers you'll need. You'll also find your employment papers and insurance forms, which I'll need you to complete and return to me no later than tomorrow noon so that we can add you to the payroll for this pay period. When you're ready, I'll walk you down to the armory where the sergeant will issue your service weapon. The motor pool will assign your car, just dial three on your desk phone and someone will bring it around. I suggest you meet with Darryl first and get logged into the system. Shall I send him in?"

He looked at her for a moment, trying to remember who Darryl was, and then blinked. "Lydia," he said with an effort, "I appreciate all your hard work. This is all very... organized. But I've been awake since 6:00 a.m. yesterday and it's all I can do to keep from seeing two of you. Could you just give me a minute?"

"Of course, sir. Do you still take your coffee black with one sugar?"

She had served him coffee once three months ago. He wasn't about to ask how she had remembered that. He nodded slowly, and she made a note on the pad she carried.

"Also," she said, "in your top desk drawer you'll find a collection of take-out menus that the former chief found helpful. If you'd like to make your selection now, I'll go ahead and place your lunch order. Or I can send someone across the street to the sandwich shop, if you prefer. Chief Aikens was particularly fond of their BLT."

He was about to say that he didn't expect to be here through lunch, but then he noticed the sudden mirror-sheen of tears in her eyes behind the glasses and the pinkening of her nose. He said quietly, "Lydia, I am so damn sorry it happened like this. I'm not going to pretend to know how you feel. You worked for Billy a long time. If you need a few days off, I understand."

She lifted her chin, banishing the tears with a single blink. "Thank you, sir. I'm fine." She turned to leave, and then glanced back. "You should look at the menus," she advised simply, and crossed the room to her office, closing the door quietly behind her.

Buck moved around the desk and sat down in the worn leather office chair that was clearly molded to someone else's body. He could feel the beady eyes of the alligator looking over his shoulder. He absently moved the mouse of his computer, but nothing came up on the screen but the police department logo. He flipped open the file folder on his desk and the first things he saw were the crime scene photos: Billy's body after it had been pulled from the river. He closed his eyes, and the folder.

He leaned back in the chair and slid open the top drawer of the desk. Inside were an unopened package of felt-tipped pens, a legal pad, and the menus Lydia had promised—Chinese food, pizza, barbecue, Denny's, Chick-fil-A. On top of them was a sealed envelope with his name written on it in bold black script: Buck Lawson.

Buck slit open the envelope with his thumbnail and unfolded the single sheet of paper that was inside. The letter was handwritten with a black felt-tip pen in the same confident hand that had scrawled his name on the envelope. It was dated May 3, three weeks earlier.

Dear Buck,

I read somewhere that every time a US president leaves office, he writes a letter to the incoming fellow, turning over the reins and welcoming him on board. God knows I'm no Commander in Chief, but I thought it was a nice tradition. Welcome aboard, Buck. I hope this town will be as good to you as it has been to me.

In this job you're going to have some good days, some bad days, and some very bad days. You know that. You're going to have to make some tough decisions, the unpopular kind, and sometimes even the kind you don't sit easy with in your own bones. Maybe you'll have to choose between the greater good and the lesser evil more often than you'd like. These are the times we live in. This is the job that was given to us. Don't be a hero. Play the long game. Keep your priorities straight.

I hope I'm not leaving you too big a mess. I've got a few things to clear away before you take over; we'll be talking about that before I leave. I'll get out of your hair for a few weeks while I visit my daughter in Maryland, and give you a chance to settle into the job, but I want you to know I'm only a phone call away. There's nothing I wouldn't do for this town. In time, I hope you'll come to feel the same way.

Welcome home, Buck—
Billy Aikens

Buck took in a deep breath and blew it out. "God damn, Billy," he whispered. "God damn."

He folded the paper and returned it to its envelope. Then he sat forward and opened the homicide file on Billy Aikens.

CHAPTER NINE

Buck turned over the last page of the report, frowning, and closed the folder. He sucked in a breath to call for Lydia, then realized that, based on what he had seen so far, that probably was not the way they did things here. He'd just picked up the receiver of his desk phone and was searching for the intercom button she'd told him about when there was a light tap on his door and she entered with a big mug of coffee.

"I'm sorry it took so long," she said, setting the mug on his desk. "We made a fresh pot."

"Lydia," he said, "I need to see my investigative team right away. And can you get me a copy of the duty roster for the upcoming month?" He picked up the coffee mug and took a sip. "This is good coffee," he said surprised. "Thanks. I also need to set up interviews with each of the officers starting tomorrow. Who do I talk to about that?"

She was jotting notes on her pad. "I'll take care of it, sir."

He took another sip of coffee, starting to feel more like himself. "I want to touch base with everyone on the force before the end of the week, and I'll need to see their personnel files before the interview. And can you get that lawyer—what's his name? Jefferies? Do you know who I'm talking about? I think he handled Chief Aikens's estate. Can you get him on the phone?"

"Right away, sir. You'll be able to access the personnel files from your desktop, as well as the duty rosters, past and present, as soon as you're set up. Shall I send Darryl in to get you started?"

Buck frowned. He knew IT guys; once you let them in the door you could kiss your afternoon—or your morning, as it happened—goodbye. "Yeah," he said, "As soon as I finish with the detectives."

He had spent the last month studying the Mercy Police Department's employee handbook—as well as the city charter and ordinances, policy and procedures, and even the Georgia Code, when he had time. He knew his investigative team consisted of two detectives, which was plenty for a town this size that mostly prosecuted shoplifting, domestic violence, and minor drug charges. Francine Moreno had signed off as lead investigator on Billy's case, but her partner Craig Teller had done most of the interviews. Buck was not particularly pleased when, a few seconds later, Lydia opened his door and said, "Detective Francine Moreno, Chief Lawson"—and Craig Teller was not with her.

Francine Moreno was a short, square woman with a plain face and no makeup. Her curly mouse-brown hair was cut in a practical, if unattractive style, short behind the ears and longer on top. She wore a blue Oxford shirt and tan slacks that reminded Buck, unaccountably, of a retail store uniform. She carried a slim file folder in her hand, much like the one he had open on his desk.

He stood and she crossed the room to shake his hand. She had a firm grip. "It's a pleasure to meet you, Chief. I'm sorry Craig isn't here. There was a robbery this morning at a convenience store and he's interviewing witnesses."

She delivered this information in a perfectly deadpan manner, and Buck regarded her curiously, uncertain whether or not she was being facetious. "He might have started with me."

"Yes, sir." Still deadpan.

He gestured her to be seated as Lydia left the room, closing the door behind herself. Buck took a sip of his coffee and settled back in the chair, studying her for a moment. "So, Detective Moreno…"

"Frankie," she volunteered. "People call me Frankie."

He nodded, keeping his expression as pleasant as possible. "Okay, Frankie. Sully seems to think that the convenience store robbery was an inside job. That the owner—I think his name is Dash?—set it up for one of his relatives to rob the place as kind of a cash bonus."

She nodded. "That's what it appears to be, yes, sir. We arrested…" she opened her file folder and checked a paper inside. "Farhan Singh, age twenty-five, nephew of the store owner, Daksh Patel, and a former employee. We recovered $5,683 stolen from the property, still in the original bank bags."

Buck frowned. "Five thousand? I thought Sully said eight thousand."

She checked her paper again. "He may have misunderstood, sir. This is what we recovered, and this is what Mr. Patel reported stolen. I have his signed statement." She took a paper from the file and passed it to him.

Buck glanced down at the typed statement and murmured,

"Maybe I heard him wrong." He was certain he had not. He returned the statement to her. "Does Mr. Patel read English?" he asked.

She blinked. "Well, of course. He runs a business."

"A lot of people run businesses who can't read in their own language," Buck pointed out, "much less a foreign one. You should have asked before you had him sign this statement. And I don't see anything here about who turned off the security camera."

She tucked the statement back into her folder, stiffening her shoulders. "I don't understand."

"Why would Patel turn off the security camera if it was an inside job? He needed the camera to corroborate his story that he was robbed."

Her lips tightened, but she had no reply.

Buck picked up his coffee mug, sipping from it, watching her. "So is this how you investigate, then? The officer on the scene decides who's guilty, and you work backward from there trying to prove it, ignoring any evidence that might get in the way?"

He could see her trying to hide her resentment, and her unease, and doing a pretty poor job of both. She forced something resembling a smile. "This is a small town. We almost always have a suspect in mind as soon as the crime is committed, and we're almost always right. Sometimes we might miss dotting an 'i' or crossing a 't,' but we always get our man."

Buck put down the coffee cup and opened the folder before him. "Explain to me how you knew it was Carl Tucker who killed Chief Aikens, because I'm having a hard time figuring it out from what I see here. You've got a statement from the witness who found the car, but no report from the first officers on the scene. You've got an interview with Carl

Tucker who says he hadn't seen Billy since Billy arrested him three days previously, and a corroborating statement from Tucker's wife. There should be a copy of that arrest report here. I don't see any witness statements from neighbors who might have seen Tucker leave his house that day. So tell me again how you came to suspect Carl Tucker."

The ruby stain that crept across her cheeks was not attractive. She said, "We have fingerprint evidence and a ballistic match on the gun. Those reports are in the file."

"Witnesses to testify to the time Tucker left the house and the time he returned?" Buck prompted, flipping a page. "I don't see anything here. What about his clothes? Were they taken into evidence? Did the bloodstains match the victim?"

A muscle knotted in her jaw, but she said, "We found a pair of work gloves at the scene, as you'll see on the evidence list. We believe the perpetrator used those to transport the victim to the water. We didn't find any bloodstained clothing, but we weren't able to obtain a search warrant until forty-eight hours after the shooting. There should be a report to that effect. I'll take care of that right away and make sure it's included in the file. Along with this." She opened the folder in her lap and took out a sheet of paper, passing it to him.

"What's this?" Buck glanced at the paper.

"It's Carl Tucker's confession," she said. "It came in this morning."

Buck sat forward and read the statement with interest. According to it, Carl Tucker had been out crabbing off the abandoned pier at Lost Creek when Billy spotted him and started hassling him about a fishing license. Carl had his pistol with him for copperheads, which were notorious for nesting under the pier, and his work gloves for stacking the crabs in the cooler. He'd been drinking beer all day and it was hot and he was still mad at Billy for dragging him off to jail the other day over a fight he'd had with his wife. So when Billy started threatening to write Carl a ticket for a fine he couldn't afford they got into an argument. Billy walked back to his car to get his ticket book and Carl picked up his gun, which was lying on top of the cooler, and shot him in the head. He dragged the body to the creek and threw his weapon in the weeds, along with his gloves, which were covered in blood. Then he walked home, approximately a mile away.

Buck looked up at the detective. "This is part of a plea deal?"

She nodded. "Apparently the prosecutor and Carl's attorney worked it out over the weekend. Life with parole after thirty."

Georgia was a death penalty state. That was a damn good deal for killing a police officer. He said, "Prosecutors don't usually make a deal like that if they think they can prove their case."

She knew that. The knot that reappeared in her jaw told him so.

"Frankie," Buck said, not unkindly. "Did you conduct any interviews with any of these witnesses?"

Her nostrils flared with a quick breath. "No, sir, I did not."

"Did you sit in on any of them?"

"No."

"Yet you signed off on everything."

"Detective Teller and I have found it usually works best if he handles the legwork and I do the paperwork."

Buck nodded and leaned back in his chair again, drumming his fingers on the open file folder. "Somebody didn't do a very good job this time. It's hard to tell who that was."

She said, "Chief Lawson, I'm sorry the file is incomplete.

I'll rectify that immediately. But Carl Tucker is guilty, everyone knows he's guilty, and now he's confessed to being guilty. This is a good outcome."

Buck regarded her silently for a moment, then closed the folder and slid it across the desk to her. "Get this case file in shape and make sure a copy is on my desk first thing tomorrow morning. And Detective," he added as she took the folder and stood. "Never try to cover for a sloppy colleague. It's a good way to ruin a career."

The dark red stripes across her cheeks had almost faded, but now they grew bright again. She said, "Yes, sir." But just before she reached the door she turned back, her shoulders square.

"I'm a good detective, Chief Lawson," she said, lifting her chin. "I just need a chance to prove it."

She turned and left the room before he had a chance to reply.

Buck rubbed his fingers over his eyes and picked up his mug again. He took a deep gulp and then called, "Lydia!"

She was there almost before the last syllable left his mouth. "Ken Jefferies is on line one," she said. He must have looked confused, because she added, "The lawyer."

"Right," he said. "Thank you." He held out the mug. "Is there any more...?"

"Right away, sir."

She swept the mug away and was gone before he could even find the button on his phone that connected him to Ken Jefferies.

"Chief Lawson!" the voice boomed genially as soon as Buck identified himself. "I didn't expect to hear from you today. I was going to have my girl set up a meeting next week, after you'd settled in. Maybe lunch at the White Horse Inn? Or, tell you what, even better, do you play golf?"

Buck admitted that he did not.

"Well, if you ever decide to learn, my club is just a twenty-minute drive outside town and the pro there is top-rate. He'll fix you right up—equipment, lessons, the works. First year's membership is free for city officials."

"That's good to know," Buck said. "Listen, what I was calling about..."

"Right." His tone sobered. "I guess the Carl Tucker plea deal hit your desk this morning. Hell of a way to start your first week. You'll be getting calls from the press—no matter how hard you try to keep these things quiet, something always leaks. But the official word is we have no comment until the judge gives us a preliminary approval on the deal. That might come as soon as Wednesday. Then I figured we'd hold a press conference—you, me, Lyle Brighton from the DA's office. Will that give you enough time to get up to speed?"

Buck cursed himself for letting Frankie walk out of the office with the case file. "I'm sorry," he said. "I only had a minute to glance over the file. You're representing Tucker?"

"Actually, Dobie Jones is the attorney of record, a junior associate here. He does most of our pro-bono work, and just about all the criminal cases, not that we get that many. Damn smart kid. And I'll tell you, Chief, he did a hell of a job for that no account piece of swamp trash Tucker. Most folks around here would have gone to his hanging and thrown rocks at his corpse. And that's another reason we want to control the narrative on this, if you get my drift. More emphasis on the confession, less on the fact that he's sliding out of the death penalty."

"Right," Buck murmured. He scribbled the name *Dobie Jones* on one of the freshly opened legal pads. "Is Tucker still being held in county detention?"

"For the time being," Jefferies said. "Private cell, TV, catered meals." He sounded bitter. "That'll change as soon as we set a hearing date and the judge pronounces sentence. He's off to Reidsville."

Buck said, "Okay, thanks."

"You bet. We'll do that lunch. I'll let the girls work it out."

Buck was about to hang up when he remembered what he had actually called Jefferies about. "Say, wait. I need to ask you something. Mayor Watts said that Billy wanted me to have that big mounted marlin that hangs in his study. Said he even put a codicil in his will."

Jefferies chuckled with rueful affection. "That Billy could be a character, all right. He said you'd understand when you got here."

"I was wondering if you remembered when he did that. Changed his will, I mean."

"I can look up the exact date for you. But I recall it was only a few days before he died, less than a week. It always gives me a chill when something like that happens—a man comes in to change his will, and a few days later, he's gone. Almost like they had a premonition or something."

"Right," Buck murmured. "Or something."

When they hung up, Buck slid open the drawer of his desk again and unfolded Billy's letter. It was dated May 3. On May 3, Billy was looking forward to retirement and an easy transfer of power. The next week, he was making plans to die. Buck read over the letter again. "… a few things I have to take care of…" he'd said. Was one of those things the one that had gotten him killed? And had Billy known it might?

"Damn it, Billy," Buck whispered.

There was a light tap on his door and Lydia entered, placing another steaming mug of coffee at his elbow. "Darryl is waiting," she said. "Shall I send him in?"

Buck slid the drawer closed and looked up at her, forcing a smile. "Absolutely," he said, and picked up his mug. "Let's get this party started."

CHAPTER TEN

Passwords. Security codes. Spreadsheets. Payroll forms. Service weapon. Office keys. Building keys. Facebook profile. Twitter profile. Emergency authorization codes. By three thirty Buck had everything except the personal cell phone number of the president of the United States, and he had to double-check to make sure someone hadn't forgotten to give him that. He used to think "drunk with power" was a metaphor. He now knew it was a perfectly accurate description of what happened when a person was given too much responsibility with too little preparation and far too little sleep. If he had been a patrol officer at a bar, he would have taken his own keys. The fact that this random thought made perfect sense to him was exactly why he needed to get out of there.

As soon as Darryl left, Buck turned off the computer, gathered up his phones, keys, and passes, and poked his head inside Lydia's door. "I'm calling it a day," he said. "Do I lock up or do you?"

"I'll take care of it," she replied, as she had done perhaps a dozen times that day. She took a sheet of paper from her desk and offered it to him. "Do you want to see your schedule for tomorrow?"

"No."

She tucked the paper back into its folder. "I'll e-mail it to you."

"I won't read it."

"Have a good evening, Chief." She turned back to her computer.

He leaned against the doorframe, gathering his strength for departure. "I probably shouldn't have come in today," he said.

"Probably not," she agreed.

"Well." He pushed away from the door. "Thanks for all your help. If you need me…" He hesitated, and finished, "Don't need me."

He started to leave, and then looked back. "Oh, and Lydia…"

She glanced up.

"Can you call somebody about getting rid of that…" He jerked his thumb over his shoulder at the alligator leering from the wall behind his desk. "Thing?"

He might have imagined it, but he thought she looked relieved. She picked up the telephone receiver. "Dialing, sir."

"Thanks."

"Chief," she said.

When he glanced back she was actually smiling. More or less.

"Good first day," she said.

He smiled back wearily and left.

The inside of his truck, which had been sitting in the sun all day, was like a blast oven when he opened the door. He knew he wasn't going to make it to the Comfort Inn, so he took the left, and then the right onto Magnolia Avenue. The air-conditioning hadn't even had a chance to cool the cab before he pulled into the gravel driveway beside the historic Aikens House, built in 1853.

He was too tired to try to figure out which one of the keys on the ring Corinne had given him fit the garage, so he left his truck in the driveway and carried his duffel, his laptop, and his cooler across the short path between the hedges to the house. He entered through the kitchen, where the air-conditioning enveloped him like a spring-fed lake. It got hot in the mountains, but this kind of heat was going to take him some time to get used to.

He left his things on the floor and splashed cold water on his face, drying off with a paper towel. Then he took a beer from the slush of ice water in his cooler and a chicken leg from the platter in the refrigerator and went back out onto the screened porch. Immediately he regretted the decision. The muggy air was almost too thick to breathe and the smell from the river made him wrinkle his nose. He finished off half the beer in one long draw. He found a switch on the wall that turned on an overhead fan, but that only stirred the hot air into a soup. Nonetheless, he did not have the ambition to go back inside, and he was hungry enough that even the river smell didn't dampen his appetite. He sat in one of the rocking chairs and finished off the chicken leg and the beer while staring mindlessly out at the shadowed riverbank. A white bird swooped in from nowhere while he watched, dived down behind the trees, and came up a moment later with a fish in its beak. That almost made him smile, thinking about how much Willis would have loved that.

He took out his phone, selected video chat, and called home. It rang for almost a minute before the image of a grinning little boy with corkscrew curls and dancing eyes appeared, exclaiming, "Buck!" The image wobbled as he called over his shoulder, "Mama Eloise! Look, it's Buck!"

Buck had given Willis the iPad for Christmas, even though Jolene hadn't approved and was still—in Buck's opinion—too strict with her son's screen time. He hadn't known then that this might someday be the only way the two of them could see each other, or that it would matter so very much that they did.

Willis's grandmother appeared upside-down in the frame. "Hi, sweetheart! Good to see you safe and sound. Was it a bad trip?"

Buck said, "It was fine. It's hot here, but the people are nice. They left fried chicken and potato salad in my refrigerator. And," he added, remembering, "a lemon meringue pie."

"What kind?" she demanded suspiciously. Still upside down. "Shortbread crust or graham cracker?"

"I haven't had a chance to check," he admitted, "but I know it's not as good as yours."

"It'd better not be." He could hear the smile in her voice, even though she pretended to be stern. "But I'm glad you got there safe, Buck. I worry about you, you know, all by yourself."

Buck started to reply, but Willis called, "My turn!" and his image replaced that of Eloise.

"You take care, Buck!" she called.

Buck told Willis, "Tell your grandma I'll call her."

Willis shouted, "He says he'll call you!" The screen began

to bounce and sway wildly with his running steps as he cried, "Buck, look what I did! Wait'll you see!"

Buck, who a moment ago had been too exhausted to lift his head, was wide awake and laughing softly to himself as he watched the six-year-old's progress through the familiar rooms of the house. The screen door opened and slammed, and Buck heard Eloise call, "Jeremiah Wilson Smith, what did I tell you about slamming that door?"

"Yes, ma'am!" Willis called. "I'm sorry!"

He turned around, and Buck got a view of a pair of scuffed child's sneakers as he heard the screen door creak open and close again, more softly this time. Buck laughed out loud. God, he loved those people. And missed them.

Willis's image bounced down the back steps and across the yard, past a blurred tilted tricycle and half a plastic fort, coming to rest at last on a pile of stones and mud that Buck could only assume was Willis's version of a fire pit.

"Wow, buddy," he said, admiring it. "That must have taken you all day. Good job, my man!" He raised his palm for a high five ad Willis, grinning, slapped the camera.

"Mama Eloise said we can roast marshmallows tonight if Mom says it's okay, just like we did in the woods. Gosh, Buck, that was fun. When can we go back?"

"That was fun," Buck agreed, although he felt hollow at the thought of how long it might be before he and Willis went camping in the Nantahala again. "One of the best times I've ever had. But, hey, you know what? We've got so many fun things lined up to do it might be a while before we make it back to the woods. I mean, you don't want to just do the same thing over and over again, right?"

Willis's expression fell. The camera bounced as he sat down hard on the grass. He gave a sorrowful shake of his head and pronounced solemnly, "It doesn't look like I'll be doing many fun things any time soon, Buck."

Willis—so nicknamed by his father before he was even born—was one of those kids over whom adults shook their heads in delight and confusion, an old soul in a miniature body, a wonder and a phenomenon. Named for Jolene's father, Jeremiah Smith, a firehouse captain who had died on 9/11, and his own father, Bobby Wilson, who had died in Afghanistan three weeks before his deployment ended, Willis had a tendency to take life very seriously. Buck thought the best gift Bobby had given his son was the nickname; it reminded him to smile.

Buck said, matching his somber tone, "Uh-oh. How come?"

Willis sighed heavily. "Mom says I have to go to Vacation Bible School. She says I need to spend more time with boys my age."

"Oh, yeah? And you don't think so?"

He shrugged.

Buck asked carefully, "Don't you like the other boys, Willis? Are they mean to you?"

"Nah, they're okay." He poked at the ground with a stick and added ingenuously, "They know my mom's a cop."

Buck grinned. "Well, I loved Vacation Bible School when I was a kid. We had peanut butter and jelly sandwiches for lunch every day and built an ark out of popsicle sticks. Maybe you should give it a try."

He said glumly, "It lasts two weeks."

"That's not very long."

Willis looked at him with big, anxious eyes. "When are you coming home, Buck?"

Buck did not believe in deceiving kids, even if that was

sometimes the easiest—or even the kindest—thing to do. He admitted, "That's a tough one, bud. I've got some things to do here that can't be put off. I don't know how long it will take."

Willis sounded worried. "Are they very big?"

"Are what very big?"

"The dragons," he replied. "Mom said you were off fighting dragons like heroes always do. I heard her telling Mama Eloise. She was crying when she said it."

Buck could barely prevent the grimace of pain that he felt from showing on his face. He had made Jolene cry. She was the strongest woman he had ever known, and he had made her cry. He had promised to bring her nothing but comfort, protection, and contentment. Instead, he had broken her heart.

He said a little gruffly, "No, my man, they're not very big. I'll have them whipped into shape before you know it."

Willis answered in a small voice, "My dad was a hero. And he died."

Buck sucked in a breath. The headache that had been threatening all day was more than a promise now. "Willis," he said firmly, "listen to me. I'm not a hero, and I'm not going to die. Not this time around, anyway."

Willis said tentatively, "You promise?"

In the back of his head he could hear Jolene, who had kissed her father goodbye one morning before school and had never seen him again, saying, *First responders don't make promises about things they can't control.* He ignored the voice determinedly. "I promise. I'm going to see you real soon, and when I do, guess what we're going to do? Go fishing."

Willis brightened. "In a boat?"

"I think that can be arranged." He added, "But listen, before you set up that marshmallow-roasting party, you need to check the burn conditions for tonight. You can do it online. Here's how. Ready?"

"Ready!" Willis declared.

Buck spent the next few minutes walking him through the website, aching to be there in person, showing him. It shouldn't have happened like this. Damn it. It shouldn't have.

Eventually he said, "Listen, little dude. I've got to go. I've got a big day tomorrow and so do you." At Willis's crestfallen expression he added fiercely, "Hey. Who are you?"

Willis puffed out his chest, threw back his shoulders, and replied, "My name is Jeremiah Wilson Smith, and I'm a heck of a boy."

Buck grinned and held up his closed hand for a fist bump. "Yeah, you are."

Willis punched the screen with his fist.

Buck's chest tightened, almost beyond the point of normal breathing. He said, "I love you, bud. And I'm proud to know you."

Willis grinned back. "I'm proud to know you too, Buck. Bye."

Buck stared at the blank screen until his forced smile faded into a bleakness so empty that even looking at his reflection on the screen made him depressed. Then he got up, put the phone away, and walked across the yard to the river, waving away clouds of gnats as he went.

Where he came from, rivers were wild and noisy, accessed via steep banks and big boulders. Here the land sloped so gently toward the river that it was barely noticeable. He walked down a short, mulched path flanked by purple hydrangeas that led from the lawn to the river, and there he was, standing on a wooden pier and looking out over a dark green mirror of wide, still water. The river was much broader than he had expected, maybe a quarter of a mile across, and the opposite shore was lined with nothing but cypress and marsh brush. The pier extended about twenty-five feet into the water and he walked the length of it, finding the gnats were less bothersome there. It was a little cooler, too. There was a bench there, perfect for watching the sunset or sitting and holding a fishing pole, but Buck did not take advantage of it. To his left he could see part of a neighboring pier, and to his right a portion of a boathouse, although both were too far away to really be called neighbors. Somewhere in the distance a trolling motor droned, and closer by, some kind of bird squawked. Otherwise, it was silent. Beneath him, the water was so still it looked as though it had been painted onto the ground. Even in the middle of the day with the sun shining somewhere overhead, the place felt desolate. Buck turned and started back toward the house.

Just as he stepped off the pier onto the mulched path, he spotted an unwelcome shape coiled up under a hydrangea bush a few feet away. He stopped dead, staring at it. The snake returned his stare with mean, beady eyes and rattled its tail in low warning.

"Sorry, man," Buck muttered, his heart pounding from the surprise, "but I'm having a really bad day. And you picked the wrong damn yard to crawl into."

He drew his Glock from its holster and blew the snake's head off.

From the Diary of The Marsh Dragon
May 1, 2021

When I was a little kid, I heard a story—or maybe I saw it on a cartoon—about this sleeping dragon. The great thing about sleeping dragons is that you never know when they might strike. When they're asleep, they're easy to overlook, just part of the landscape, fading into the scenery, snoring away. People down in the village forgot about them. They went about their paltry little lives, plowing fields, raising kids, herding sheep, going to the market and thinking everything was just fine until one day, *pow!* The dragon woke up. And when he woke up, he woke up hungry. He was ready to rain down a world of hurt, and rain he did. The people of the village who thought their plain, quiet little lives would go on being plain and quiet forever… well, they were wrong.

That is, of course, the beauty and the cleverness of dragons, and the reason they're so hard to destroy. They're unpredictable. They never fall into a pattern. Most of the time they're sleeping in plain sight, but they're never found where you think they'd be. And you never know what might wake them up. Could be a pair of headlights, moving down an empty road in the dead of night. Could be a pair of pretty green eyes, looking back at you from a Facebook photo. Could be a smart-ass word from a hard-mouthed woman. Could be just about anything.

Some folks say that alligators are the descendants of prehistoric dragons. Maybe they're right. Wouldn't that be something? The old swamp gator, come down from a line of fire-breathing earth-scorchers. It makes sense, in a way. Who would suspect a muddy old alligator is really a sleeping dragon? They just lie there all day just beneath the surface of the water, looking just like a log or a shadow, snoozing away… until they're not.

I like to think about that when I'm standing on the bank, tossing pieces of meat to them, watching how they strike the surface, lightning quick. Man, it's something to see.

They like the fingers best.

CHAPTER ELEVEN

Hanover County, North Carolina
Five months earlier

"Georgia?" Jolene had repeated incredulously when Buck first told her about the job opening. "But you hate Georgia!"

He shrugged it away. "I don't hate it."

"You're all the time talking about how stupid those Georgia boys are and how you can't trust a thing they say."

He scowled uncomfortably. "A few dumb cops. But the state itself has never done anything to me."

She'd let it go because she didn't think he was serious about applying for the job, and because they were at the sheriff's office Christmas party and she had enough to worry about with the way everybody was looking at them. They weren't trying to keep anything a secret, and it wasn't as though there was any rule against the chief deputy dating the county investigator. But she was the newcomer who had stolen the affections of the hometown Golden Boy, and she couldn't help feeling defensive about it. It didn't help her self-confidence to learn that, a mere matter of weeks into their relationship, he was already thinking about leaving.

Shortly after New Year's, she stopped by his office and he turned the screen of his computer around to show her the starting salary offer for the Mercy, Georgia, police chief.

"Holy crap," she'd breathed, staring. "That's more than the governor makes!"

"Not quite," he said. "But close. Municipal salaries are a lot different than county ones."

She sat down hard on the narrow visitor's chair in front of his desk. "Damn," she said. "Maybe I should apply for the job."

He smiled. "You'd beat me out, for sure. So do me a favor and don't."

She grew serious. "Really? You're really going to do this?"

His eyes took on that restless, troubled expression with which she had grown all too familiar these past months. "I've got to do something, Jo," he said. "I can't go on like this. And you know the old saying—nothing changes until something changes."

She examined him carefully. "You got shot," she pointed out, "lost your spleen and part of your lung, almost lost your leg, spent six months in PT and started sleeping with the hottest woman in town. That's not enough change for you?"

His smile was wan. "That's the thing. I think all of that was just the beginning. Like a sign, telling me to move on. I don't belong here anymore."

"Jesus, Buck," she replied, exasperated. "You were born and raised here. You've got these mountains in your blood. If you don't belong here, then where?"

"Don't know." He shrugged. There was a sad, faraway look in his eyes. "Maybe nowhere." But then he'd smiled, closed down the web page, and said, "You ready for lunch?"

She'd thought that was that. Three weeks later when he told her he was going to Georgia for the job interview, they'd had the biggest fight of their lives.

"Damn it, Buck," she cried. "I let you into my life! I let you into Willis's life! I *trusted* you. And this is what you do? You just *leave*?"

"I'm not leaving." He tried to sound rational. "It's just an interview. The police chief there, the one who's retiring, he's called twice trying to set up an appointment. He sounded real nice on the phone."

They were at his house, having pizza for dinner after work. Sleet was pinging against the windows and she had planned to stay the night. Now she grabbed her coat from the hook by the door and shot back, "Do you think I give a *crap* about how nice he sounded? Damn it, it's not like I didn't know better. But I took a chance on you, I *believed* you…"

He caught her arm as she tried to struggle into her coat. "Jo, just listen a minute, will you?"

"Let go of me!"

She swung around with her closed fist and hit him in the chest. She saw his lips go white and he bent over, staggering a little. She felt the breath leave her own body; her gut went hollow. She'd punched a man in the chest who'd just had lung surgery, and whatever pain she had caused him, hers was twice as bad. She dropped her coat to the floor and rushed to take his shoulders, whispering, "Oh God, oh God, Buck, are you okay? Here, sit down. Take a breath."

"Damn it, Jo." He tried to push her away, but not very hard, and she could tell he was struggling for breath.

"Hold on," she said, terrified. "I'm calling 911."

He wrapped his fingers around her wrist as she fumbled for her phone and held up his other hand for patience. "I'm okay." Wheezing. "But *damn* it... did you have to hit me... so hard?"

He did sit down, and she sat beside him, rubbing his back, looking at him anxiously. After a time, when he was breathing easier, she lay her head against his shoulder.

He said at last, making an obvious effort to keep his tone even, "I'm not leaving you."

"Buck," she said wearily, "it's what you do. You've been married three times. You've slept with every woman in this town and then you've walked away. It's what you do. I've always known that."

"It's what I *used* to do," he corrected her firmly. "That's what I've been trying to tell you. I'm not that person anymore."

He took her shoulders, trying to coax a smile. "In the first place," he said, "how stupid would I be, to think I could do better than this? Look at you. Miss New Jersey, 2007."

She jerked away and looked around in real alarm, just as though there might actually be someone there to overhear. "I told you that in confidence! I swear to God, Buck, if that ever gets out..."

He laughed softly and kissed her. She settled back against his shoulder. "You *would* be stupid," she agreed after a moment, "to think you could do better."

He smiled and squeezed her shoulders, and then the silence between them grew heavier, more thoughtful. At last he spoke, carefully, almost as though thinking the words through for the first time. "I'm serious. I'm really not that guy. Not anymore. That's not what I do anymore." Another silence.

"I fell in love with Raine when I was sixteen. Married her because I never imagined doing anything else. Married her again because I couldn't stand to be alone. By the time I realized I loved her more like a sister than a wife, I'd already screwed up both our lives." A pause. The pain of the next sentences tightened his muscles, shadowed his eyes. "Wyn was pregnant. We got married because of the baby, everyone knew that. And when we lost it… I couldn't look at her without feeling guilty, and she couldn't look at me without blaming me. Eventually all that blame and guilt ate up everything else between us until there was nothing left. So, yeah. There've been a few women. I've made mistakes." He drew a breath. "But I can't spend the rest of my life *being* my mistakes. I think… I think that's why it feels so weird, being here. I can't go back to being who I was. But I can't move forward, either. I'm stuck." He turned to look at her. "I want you to come with me."

She lifted her head from his shoulder, staring at him. "To Georgia?"

"The beach is two hours away," he persuaded. "We could make a long weekend of it, just the two of us. We've never had a vacation together before. Just think about it."

In the end, she agreed—not to accompany him to the job interview, but to meet him at the beachfront hotel for a four-day weekend. She also insisted on driving her own car, which both amused and annoyed him, because that made her feel less like she was being swept away and more like she was exploring her options. And because, as she told her mother while packing her bag, "I'm a grown-ass woman with a steady job and a son and two combat tours under my belt and I can go away with a man for the weekend if I want to."

Her mother refolded a silky little top that Jolene had carelessly tossed into her bag and replied mildly, "I didn't say you couldn't."

"It's seventeen degrees outside," Jolene went on, tugging open a drawer. "I've got a nice guy who wants to buy me a seafood dinner on the deck of a restaurant overlooking the ocean, and I'm okay with that."

"I don't blame you," her mother agreed. "I'd snap up that offer in a heartbeat."

"I just need you to make sure Willis gets to school on time and does his homework. I'll call him every night."

"No problem at all. It sounds a lot like what I've been doing the last three years."

Jolene spun around to face her mother, demanding, "Why are you looking at me like that?"

Eloise smiled and shook her head. "Jojo, honey, you know I like Buck. Any fool can see he's crazy about you, and God knows I've never seen a man more devoted to a child than he is to Willis. But I don't want you to get hurt, and, sweetheart…" She looked at her daughter with aching eyes. "He's broken in places you can't even see."

Jolene said quietly, "So am I."

Her mother came over to her and slipped an arm around her waist, hugging her briefly. "As long as you know what you're getting into, baby. Because there's nothing sadder than a woman who thinks she can fix a man."

Jolene sighed and turned back to her packing. "Don't worry, Mama. I know he's unfixable. It's just that…" She looked at her mother helplessly, her eyes suddenly bright with tears. "I'm going to miss him so damn much when he leaves."

CHAPTER TWELVE

Buck finished unloading the truck, stacking boxes on the kitchen floor, and was drenched with sweat by the time it was done. He went upstairs and found a roomy blue-and-white tiled bathroom with fluffy white towels folded on a rack and banded with a strip of paper, hotel-style. There was even a fresh bar of soap in the shower. Adjacent to the bathroom was a big bedroom with a walnut four-poster and matching highboy. Double doors opened onto a small balcony that overlooked the river, and the view, what he could see of it, was impressive. He didn't go out there, though. It was too damn hot.

Buck showered and changed into a fresh tee shirt and jeans, but that proved to be a mistake because, as tired as he was, he was now also wide awake. He went back downstairs in his bare feet, the old floorboards creaking and echoing with his every step. Sunshine still slanted through the front windows, catching motes of dust here and there. Somehow that only emphasized the bigness, the emptiness, and the quietness of the house.

He retrieved his phone from the kitchen counter where he'd left it and thought about calling Jo again, but she only had a couple of hours left in her shift and, having once held her job, he knew how crazy those last hours could be. So he took another beer from the cooler and the lemon meringue pie from the refrigerator. He found a fork and sat down at the kitchen table, surrounded by boxes, and ate from the pie plate. It was good, but nothing approaching Eloise's. Graham cracker crust. He'd have to remember to tell her.

He put the rest of the pie back into the refrigerator and methodically washed and dried his fork. The beer tasted foul after the tartness of the pie, so he poured it down the drain. He wandered back down the hall and into Billy's study, where he found himself standing in front of the marlin, gazing at it absently. It provided no more answers than it had this morning, when he had first seen it.

Buck turned around, noticing for the first time a credenza with a silver tray on it. Upon that tray were several cut-crystal decanters partially filled with liquid and some highball glasses. Flanking it were burnished wood bookcases that looked original to the house, and these shelves, unlike the ones at work, were filled with books a man might actually read—Grisham and Clancy and Stephen King. He took the stopper off one of the bottles on the credenza and sniffed it; it smelled like bourbon. He wasn't much of a hard liquor drinker, but he liked bourbon. He poured a measure into one of the glasses and took it over to the desk.

He sat down in the leather chair and put his phone on the desk beside him, leaning back, stretching out his legs. He took a sip of the bourbon, and it was good. The air-conditioning hummed softly. He slid open the top drawer of the desk, vaguely hoping to find the remote control for the television, but there was nothing there but the usual detritus of a man's life: Walmart and CVS receipts, a postcard from his dentist reminding him to book an appointment. It made Buck feel sad and hollow, just looking at the scraps of paper, the things Billy had meant to do. He picked up a field notebook and flipped through it, but it contained nothing but columns of dates and numbers that could have been lottery numbers or the odds on horse races. Billy was an eclectic fellow; maybe he had a gambling habit. Buck put the notebook aside.

Far at the back, underneath the clutter, was a photograph. He didn't recognize the subjects, but he knew who they were: Billy, forty years younger, with a woman in a 1980s' hairdo and two little kids, a boy and a girl, posing beneath the very magnolia tree that now stood outside the window in front of which he sat.

Buck sipped his bourbon and gazed at the photo for a long time, feeling the weight of the house, the town, the past, and everything he didn't know pressing down on him like a vise. "Well, hell," he muttered, raising his glass to nothing in particular. "Here I am sitting in a dead man's chair, drinking a dead man's bourbon, looking at a picture of a dead man's family." He took another gulp of the bourbon, this one big enough to burn his throat. "Thanks a lot, Billy. Not exactly what you promised."

From a corner of the room beyond Buck's shoulder, there was a soft chuckle. "If you think it sucks from where you are," Billy said, "you ought to try things from my point of view."

Buck sat up straight and whirled around, almost spilling the contents of the glass, as Billy stepped out from the shadows.

"Jesus Christ!" Buck lurched out of the chair, staring, gasping. Billy Aikens stood before him in khaki trousers and an open-necked red plaid cotton shirt, untucked, a few gray chest hairs showing at the throat. Beard perfectly trimmed, silver hair shiny, blue eyes twinkling. Buck took a step back and almost tripped over the chair. "You're supposed to be dead!"

And even as he said that there was a brief moment of soaring joy, of relief, that Billy wasn't dead, that this could all be fixed, that this wasn't, after all, now Buck's life. And then Billy assured him, "Oh, I am."

Buck set the glass down on the desk and heard it thunk. He said carefully, "You look pretty good, for a dead guy."

Billy grinned and spread his arms. "You know what they say: live hard, die young and leave a good-looking corpse. Two out of three's not bad." Then he shrugged and moved forward into the room, into the shafts of light that came from the windows. "It's not so bad here," he added. "Pretty much what you make of it, like everything else. Something to keep in mind when your turn comes."

Buck looked down at the half-empty glass of bourbon on the desk. He was drunk, he understood that now. Nothing to do but go with it. He said, "What are you doing here?"

Billy walked to the center of the room and thrust his hands into the pockets of his khakis, looking around with satisfaction. "Well, good for them. They kept the place exactly as I wanted it. You never know," he added, sliding a confidential glance toward Buck. "Kids and lawyers. Can't trust either of them."

Buck repeated, "What are you—"

"I told you I'd be here for you," Billy replied, cutting him off. "And here"—he spread his hands open wide, smiling—"I am."

Buck sucked in a breath through his nose, blew it out. "You left me a hell of a mess, Billy."

"Yeah, I know." Billy's expression grew solemn. "It wasn't the way I planned it, believe me." Then, turning, he gestured around the room. "So, what do you think of the place?"

"It's creepy, living in somebody else's house," Buck said. "And your river stinks."

Billy chuckled. "I know."

"Do you ever catch anything out of it?"

"Oh, sure. Pretty good eating, too. Nothing like the big trout you're used to where you come from, but bream, catfish, bass. Many's the fine summer afternoon I spent sitting on the pier with a fishing pole in my hand. With my dad, with my son, all by myself. Things like that make memories, Buck." His expression softened appreciatively as he walked over to the window and looked out, his hands clasped behind his back. "I wish you good memories, and lots of them. Because in the end, that's really all you've got worth holding on to."

He stood there in silence for a moment, drinking in the view. Then he turned to Buck, all business now, and said briskly, "So. I guess somebody told you about Mirabelle's Magic Formula?"

Buck shook his head dumbly.

"It's an insect repellent, local remedy. Don't know what's in it but it's the only thing in the world that'll keep the damn no-see-ums away. We buy it by the case for the department. Tell Lydia to fix you up. What else? Oh, the upstairs toilet leaks. You have to jiggle the handle. And don't try to use the toaster and the microwave at the same time. They're on the same circuit and it trips the breaker every time. The timer on the sprinkler system out front is broken. You have to turn it on and off by hand. I figured I'd get around to fixing things like that when I retired." He gave a rueful grunt of laughter. "Never put off until tomorrow, huh?"

His expression sobered as he added, "I meant to fix a lot of things before you got here, Buck. I thought I had more time. I guess you always do."

Buck said, "That was a nice letter you left me. I appreciate it."

Billy replied, "It was supposed to be a gesture. If I'd known how things were going to turn out, I would've gone into a little more detail." He walked over to the bookshelf, running his fingers over the spines of the books absently. "I wish I'd had a chance to show you around a little, help you get to know the town. There's a lot of history here." He took a book from the shelf and opened it, turning the pages with a fond look on his face. "You can learn a lot from the past. In fact, I'd say just about everything you need to know."

"Except that it's not my history," Buck pointed out, "it's yours." He jerked his head toward the mounted marlin. "Thanks for the fish, by the way. But do you mind telling me what I'm supposed to do with it?"

Billy glanced up from the book, his eyes twinkling. "Whatever you like."

Buck frowned. "The house, I understand. You figured to be living here yourself another twenty or thirty years, tax free, and if your kids didn't want it, what did you care who got it after you died? But the fish… you changed your will just for that? Why didn't you just wait until I got here and give it to me then?"

Billy shrugged and closed the book. "Maybe I was afraid that by the time you got here, it would be too late."

"That doesn't make any sense."

"Most of the time," Billy said, "the answers you're looking

for are right in front of you. As a lawman, you know that. Remember, we talked about that, that day in the park."

He turned and put the book back on the shelf. "I think you're going to like it here, Buck. It might take some time, but give it a chance. You'll find your place." He nodded toward the desk. "Are you going to get that?"

"What?"

"The phone."

Dimly, Buck was aware of a rhythmic buzzing in the background, and when he looked, he saw the screen of his phone was lit up. He reached for it.

Buck came awake with a jerk. The day had faded to deep twilight, and when he swung his head around, looking for Billy, he was no longer there. He flung out his hand for the buzzing phone and this time he really did spill his drink. He swore and looked around for something to blot the mess while he snatched up the phone.

"Yeah." His voice was husky with sleep and he cleared his throat. "Lawson."

"Mr. Lawson, this is Trooper Jim Marchetti from the Georgia State Patrol."

Buck squinted at the phone, coming slowly more awake, wondering why the state patrol would be calling him on his personal phone. He was sure it was his personal phone because it had the black faux-leather case with the Star Wars insignia on it, the one Willis had given him for Christmas. He said, trying not to sound too stupid, "State patrol?"

"Yes, sir. We're investigating an abandoned vehicle here on Highway 62 about twenty miles north of Mercy, Georgia, and we found your card on the floorboard of the vehicle. Buck Lawson, Hanover County Investigator, is that right?"

"Right. I mean, no." Buck rubbed his face over his face, still groggy. "That's an old card. I work for the Mercy Police Department now. In Georgia. Who did you say you are?"

"Trooper Jim Marchetti," the other man repeated patiently, "Georgia State Patrol. Sir, do you have any idea why your card would be in a vehicle registered to…" He paused and appeared to check a reference. "Peyton McGilroy?"

Now Buck was wide awake again. "Say that again?"

There was a pause while he double-checked. "Peyton McGilroy, age twenty-one, seems to be from Savannah, Georgia."

Buck ran his fingers through his hair, stifling a groan. This day just got better and better. He said, "She was a witness to a robbery this morning in Mercy. I interviewed her and gave her my card, which turned out not to be necessary since we apprehended the suspect a few minutes later. She said she was a student at Mercer University."

"I see." There was a pause while he finished making his notes. "Sorry to bother you, sir. We tagged the car, but since it was found fully operational with the keys in the ignition, I thought I'd better follow up just in case there were any extenuating circumstances we should be aware of."

Buck frowned. "Wait. It wasn't a breakdown?"

"It doesn't appear to be, no."

"And all you found was my card?"

"On the floorboard, yes, sir. And it looks like there was a backpack in the back. No wallet or other personal belongings except a phone in her backpack. We traced the name of the owner through the vehicle registration, and we'll send a notification to the last known address that the car has been impounded."

"Why would a person just leave the keys in the ignition

and abandon a perfectly operational vehicle on the side of a highway?" Buck wondered out loud.

"I couldn't tell you, sir," replied the trooper. "You see all kinds of things in this job. Well, thank you for your time."

"Right."

Buck disconnected and sat there another moment, frowning, until the spilled bourbon began to drip over the corner of the desk and onto his clean jeans. He got up and made his way to the kitchen, fumbling for light switches as he went, and grabbed a handful of paper towels to clean up the mess.

He didn't think he'd sleep again that night, but he was wrong. He went upstairs to the room with the walnut four-poster and found the linens fresh and crisp, the mattress firm. He was asleep the minute his head hit the pillow, and he didn't open his eyes again until sunshine glinting off the river woke him.

CHAPTER THIRTEEN

At 7:30 the next morning Buck walked into the Stop-and-Go, filled a paper cup with coffee from the dispenser, and picked up a cruller in a cellophane bag. There was a display of Mirabelle's Magic Formula on the counter, which made him smile a little. He must have noticed it yesterday, which was why he'd dreamed about it. He took one of the spray bottles and placed it on the counter with his purchases. When the woman at the register finished with the customer in front of him, Buck took out his badge and showed it to her.

"I'm Buck Lawson," he said, "the new police chief. Is Daksh here?"

She was dark skinned and dark haired, wearing a multilayered orange sari that seemed to float when she moved. She looked at him with cold eyes. "He is my husband. He's not working today."

Buck nodded, unsurprised. "I wanted to talk to you a minute about the robbery yesterday, if I could."

"I know nothing," she said. "I was not here."

"I know that," Buck said pleasantly. "But this is a family business, isn't it? I just wanted to clear up how much money was taken. There seems to be a discrepancy in the report."

She cast him a quick suspicious look and began bagging his purchases. "We paid our fine," she said shortly. "We're even. We don't owe anything."

"Fine?" Buck repeated, puzzled. As far as he'd been able to tell from the garbled police report, the owner hadn't been charged with anything. And he didn't see how the suspect could have been arraigned and released overnight, not on an armed robbery charge. "Do you mean to a judge?"

"To the policeman," she said, thrusting his package at him with one hand and the coffee cup with the other. "The detective with the gum and the notebook. We're done."

Buck took the sack and the coffee, watching her carefully. "You paid a police officer?"

She nodded impatiently. "From the money in the bank bags. That way Daksh doesn't go to jail and we stay open. We owe nothing."

Buck said, "How much did you pay him?"

"Twenty-five hundred dollars," she said firmly. She hesitated. "The rest of it, the money from the safe... the policeman said we would get it back."

Buck kept his expression carefully neutral. "That's right."

"When?"

"I'll check on that for you." He reached for his wallet, indicating the bag in his hand. "How much do I owe you?"

"No charge for cops," she said. Already her eyes had moved over his shoulder, beckoning the next customer forward.

Buck took out three twenties and placed them on the counter. "I owe you for beer and gas from yesterday," he said.

He started toward the door, then looked back. "One more thing. Does your husband read English?"

"No," she told him and lifted her chin. "But I do."

"And did the police ask you to read anything to him yesterday before he signed it?"

She replied, as he'd known she would, "No."

Buck nodded his thanks and smiled at her. He could feel her staring after him as he pushed through the door, the chime echoing in his wake.

Lydia was waiting for him when Buck strode through the door at 8:05.

"Good morning, Chief," she said, handing him a sheet of paper. "Captain Sullivan wanted me to let you know he's in his office if you need him. The overnight incident reports have been logged in and are ready for your review. Let me know if you have any trouble accessing them. Mr. Jefferies's office e-mailed to set up lunch on Wednesday, and Sheriff Tyler called to set up a meet-and-greet in his office on Monday before the monthly LLE luncheon."

Buck glanced up from the paper in his hand, which appeared to be his schedule for the day. "LLE?"

"Local Law Enforcement," she clarified. "Representatives from the sheriff's department, Fish & Game, the municipal police departments, and the state patrol get together once a month to discuss procedure and coordinate policy. There's usually a speaker."

"Sounds good," Buck murmured, turning back to the schedule.

"You're it this month," she informed him.

His expression turned sour. "Terrific."

"Mayor Watts's office called for a report on the extra security for the Memorial Day festival on the river," she went on. "If you'll just approve what I left on your desk, I'll send it over. I set up the first four of your personnel interviews, allowing twenty minutes for each one, beginning after lunch. I've scheduled them alphabetically by shift, unless you have another preference. Also, I really need a decision on your uniform."

Buck was wearing khakis and a white buttoned-down shirt with the sleeves rolled up—untucked to cover his back holster, but nonetheless as close to regulation as he would get until his work shirts arrived. He said, "What about it?"

"The collar stars on your dress blues," she explained patiently. "Do you want four or five?"

He was confused. "What do you mean, I get to choose? I thought they were assigned. Like for years of service or something."

"No, sir, they're purely decorative." She stood poised with her pen over her notebook. "Four or five?"

"How many did Billy have?"

"Five."

Buck said, "I'll have four."

He thought he saw the faintest twitch of a smile touch a corner of her lips. "Good choice, sir. It will be delivered Friday." She made a note on her pad. "Amos Solby is coming to remove the taxidermy this afternoon at 4:00. Have you thought about what you'd like to hang in its place?"

It took him a moment to realize she was referring to the alligator. "Oh," he said. "I don't know. You pick something. I liked that picture in the mayor's office of the marsh."

"I'll see if I can find a print," she said, making the note.

"However, you might have to live with a blank wall for a day or two. I've scheduled the decorator for 10:00 a.m. tomorrow. She might be able to suggest something."

Buck glanced at the clock on the opposite wall. "You've been at work, what, seven minutes?"

"Eight," she corrected.

"You are a treasure and a wonder, Lydia."

"Yes, sir. I expect we'll be receiving more calls from the press this morning. I referred yesterday's calls to the district attorney's office, but that won't hold them off for long. What would you like me to say?"

Buck hesitated. "Tell them I'll be holding a press conference in a few days. Meantime, don't confirm or deny anything on behalf of this office."

"Yes, sir. Shall I set that up for you?"

"What's that?"

"The press conference."

"No," he replied. "But you can set up a meeting with the prosecutor on Billy's case. First available."

She made the note. "Yes, sir."

He turned toward his office with his schedule in hand. "I need to see that detective, what's his name?"

"Detective Teller?" she suggested.

"That's it. I want him in my office right now, I don't care if you have to pull him out of the john to get him. Ask Sully to join us. And some coffee would be great." He had poured the foul concoction from the convenience store out the window after one sip.

"On your desk, sir. And Detective Teller is waiting in your office."

He looked at her in muted amazement. "A treasure and a

wonder," he repeated, and this time he was sure he saw her smile as she turned away.

Craig Teller had made himself comfortable on the plaid sofa in Buck's office, one foot resting on the coffee table, chewing gum that smelled faintly of cinnamon while he perused a copy of *Guns and Ammo.* There was a file folder on the sofa beside him. To his credit, he got to his feet immediately when Buck came in and extended his hand with an easy grin.

"Chief Lawson," he said. "I'm Craig Teller. Sorry I didn't make it by yesterday, but I was out in the field."

Buck ignored his offered hand and went behind his desk. "Did you close the case?"

Craig's smile faded a little as he reached for the folder on the sofa. "We arrested Farhan Singh, age twenty-five, who was found in possession of two bank bags filled with cash about eight miles from the scene of the robbery." He passed the file to Buck, who took it without comment.

Buck sat down and opened the file, which appeared to be considerably better organized than the one on the Aikens case had been. He thought Craig probably had Frankie to thank for that. When Sully tapped lightly on the doorframe, Buck glanced up only long enough to wave him in. He took his time reading through the reports, particularly the ones from Baker and Torrance, both of which carefully omitted identifying Buck by name but referred to him only as an "off-duty law officer legally authorized to carry a weapon in the state of Georgia." The wording was so identical in each report that he doubted either officer had written his own statement. Peyton McGilroy's statement was equally as sketchy, and it was, of course, unsigned.

He looked up. "Captain Sullivan, how much money did the store owner tell you was taken from the vault?"

Sully took his field notebook from his pocket and consulted it. "Eight thousand three hundred twenty-three dollars," he said. "At least that's what he had written on one of his cash deposit slips."

Buck turned a page in the folder. "But his statement less than two hours later says only $5823 was taken. That's also what the evidence receipt reads."

Neither man said anything. Craig munched on his gum, though with slightly less enthusiasm now.

Buck leaned back in his chair, looking at Craig. "Mrs. Patel told me that a detective who chewed gum and carried a notebook took $2500 from one of the bank bags and called it a fine. Would that officer have been you, Detective Teller?"

Craig stopped chewing. He shot a glance at Sully, whose jaw knotted, but Buck couldn't tell whether it was from anger or fear.

Buck's gaze was relentless. "She also said they paid the money to keep her husband out of jail, so that he could keep working."

Craig cleared his throat and smiled nervously. "Well, that's just not what happened, sir. Not at all."

"Then why do you suppose she said that?"

A person didn't have to know much about human behavior to tell that Craig was debating whether to lie. But he glanced again at Sully, who was now clearly furious, and made a better decision. "Look," he said, opening his palms. "Patel gave me the money, okay? They do that sometimes. He was behind on his tax, and he thought that would square it and keep him out of jail. I wrote him a receipt and turned the money over to City Accounting."

Buck felt as though he had one foot in the rabbit hole and was about to tumble through. He stared at the detective. "Since when are police officers tax collectors? And why is there no mention of this in your report?"

Craig said stiffly, "That's on me. I'll correct that right away."

Buck drew a sharp breath for a reply but Sully interrupted with, "Chief, if you'll permit me?" He turned to Craig. "Get a copy of the receipt you gave Patel and the receipt from accounting and attach them both to the incident report you're about to write. One copy on my desk and another in the file, got that?"

Craig replied, "You got it. Right away." He spun toward the door and then paused, looking back at Buck anxiously. Buck waved him away with a curt gesture, and he left, his jaw working visibly as he smacked his gum.

Buck stared at Sully. "What the..."

Sully sank into the chair in front of Buck's desk. "I know it sounds bad."

"It sounds like something out of a 1930s' gangster movie," Buck corrected, struggling to keep his tone even. "It sounds like Mercy police officers are collecting protection money from small businesses."

Sully gave a small, brief grunt of laughter. "You're right. It does."

"I hope to God," Buck said without any hint of humor whatsoever in his voice, "that you have a better answer than that."

"I do." Sully straightened up and ran a hand over his bald head. "The city provides fire and police services for all residents inside the city limits. Outside the city limits they can either rely on the county or contract with us separately. Most businesses choose to contract with us because the response time is faster. The big box stores, hotels, and chain restaurants pay tens of thousands of dollars in special assessments that go directly to the police department. The smaller business, slightly less."

"I know that," Buck said impatiently. "And none of it explains why one of my officers would ever be justified in taking money from a citizen."

"No, sir," agreed Sully firmly, "it absolutely does not. The problem is that since the assessment is paid directly to the police department, some of the small business owners, particularly those from other cultures, look at this a kind of fine they can pay a police officer in order to ensure their safety. And unfortunately, some of the officers are incentivized to let them go on thinking that."

Buck glowered at him. "What do you mean, incentivized?"

Sully shifted his weight uncomfortably. "Mayor Watts pays a bonus to any officer who brings in overdue assessments." He paused a moment, as though debating whether to elaborate, but he clearly had no choice. "There are also bonus incentives for other kinds of revenue brought into the treasury, like property forfeiture and citation fines over a certain dollar amount."

Buck did not blink. "That's graft."

"No, sir, boss, it's not," Sully corrected him politely, "if it's public policy."

Buck allowed several beats of silence to pass. Then he said, "You know as well as I do that Daksh Patel didn't give Detective Teller $2500 in cash from the bank bags. Once the bags were recovered, they were taken into evidence and no one saw them except members of this police department. So Craig Teller helped himself to the cash then altered the report about how much money was stolen. Whether or not he did so in accordance to *public policy…*" Buck bit out the words. "He tampered with evidence, falsified a report, and altered a witness statement—a statement you're going to have to throw out, by the way, along with most of your case, because, according to his wife, Patel can't read English."

Buck did his best to keep his voice from rising with this last, and he drew a breath, taking another few beats to tamp down on his temper. Then he said, in a much calmer tone, "You know something, Sully? This is one headache I do not need right now. So I'm going to make it simple for everybody. As of this moment, official policy is that no member of this department is to accept cash, goods, or services from any member of the public for any reason whatsoever. And I mean not so much as a free cup of coffee. I'll have it typed up and distributed within the hour."

Sully lifted an eyebrow. "I'm going to miss those Huddle House breakfasts."

Buck did not smile. "There's something else. One of the witnesses in this piss-poor excuse for a police investigation—the girl, Peyton McGilroy—might have gone missing. "

Sully stared at him. "What?"

"Her car was found abandoned on the side of the highway yesterday with the keys still in the ignition and her backpack and phone in the backseat."

"Shit," said Sully, sitting back heavily. "What are the odds?"

"All I can say is we'd better hope she's been found curled up with her boyfriend safe and sound somewhere by now. Because if there's an investigation, somebody is going to want to read the report of the robbery, and according to the only statement we've got from her—an unsigned statement, by the way—it would appear nobody from this office even bothered to ask her what she was doing here in Mercy or how she happened to end up at the scene of a crime. We're going to look like a bunch of jackasses."

"Shit," said Sully again.

Buck held his gaze. "Exactly."

Sully drew a breath. "I'm going to write Craig up for failure to follow procedure, and he's got a good ass-reaming coming from me personally, too. Anything more than that is up to you. If you want my opinion…" He waited until Buck gave him the very slightest nod of affirmation to go on. "Craig is sloppy, he's lazy, and between you and me, not all that smart. But I've got to tell you, Chief, I'd be very surprised if he had anything illegal in mind when he took the money, and you're going to have a hard time proving that he did if you bring him up on charges."

Buck regarded him silently for a moment, and then came to a decision. "Okay," he said. "I appreciate your input. Let me think about it." He picked up his coffee cup and sat back. "What are you doing in today, anyway? Where I come from, we get two days off for working a weekend of nights."

"Same here," Sully admitted, "but I thought you might need me. Also…" The beginnings of a sly grin quirked his lips. "I needed to tack on a couple of extra days next weekend for a trip to Disney World I promised the kids so…" He shrugged. "It worked out."

Buck said, "Yeah, it did." He pulled the schedule Lydia had given him closer with one finger and glanced over it again briefly. "Listen, have you got anything you can't push back this morning?"

"Not a thing," Sully replied. "What do you need?"

"I need you to take me on a little tour," Buck said. "There are some things I'd like to see for myself."

"No problem." He stood. "Where're we going?"

Buck thumbed through the file folders on his desk until he found the one he was looking for—the updated case file on Billy Aikens. He'd had a feeling Frankie would come through, and he was gratified to know he'd been right. He turned a page. "Thirty-four Bob Cramer Road," he said. "But first, the pier at Lost Creek. Give me about an hour to take care of some of this paperwork and meet me back here."

Sully showed no reaction to the familiar locations. He simply nodded and replied, "Yes, sir."

As soon as he was gone, Buck called, "Lydia!"

She appeared in a moment, pad in hand. "There's an intercom, sir."

"Right. Sorry." He slid the schedule sheet across the desk to her. "Clear everything before noon. I'm going out. I can see the fire chief at twelve and the council chair at twelve thirty."

She looked disapproving. "It's best to keep regular office hours, sir."

"I know." He tried to look chagrined. The last thing he wanted was to have Lydia annoyed with him. "I'll do better, I promise. In the meantime, can you tell me how to write a new department policy?"

She replied, "You can't actually write policy, sir. But you can issue a directive that will go into effect immediately and, after it's been implemented for three months, will be approved by the city council and become policy. A full explanation of that procedure is covered in the city charter. Shall I get a copy of that for you?"

He waved the offer away. "How do I write a directive?"

She stood with pen poised over the pad. "I'll take care of that for you, sir. Just tell me what you want it to say."

That was exactly the response he'd hoped for.

CHAPTER FOURTEEN

Hanover County, North Carolina
Ten weeks earlier

"Listen to this," Jolene said, scrolling down a page on her laptop. "In 1976, Corley County Sheriff Hiram Kissick disappeared during a routine patrol. Despite an intensive two-year investigation, no sign of him was ever found—until 1988, when a record drought caused water levels in the marshes fed by the Blood River to drop to historic lows. A Corley County Sheriff's vehicle was recovered from the receding silt outside of *Mercy, Georgia*..." She emphasized those last two words and glanced up to gauge Buck's reaction. He gave none. "In the trunk of the car, skeletal remains were found that were later proven to be those of the missing Sheriff Kissick." She sat back triumphantly. "What do you think of that?"

Buck thumbed a page on his phone. "Before my time, babe," he murmured.

They were at Jolene's rental house on Greene Street, sharing the sofa in front of the low-rolling glow of flames behind the glass door of the wood-burning stove. Willis had been asleep for hours; Eloise was not far behind. The television flickered blue lights on the wall, tuned to some celebrity game show with the volume turned down to a comfortable murmur in the background. Jolene's feet, clad in thick wool socks, were in his lap, and he massaged her toes absently. They spent many an evening like this, watching television, eating popcorn, reading, talking, just being together. Out of respect for her mother and her son, Buck never stayed over. But they felt like a family, nonetheless.

"All right." She clicked another page. "June, 1992."

"When I was eight," he pointed out absently, not looking up.

She ignored him and read on, "Twenty-three-year-old Melissa Hardwick, a waitress in the Mercy, Georgia, Four-Way Cafe, failed to return home after her shift. Her car was later found abandoned with a flat tire along State Road 62. The case was never closed. March, 1998. Amelia and Jarred Laker, ages twenty-eight and thirty-three, respectively, were driving home to Atlanta from Florida and stopped overnight at the Mercy Day's Inn. Two days later their bloodstained car was found in a used car parking lot fifty miles away. Jarred was eventually found in a wooded area adjacent to 1-75, a victim of multiple stab wounds and genital mutilation. And, get this—on a nearby tree, written in blood, was the word 'Mercy.' His wife was never found."

Buck looked up from his phone, his expression one of

mild revulsion mixed with amused skepticism. "Jesus, Jo, where are you getting this stuff?"

"VICAP," she replied. Then she admitted, "Well, some of it's from VICAP. Some is from a book called..." She checked another page. *"Tales From the Swamp: a Tour of the South's Most Infamous Mysteries."*

He grunted and turned back to his phone. "Catchy title."

"In 2016," Jolene went on determinedly, "the city of Mercy made over 1500 traffic stops, prompting a warning from AAA to its customers about a speed trap. In 2018, a twenty-two-year-old Black female was pulled over in the early hours of the morning for an illegal lane change and claimed that the officer involved offered to dismiss the charges in exchange for sexual favors. The case never went to trial. In 2019..."

"Baby." Buck regarded her patiently. "What are you trying to prove?"

"That this place is messed up," she said. There was a stubborn jut to her jaw. "You need to know what you're getting into."

"Yeah, well, I hate to think what you'd find if you googled Hanover County, especially after the year we've had here," he replied. "The difference is that in Mercy..." He thumbed a page on his phone. "You can get a four-bedroom, three-and-a-half-bath house with a pool for $1200 a month." He turned the phone to show her the picture on his screen.

She scowled. "What do you need with four bedrooms?"

"Or here's one with a mother-in-law suite with its own entrance. It even has little garden out back. Your mom would love that. Walk to schools and parks."

She didn't blink. "What has my mother got to do with this?"

He dropped a hand to her wool-clad ankle, caressing

gently. His gaze was steady. "You know I'm not doing this without you, Jo. Come with me."

"Oh, please." She pulled her feet out of his lap and sat up, inching to her corner of the sofa. "I just moved here. Dragged my mother and Willis all the way down from Raleigh. We've got boxes we haven't even unpacked yet! And you expect me to pick up and move to some godforsaken town in south Georgia with a Confederate statue in the park because some man crooks his finger? Seriously?"

"It's not entirely godforsaken," Buck replied reasonably. "You said yourself it was cute."

In February, Jolene had ended up meeting Buck at the Comfort Inn in Mercy on their way to the beach. While he took the grand tour with Billy Aikens, she had shown herself around, wandering the springs, taking a pontoon boat ride on the river, walking through the historic district and buying a sun hat and a couple of cute tee shirts from the Main Street shops. She gave the aesthetics of the town her qualified approval. Nice place to visit, but who would want to live there?

She said pointedly, "I've got a job, Buck. Willis has just settled into a new school."

"First grade," Buck replied pointedly. "It's not like he'd be blowing his chances at a college scholarship. And you can come work for me."

Now her glare grew dangerous. "I will never work for you again, Buck Lawson."

"Okay," he agreed quickly. "There are plenty of other law-enforcement agencies in the area. The sheriff's office, three police departments within a forty-minute drive…"

"Not hiring," she said briefly.

He tried to mute the surprised pleasure that sparked in his eyes. "So, you've thought about it."

"I've thought about it enough to know it's not happening," she answered shortly. "I'm a chief deputy and a top K-9 handler with a background in Homeland Security. I'm not going to give that up to be a beat cop in a town that barely pays its patrol officers minimum wage."

Jolene's canine partner, Nike, had been returned to Homeland when her contract had expired a few months ago, and while Jolene pretended to take it in stride, she had been at loose ends ever since. The sheriff assured her he was trying to find the funding to reactivate the K-9 program and get her another dog, but no progress had been made in that direction so far. Jolene was a good chief deputy and she liked her job, but whether she would admit it or not, Buck knew she was bored. There was nothing keeping her here.

Buck felt compelled to say, mostly just to needle her, "Mercy pays well above average. Full benefits after six weeks."

Her fierce expression did not change.

He tried one more time. "Jo." He reached out to stroke her knee. "Did you ever think that maybe there's a reason you haven't unpacked those boxes? You told me one time that the military had taught you never to get too comfortable in one place. But it's really not about where you are. It's about who you're with. You don't have any friends here. You don't even know anybody outside of work. But you and Willis and your mom—you're my family. Maybe we could all find our place, wherever it is, together."

The defensiveness went out of her expression, leaving nothing but vulnerability in her eyes. "You really want to do this, don't you?"

"Yeah," he said. The admission seemed to surprise him. "Yeah, I think I do."

She nodded, but her eyes were sad as she laid her hand atop his. "Buck," she said quietly, "try to understand. This is your dream, not mine. And I don't do other people's dreams."

He looked at her thoughtfully for a long moment, then squeezed her fingers. "Okay," he said simply. "I'll call Billy in the morning and turn the job down. He's still got plenty of time to find somebody else." He turned back to his phone.

She stared at him. "Now what are *you* trying to prove? That you're a better person than I am?"

A corner of his lips turned up in a half grin. "Nah. Just that I'm a better person than I used to be. Or at least that I'm trying." When she did not respond, he looked at her and released a small breath. "Look," he said. "I thought a new place would help give us a new start, that's all. But if I choose what I want—or think I want—over you and what we're building together, that's just another version of the same old song. So, this time, I'm making another choice. I've got to start somewhere."

She looked at him for a long time, her expression inscrutable. "'I could not love you half so much, dear, loved I not honor more,'" she murmured softly.

He gave her an amused look. "What's that?"

"Just some poem we studied in high school. Wordsworth or Longfellow or somebody. I don't know why it's always stuck in my head."

"You had a much classier education than I did."

"I know." She held out her hand. "Let me see your phone for a minute."

He handed it over, the screen still open to the Mercy,

Georgia, real estate listings. She thumbed a couple of pages and then started to type.

He said, "What are you doing?"

She finished typing, and then read what she had written.

Dear Chief Aikens,

Thank you for your patience while I considered your offer for the position of Mercy Chief of Police. I've enjoyed our conversations and have taken them all into account while I thought this over. As you know, this has been a difficult decision for me, but I have come to the conclusion that this change can only benefit us all. I therefore gladly accept your offer upon the terms we discussed. You can e-mail the contract to me at this address or send it USPS to the address you have on file. Let's talk later this week.

All best,
  Buck Lawson

She looked at him. "What do you think?"

He lifted an eyebrow. "I'm impressed. You caught my style better than I could. What is this, some kind of psychology exercise? Like, how does it feel to make the leap?"

She said, "So how does it feel?"

He thought about it for a minute, then shrugged one shoulder. "If I'm honest, kind of exciting." He smiled and slid closer. "But more exciting to be here with you. So we're good."

"Glad to hear it," she said, "because I just clicked send."

He sat up straight and snatched the phone from her. "What?" He stared at the screen. "Jesus, Jo, what did you do?"

"What you should have done three weeks ago," she said.

"Christ!" He scrolled down frantically. "Where is 'unsend'?"

"Because when you make a commitment," she went on calmly, "whether it's to a friend, a lover, or a principle—or even to yourself—you have to keep it. You made a commitment to yourself. If you don't keep it, you'll never believe you deserve to be loved by me, and I guess you'd be right. That's what that stupid poem meant. I finally figured it out, after all these years. And there's no 'unsend.'"

He stopped scrolling and looked up at her, confused and uncertain. "I don't want a long-distance relationship."

"It's better than no relationship at all, isn't it?" she challenged. And then she added reasonably, "We'll work it out, Buck. We've got time to work it out." She sighed and sat back, her shoulders relaxed. "Who knows? You might get down there and decide you hate it. Maybe you won't even stay. One thing's for sure, though. It's a whole lot easier to get on the right road when you know where you're going."

She took up her laptop again. "In 2018," she read, "eight, count them, eight complaints of excessive force and/or assault were brought by citizens against Mercy police officers. All settled out of court."

Buck looked at her for another moment, then returned to his phone. "Gee, we only had six complaints in Hanover County this year. Of course..." He slanted her a glance. "Five of them were against you."

She darted him a dark look, then turned back to the screen. "In 2019. A woman complained that a Mercy police officer attempted to rape her during a traffic stop in a deserted parking lot after midnight... Oh, wait. Turned out to be a cop impersonator. Never mind."

Buck said, "Three bedroom, three-and-a-half-bath, fenced

half-acre, screened porch, hot tub, overlooking the marsh. Gourmet kitchen."

"You don't even cook."

"Your mother does. She says the kitchen is her happy place." And before Jolene could draw a breath, he pointed out, "With what I'm going to be making, you can take your time looking for a job, Jo. We can have a nice house, big enough for everybody. There's no need to make this hard."

She replied impatiently, "I told you before, I'm not the kind of woman who follows a man from pillar to post. I wouldn't do it for Bobby and I'm not going to do for you. You're going to have to marry me first."

He replied, "Okay."

She clicked the mouse on her laptop. "Here's one. In 2017. A kayaker navigating a creek in the marsh outside of Mercy, Georgia, discovered a human tibia…" She looked up, her face suddenly still, her gaze sharp. "What did you say?"

He smiled and moved closer, cupping the back of her neck with his hand. In his other hand, he held a small box, open to reveal the ring inside. "I said, okay. Let's do it. Let's get married."

She looked at the ring, and then at him. She couldn't speak.

He said, "I've been carrying this thing around for weeks. Doesn't look like I'll get a better opening than this." He smiled a little uncertainly. "I'd get down on one knee but I don't think I could get up again."

His expression sobered, and he took the ring from its velvet cushion. "You know what you're getting, Jo. A man that's broken and scarred and has a past filled with mistakes. I can't promise you much. But if you'll let me, I swear I'll spend every day of my life loving you, and every waking moment doing my damn level best to be the kind of husband you deserve, the kind of father Willis needs. I want to build a home with you. I want to be a family. What do you say?"

She looked at him for a long time, searching his eyes, his face, his soul. And of all the crazy things that might have come out of her mouth in reply, the last one she expected was the one that did. "Okay," she said.

She held out her hand, and he slipped the ring on her finger.

It should have been that easy. But, of course, nothing worth having ever was.

From the Diary of The Marsh Dragon
May 4, 2021

My daddy used to tell the story about when he got back from Sand-Land, how his unit came up on the A-Rab encampment —that's how he used to say it, A-Rab—and how he found this one towel-head that was on his knees, whimpering and begging for his life, and how he just walked right up to him and slit the son of a bitch's throat. He had him by the hair and was about to take his scalp when his captain walked up and put a stop to it. They sent him home for that, and he hated the sight of a uniform ever since.

Ha. Wonder what he'd think of his son if he could see me now?

So anyway, naturally, the first thing he did when he got back here—to hear him tell it anyway—was he slit his own daddy's throat in his sleep, just so he could have the place to himself. Then he cut off his head and tossed it to the gators.

Hell, I don't know if it's true or not—probably not—but it sure makes a good story. And ever since I heard it, I've got to say, I've been a little obsessed with that whole scalping thing. How would you do it, anyway? I mean, are there tendons and things? Or is it like skinning a squirrel or a possum? What kind of knife would you use? And how long, I wonder, will she live afterwards? I hear there are a lot of blood vessels in the scalp.

I've been studying on it, and today is the day. I think I'll start at the ear and work my way around.

CHAPTER FIFTEEN

It was good to be back in a patrol car again, even if someone else was driving. The smell of leather, sweat, and fast food was like home to him, the radio chatter background music. "Sweet ride," Buck remarked as he swung into the Interceptor SUV that was waiting for them out back.

"Top of the line," agreed Sully, taking the driver's seat.

From what Buck could tell, the entire Mercy police fleet was top of the line, ranging from the ever-popular Charger to the sleek Durango and, the vehicle Sully preferred, the Ford Interceptor. The official color was black, with the Mercy insignia and motto painted in pale gray script on the sides, making the vehicles difficult to distinguish in the dark. The interiors were tricked out with a state-of-the-art computer, communications and detection systems, which was about what Buck would expect from a police force that made—what had Jo said?—1500 traffic stops a year.

Buck fastened his seat belt and added, "Show us 10-7 to dispatch."

"You got it, Chief."

Sully notified dispatch their unit was out of service and muted the radio, which he probably would have done without Buck's instruction. But Buck had learned his lesson about being too casual with employees during his brief term as sheriff of Hanover County, and he wasn't going to make that mistake again.

He waited until they were on the road headed out of town to say, "I see that almost ten percent of the department's revenue comes from traffic stops. Don't you think that's a little aggressive?"

Sully replied, "About six years ago a little boy was killed getting off the school bus right past this intersection we're coming up on here. Some damn fool spring-breaker barreling down here doing sixty in a twenty-five-mile zone, wasn't about to slow down for a school bus. Right then and there Billy instituted a zero-tolerance policy for moving violations."

Buck nodded. Billy had told him the story, and he didn't disagree with the reasoning behind the policy. He had simply wanted to get Sully's take on it. "You've got a little reputation here in Mercy."

"Good," Sully said. "People get off the interstate with their cruise control set to seventy-five and don't even check the speed limit when they get on these country roads. It's dangerous. State law won't allow us to write tickets for anything under five miles per hour over the limit, but we can for damn sure get them on something else. And we want folks to know that when we do, they're going to pay some of the highest fines in the state."

"You feel good about the number of enforcement personnel you've got on the road?"

"We do okay. Pull a lot of overtime between May and July."

They talked for a while about staffing and traffic trends, but it was really just a way for Buck to warm up to the subject at hand. He suspected Sully guessed as much. Eventually Buck said, "Do you happen to know what Billy was working on before he was killed?"

Sully glanced at him. "You mean, like a case?"

"Yeah."

"Billy was more of a behind-the-desk kind of chief," Sully said. "He didn't really get personally involved in police work. I mean, don't get me wrong, he had eyes on everything that was going on in the department, but he wasn't really a boots-on-the-ground kind of cop."

"What about you?" Buck said. "You work the streets. Can you think of anything unusual that was going on in the weeks before Billy was shot?"

"Aside from the Tucker situation, no. And that wasn't even that unusual. We lock Carl up for pure meanness once or twice a year." He cast a puzzled look in Buck's direction as he made the turn onto a packed dirt road. "Are you thinking something else was going on besides what we found?"

"Just trying to get my ducks in a row," Buck replied. "I've got to give a press conference this week about a case I wasn't even here for. I don't want to get hit with any questions I can't answer."

"I'll be there to back you up, boss."

"Counting on it," Buck said.

The road was flat and straight, lined with tangled brush and straight pine trees. The occasional dirt driveway jutted off toward a double-wide or an unpainted house, but the area was largely unpopulated. They passed a hand-painted sign that read "Pupys for Sale" and another, store-bought For Sale sign affixed to an aluminum jon boat on a trailer that was parked near the road. In a lot of ways, the scenery wasn't that different from the roads Buck had spent his life traveling back home. Or that's what he thought until Sully swerved to avoid an armadillo that lumbered across the road. That was something he would never see back home.

Buck said, "I guess you tracked Billy's GPS to see where he'd been on the day he was shot."

"He was in his personal vehicle," Sully said. "The nav system in those things go all wonky out here in the swamp. Most of these roads aren't even on the map, and those that are will have you driving straight into the river if you listen to the GPS. Now, if he'd been in one of these babies…" He tapped the dashboard affectionately, "We could have traced him down to his last footstep." His expression grew grim. "Would've found him a lot sooner too."

"What about his phone?"

Again, Sully shook his head. "All he had on him was his personal phone, and it had been in the water for over twenty-four hours, completely unrecoverable. But I can pretty much guarantee he had his locations turned off."

Buck nodded. Department-issued phones had a secure tracking feature on them to make it easy to find an officer in trouble. But most lawmen were a little paranoid about turning on the GPS on their personal phones. He said, "Did you check his official phone for any unusual calls or texts?"

"Yeah. But by the time we finished going through it we'd already made an arrest. Nothing there, anyway. That should have been in the report."

"It wasn't." Buck opened the folder in his lap and checked again. Instead of a log of all incoming and outgoing calls in the weeks prior to the event, there was a statement reading, "No significant activity was noted on the victim's personal phone during the previous twenty-hour hours." He looked across the seat at Sully. "You know this is pretty sloppy police work."

Sully took a moment to reply. "The last homicide we worked was three years ago, a stabbing in the parking lot of the Wayside Motel over a drug deal. Six witnesses. The suspect was standing there waiting for us when we got there, knife in hand. Before that, it was seven years. Old Jack Mandelson shot his neighbor over a dog. He said he didn't mean to kill him, but he was dead nonetheless. The point I'm trying to make, Chief, is we don't get a lot of violent crime here, and this is for damn sure the worst one we ever worked—in my lifetime, anyhow. I know you're coming off an investigator's background and things probably look different from where you sit. But we did the best we could."

Buck said nothing until Sully made the turn onto a short, rutted road identified by a sign that read, "Entering Lost Creek Wildlife Preserve." The pine trees gave way to cottonwood and live oaks, and he could see where wild boar had dug up the shoulder of the road here and there. The undergrowth was closer here, occasionally scraping the side of the car, and the Spanish moss heavier. Even though the morning was bright, it felt dark.

Buck said quietly, "I don't mean to be disrespectful. Not to you, or the department Billy ran. But there are some things about his murder that don't add up. And I think... this might sound crazy, but I think Billy hired me because he knew I was the kind of guy that would spot those things. I'm just trying to do what he would've wanted me to."

Sully looked over at him, and something about his expression had changed. Buck thought they might have reached an understanding.

The road widened into a murky beach that sloped down to the water. There was a picnic table beside the road and a pier that jutted out over a body of still, green water. Sully parked beside the picnic table. "So, this is it," he said. "The kill site."

Buck reached for the door handle but Sully said, "Hold on a minute." He took a bottle of Mirabelle's Magic Formula from a compartment in the console and sprayed it on the exposed parts of his arms and hands, then rubbed it on his face and bald head. He passed the bottle to Buck. "It's the only thing in the world that'll keep these swamp gnats away. Be sure to run some over your hair or the sons of bitches will drive you crazy."

Buck did as he was told, and then got out of the car, looking around. The smell of sulphur wasn't as strong here as it was closer to town, or maybe it was just overpowered by the herbal scent of the insect repellent. The creek, if that's what it was, lapped so gently against the pilings of the pier that the sound was barely noticeable, and then spread out wide beyond the shore into a marsh pitted with wild grasses and pale gold hillocks. It was pretty, in its way, but Buck couldn't help thinking about the tumbling, gurgling creeks and waterfalls back home.

He said, "All this is public land?"

"Right around here, yeah," Sully said. "Managed by the DNR. Of course, there's still a few houses left back in the woods on the marsh side. Shacks really. But you get three, four miles down the road where it's a little more accessible, and people are putting up half-million-dollar homes."

Buck looked around. As far as he could see there was

water, marsh grass, and wilderness. "Is it always this deserted?"

"This time of year, yeah. It's mostly a local spot, anyway. Not many outsiders know about it."

"How deep is the creek?"

"Four feet high tide, two or three low," Sully answered. "It would've been high tide when Billy was killed."

"So you figure the tide washed the body downstream to the riverbank? How far?"

Sully pointed to the west. "Less than half a mile by boat. We found him right where the creek feeds into the river, caught up on a dead tree. If it hadn't been for the tree, we might never have found him."

Buck walked toward the pier.

"Watch your shoes, there, boss," Sully advised, following. "That black mud is like quicksand."

Buck stayed to the path, avoiding the mud, and stepped up onto the pier. "I heard y'all pulled a car out of that marsh one time."

"Yeah, I heard about that too. Of course, I was just a kid at the time. Turned out to be a homicide from something like twenty years earlier."

Buck said, "Looking at it, you wouldn't think the water was deep enough to hide a car."

"Oh, it's not," Sully said. "But the silt can be ten, fifteen feet deep in spots, and it'll suck down anything heavy in a heartbeat. More than one dumb-ass tourist has lost his life that way, I'm sorry to say."

Buck squatted down, gazing over the worn deck boards in the bright sunlight. "Ya'll find any blood spatters on the pier?"

"No, sir, we didn't," admitted Sully. "But it had rained the night before. Footprints, tire tracks, blood—all would've been washed away."

Buck walked back toward the car, and Sully showed him where the gun and the gloves had been found. "Nobody heard the gunshot or saw anything suspicious?" Buck asked, already knowing the answer.

Sully shook his head. "Nobody around *to* see or hear anything."

Buck looked around thoughtfully. "I wonder what brought Billy out here."

Sully had no answer to that.

When they were back in the car, Buck said, "All right, let's pay a visit to Mrs. Tucker. How far away are we?"

"Maybe five minutes." He started the engine and put the car in gear. "A person could walk it if he had a mind to, but who would want to?"

Buck said, "You mentioned Billy didn't usually work cases. So how come he was the arresting officer on the Tucker domestic complaint?"

"He was the closest responder when the call came in." Sully turned the vehicle back down the rutted dirt road. "My understanding is that by the time the regular patrol got here Billy had already disarmed and cuffed Carl, and Carl's wife—who had a bloody nose and an eye so swollen she couldn't open it from where Carl had hit her with a lamp base—was screaming about how she was going to sue for false arrest."

Buck grunted thoughtfully, opening the folder with the crime scene photos again. "What was he doing out here, did he say?"

"No," Sully answered. "I wondered the same thing, but all he ever said was that he was looking into something. I figured he would tell me about it if it was important, so I didn't press."

"Whatever it was," Buck observed, "it was important enough to bring him out here again a week later."

Sully glanced over at him but said nothing.

They turned onto the hard-packed road, and Sully said, "This used to be the main road to town, believe it or not. My folks lived out here until my dad got a job that paid enough to let him move closer to town, and I remember my uncle talking about the old Sinclair Station that used to be right here on the corner. Him and his buds would target practice on the dinosaur sign until the big storm took it out."

"Do many folks still live out here?"

Sully shrugged one shoulder. "About what you'd expect. Mostly fishing shacks and trailers, a few farmhouses." He lifted his little finger from the wheel, gesturing east. "Down that way," he said, "this road picks up the hardtop again, and you get into some nice neighborhoods. And down that road there about a mile…" He pointed to a sandy track between the weeds. "It opens out onto the deepest part of the marsh. We've got a few old fishing cabins back in there, a farmhouse or two. Used to be a little store, a couple of other businesses, but that would've been back in my granddaddy's time. I hear that's where they found that car you were talking about. Some old timers still like to fish back in there, but it's too tricky for me. You lose more line than you cast."

Buck turned in his seat, marking the spot. He couldn't help thinking about all the times he had been the guide, driving some visiting dignitary or law enforcement officer around his territory, trying to tell them what they needed to know, to point out what they didn't know and—if he was completely honest—resenting the hell out of it. "You don't suppose that's what Billy was doing here the day he was shot, do you? Fishing?"

"I thought about that," Sully admitted. "But we didn't find any gear, and Billy mostly liked open water. He didn't even have a marsh boat." He turned the wheel onto another dirt road beside a hand-lettered sign that read, "Wayside Trailer Court." "Here we are."

Except for the enormous banana tree that marked the entrance, the Wayside Trailer Court could have been one of any of the half-dozen or so just like it in Buck's native Hanover County. Five single-wides that had seen many, many better days were arranged in a rough semicircle connected by red dirt roads. No effort had been wasted on grass or landscaping. A mottled hound, tied to a stake outside, bayed furiously across the way when Sully pulled the cruiser up in front of a faded blue trailer with the number 34 painted on the mailbox. A shirtless man, his back a maze of tattoos and his fish-belly white gut hanging over the belt of his jeans, turned a wrench on a motorcycle two doors down and pretended not to stare at them. A couple of teenage boys leaned laconically against a battered gray sedan with the hood up, chewing tobacco and spitting on the ground. A skinny Black woman with a corona of frizzy gray hair sat on the stoop next door, smoking a cigarette and glaring at them.

Buck remarked, "Seems pretty quiet."

"Yeah, well, the residents of the Wayside Trailer Court are not known to be early risers," answered Sully. His eyes, too, were busy taking in his surroundings. "You come back tonight and you might see a different picture."

"Do you get many calls out here?"

"A knife fight a couple of times a year," Sully answered. "Overdoses, the usual. This is not one of our popular tourist spots." He put his hand on the door handle and glanced at Buck. "This is the point where I'd usually ask Chief Aikens to wait here while I checked things out, but I'm guessing you're not that kind of chief."

"You'd guess right." Buck opened his own door and got out, making eye contact with everyone he saw as he looked around. Only the old woman on the stoop refused to look away.

They went up a set of three rickety wooden steps and Sully knocked on the door. "Police!" he called when there was no answer. He waited a minute and knocked again. "Miz Tucker, open up! We're just here to talk!"

Buck looked around, noting the two vehicles in the yard—a Chevy truck with balding tires and a newer-looking Jeep Wrangler. "Are those her vehicles?"

Sully nodded. "The same ones that were here when we arrested her husband."

He knocked again, louder and longer. "Police! Open the door!"

The woman on the stoop next door remarked in a reedy voice, "She ain't been out in two days." She tossed her cigarette butt in the weeds and lit another. "Not even to get the mail."

Buck and Sully looked at each other. "I'll check the back," Buck said.

Sully tried the front doorknob, and then started checking windows while Buck walked around the side of the trailer. There was a set of sliding glass doors that led to nothing but a two-foot gap between the trailer and the dirt. They opened creakily when Buck put some force behind it.

The odor rushed out at him like a living thing. He took an automatic step backward and turned his head, flinging up an arm to protect his nose and mouth. After a couple of deep breaths of almost-clean air, he called out, "Sully!"

The answer was hoarse and muffled. "Inside, Chief!"

Holding his breath, Buck grasped the doorframe and pulled himself up and into the trailer. He put his hand on the butt of his pistol but did not draw it. He had a bad feeling that, as far as whoever was inside this place was concerned, they were already too late.

From the Diary of The Marsh Dragon
May 5, 2021

Well, that was disappointing.

She didn't last twelve hours. I don't think it was from the scalping, which was loud and messy but not that severe. More likely, dehydration and shock. Shit. And after all that trouble to get her here, too.

I hung her necklace on the Shining Tree, in memoriam. We've got quite a collection going there now, between my grandpap, my daddy, and me. Sometimes I like to drag a lawn chair out there and just look at it, all glittery when the sun hits it just right. Like a poem or something, you know? The beautiful things you don't see until you look for them.

But enough of that. I've got work to do. Time to feed the dragon.

CHAPTER SIXTEEN

Buck's peripheral vision caught a glimpse of a grimy kitchen, sink piled with dishes, take-out containers and pizza boxes spilling out of the trashcan. He met Sully in a long, dark living room where the muted television was the only light and a bloated body was sprawled out on the couch. A window air conditioner poured out a thin stream of cool air but it was ineffectual against the oven the trailer had become. A front window was open, which was apparently how Sully had gained access. The upholstery fabric of the sofa was dark with fluids that had leaked from the corpse, and a single sweep of his gaze showed Buck the two empty vodka bottles, multiple syringes, and rubber tubing that littered the floor. He tried not to inhale, but the stench of rotting flesh was seeping into his clothes, his hair, his pores.

Buck said, "Is that her?"

Sully nodded grimly. "Near as I can tell."

They both studied the scene in silence for a while, scanning the room for anything they might have missed.

Sully said, "Look like an OD to you, boss?"

"As much as anything I've ever seen." He nodded toward the door. "Let's call it in. Get the coroner and a couple of cars out here. I'll take a look around."

While Sully was on the phone, Buck donned gloves from the car and sprayed more of the herbal insect repellent on his face in an attempt to mask the smell. He walked through the trailer again but found nothing unexpected—a few packets of what was probably heroin, a cocktail of narcotics and amphetamines in a pill bottle, the usual drug paraphernalia. No weapons. He snapped photos with his phone and inventoried the items in his field notebook. He hadn't been an administrator long enough to stop carrying a notebook, and he had been a cop too long not to document everything he saw in meticulous detail.

Outside again, he showed the list to Sully. "You'll want to confiscate the drugs and paraphernalia, and make sure to fill out an evidence sheet. Did y'all find any weapons when you arrested Carl?"

"Just the Glock at the crime scene."

"Okay, the place is clean, then." Then he hesitated, frowning a little. "No ammo."

"Sir?"

He said, "Have a couple of men do another sweep of the house once the body is removed. See if they can locate any .9 mm-caliber ammunition for that handgun of Carl's."

"You got it."

Buck walked across the yard to the woman sitting and smoking on the steps. "Morning, ma'am."

She exhaled a cloud of smoke. "She dead?"

"Yes, ma'am, I'm afraid so."

"I figured. That damn woman ain't got a lick of sense. I been telling her two years you can't drink like that all day and shoot up at night. She was bound to off herself sooner or later."

"Did you know her well?"

She took a drag on her cigarette. "Nah. Seen her around from time to time, mostly when she was collecting the rent."

Buck said, "My name is Buck Lawson. I'm the new chief of police."

She looked him up and down, her contempt undisguised. "Don't care."

He insisted politely, "What should I call you?"

She drew again on the cigarette. "Anything you want. But my name's Ruth."

He said, "Could I sit with you for a minute, Miss Ruth?"

She gave an elaborate shrug of her boney shoulders. "Can't stop you."

He sat down on the stoop beside her. "Do you think Ms. Tucker wanted to take her own life?"

"How the hell should I know?" the woman replied snappishly. "I cain't see inside her head, can I?"

Buck said nothing, and she smoked a minute in silence. Then she added, "She sure talked a lot about killing other folks, though. Fact is, that's about all she did rant about ever since you all come and dragged her man away."

"Is that right?" Buck's tone was mild. "Who did she want to kill?"

Ruth gave a short, crackling laugh. "Ever one of you damn po-lice, for one. And that white-faced lawyer, the one that made Carl sign that confession when he knew damn well wasn't a word of it true. She'd stand outside her house some days, high as a kite, and scream about it for hours, until she passed plumb out."

Buck glanced around casually. "I guess you see most everything that goes on around here from where your house sits, right in the middle of the court."

"Maybe I do," she admitted sullenly. "But I ain't no narc, either."

Buck smiled. "I was just wondering if you'd noticed anything unusual going on at the Tucker place in the last day or two. Anybody visiting, that kind of thing."

She scowled. "Aside from the po-lice and that sneaky lawyer, ain't nobody been around since ya'll hauled off the old man. Not that I seen nohow."

Buck said, "Do you know where she got her drugs?"

The tip of the cigarette brightened as she inhaled. "I might."

"Will you tell me?"

"Nope."

Again, Buck couldn't prevent a smile. He started to get up, then hesitated. "Do you happen to remember Sunday a week ago, a couple of days before the police arrested Carl Tucker?"

"Maybe."

"Did the officers question you about Carl's whereabouts on that Sunday?"

She shrugged. "They mighta asked me if I seen anything. I told 'em no."

Buck nodded his thanks and started once again to rise.

"I told 'em I didn't see nothing and I didn't," she repeated firmly. "I didn't see nothing because Carl never left his house."

Buck gave her a polite but puzzled look. "How do you know?"

She nodded across the yard. "That truck of his ain't worked in six months. He drives the Jeep sometimes, but it's got a bad muffler, makes enough noise to wake the dead, not to mention that hellhound that lives across the road. He came roaring in that morning about 2:00 a.m. and got everything all riled up with the dog barking and her screaming at him, then not another peep from over there till you folks came screeching up with your lights and sirens on Wednesday, the day my social security goes in the bank. I figured she'd finally hauled off and killed him, to tell the truth. But I know he never left that house."

Buck remembered what Sully had said about being able to walk from the site of the murder to the trailer park. He suggested, "He might've walked."

Another cackling laugh was her reply, and she lit a fresh cigarette from the tip of the cigarette she was smoking before casting the smoldering butt aside. It was clear she had said all she was going to on that subject.

"Well, thank you for talking to me, Miss Ruth." Buck got to his feet and reached into his pocket for a card, but then remembered he didn't have any. "If you think of anything else, just call my office, okay?"

"Right." Her voice was thick with sarcasm. "I'll be sure to do that."

Buck walked across the yard and checked out the exhaust pipe on the Jeep. The muffler was missing, just as the old woman had said. By this time two more patrol vehicles had arrived and the coroner's wagon was on its way. Buck always hated this part of an investigation, where the police stood around in clusters, looking useless while they waited for clearance or instructions. He sent two of the men around to canvas the other trailers, although he was pretty sure he'd gotten more from talking to Miss Ruth than they would from the rest of the neighbors combined. Then he told Sully, "See if you can find the car keys and try to start the pickup." He glanced at his watch. "I need to get back. Text me as soon as you get anything from the coroner. Can you get one of your boys to give me a ride?"

"You got it, Chief." He raised his hand and his voice toward the group of officers who were standing near the corner of the trailer. "Yo, Corley!"

A chubby, curly haired officer looked up from his conversation and started trotting over to them. Sully glanced at Buck. "Listen, Chief, I get that you want to be thorough, but we're treating this like an accidental overdose, right? Or do you know something I don't?"

"Aside from the fact that Tucker's wife was his only alibi and now she's dead, no," Buck said. He took out his phone and opened his contacts. "Do you remember the name of Tucker's lawyer?"

"Do you mean Dobie Jones?"

"Jones, that's it." Buck scrolled through his contacts and found, just as Lydia had promised, the name and phone number of everyone he might ever conceivably need to contact, alphabetized by name, title, and job category. He found the attorney under J, cross-referenced to "Attorneys, private" and "Attorney, City."

Officer Corley arrived, red-faced and sweating from the brief exercise, and Sully introduced them. Buck shook his hand and said, "Give me two minutes." He tapped the icon that connected him with Dobie Jones's office.

The attorney sounded surprised, even a little nervous, to hear from Buck. But when Buck told him about the death of his client's wife, his tone immediately sobered. "Ah, no," he said. "I'm sorry to hear that." He sighed. "What a mess. I'll let my boss know, and call Lyle Brighton's office. He's the one prosecuting the Tucker case, and should be kept up to date.

Then I guess I'd better call the jail and have somebody tell Mr. Tucker what happened."

"I figured you'd want to inform him of his wife's death in person," Buck suggested. "I wonder if I could be there when you do."

Dobie barely hesitated. "Yes, of course," he said. "I have to be in court in an hour but it won't take long... I could meet you at the jail around 3:00. I'll call Sheriff Tyler and set it up."

Buck had three appointments scheduled between 3:00 and 4:00. Lydia was going to kill him. "Sounds good," he said.

"I look forward to meeting you, Chief."

Buck spent a few minutes grimacing over the revised schedule Lydia had uploaded to his phone while Officer Corley negotiated the cruiser round the worst of the potholes on the rutted dirt road. He looked up in surprise when he saw Corley's name on the schedule. "We have an interview this afternoon," Buck said.

"Yes, sir," Corley agreed. "Two thirty." He added, a little shyly, "I really liked your speech yesterday morning."

"Thanks." Buck put his phone away, feeling his shoulders relax. "I don't see any point in putting off our interview until this afternoon, do you? I just wanted to introduce myself and get to know you a little. How long have you been with the department, Officer Corley?"

By the time they reached the police station, Buck considered the interview satisfactorily completed with one slot marked off his schedule and an idea forming about how to clear the rest of the afternoon. Corley pulled up next to the steps leading to the employee entrance at the back of the building and Buck got out, thanking him for his time. He started toward the steps and then stopped dead, his heart lurching in his chest.

An eight-foot-long alligator was stretched out in the sun on the sidewalk beside him, not three feet away.

Buck drew his weapon, backing cautiously away from the walk. He sited the creature between the eyes.

"Chief! Wait!" Corley slammed open the door of the cruiser and bolted out. "Don't shoot!"

Buck did not take his eyes off the alligator, whose tail was swishing slowly, as Corley panted up.

"That's Hobo!" Corley gasped, coming up beside him. "Don't shoot him!"

"What the hell," demanded Buck lowly, his weapon unwavering, "is a hobo?"

"He's harmless," Corley insisted. "He's got to be seventy-five years old. He doesn't even have any teeth. Look!"

Corley pushed past Buck toward the gator and, before Buck could stop him, grabbed the animal's jaws. Instinctively, Buck lunged back and almost stumbled off the curb. "Jesus Christ!" he exclaimed as the officer grasped the animal's jaws and pried them open, showing him to be completely toothless.

Corley grinned up at him. "He's like the town mascot," he explained. "He's been hanging around forever, mooching off the restaurants, cooling off in the fountain in the park. The tourists love him."

Buck noticed for the first time a red stripe around the alligator's neck. "What's that on his neck?" he asked cautiously, still unwilling to lower his gun.

"A collar," explained Corley. He lowered the alligator's jaws and stood up. "So people don't shoot him. The fine is $3500," he added meaningfully, "for harming or intimidating a protected animal."

Slowly, carefully, Buck re-holstered his weapon, still

keeping his eyes on the creature in front of him. "Officer Corley," he said stiffly, "have a good day."

"You too, sir," returned Corley cheerfully as Buck resumed his ascent toward the door.

Buck thought, *I don't belong here.* Nonetheless, he keyed in his card and pushed open the door grimly, ready to do his job.

CHAPTER SEVENTEEN

Lydia was mad at him. Her gaze took on a chill when he told her his plan for rearranging his afternoon schedule and the frost in her voice was unmistakable when she replied that she would see what she could do. She brought him a chef's salad for lunch—which he had not ordered—and when he observed that there seemed to be an awful lot of lettuce, she returned crisply, "That's why they call it a salad, sir." She then added pointedly, "There was over an hour marked off on your original schedule for lunch. You could have gone out. If, of course, you had stayed on schedule."

He was not in a particularly good mood by the time the last of his interviews for the day arrived at 2:30. Officer Leon Baker, whom Buck best remembered from the weight of his foot on his back, sat in the chair in front of his desk, his uniform impeccable, his expression unreadable.

Buck said, "Thanks for coming in on your day off, Officer Baker."

The other man replied, "I put in for overtime."

Buck glanced at him briefly, but there was no hint of humor in his eyes. Buck turned back to the personnel folder open on his desk.

Usually he started with something like, "This isn't a performance review. I just wanted to take some time to introduce myself and see if there was anything I could do to make your job easier." At which point the officer in question would assure him he couldn't be happier, that this was the best-run outfit he'd ever hooked up with, that his fellow officers were all one step away from sainthood, that there'd never been any hint of corruption within the department, and so on. But the nature of his interview with Baker was different.

"You've had three complaints of excessive use of force filed against you this year alone," Buck observed. "Add mine and that makes four. And it's only May. Do you have an anger management problem, Officer Baker?"

The other man stared straight ahead. "No, sir."

"I notice all the incidents involve White males."

Baker said nothing.

Buck closed the folder and sat back, staring him down. "One more complaint and your ass is mine. Are we clear?"

"Yes, sir," returned Baker sharply and started to rise.

Buck gestured him back into his chair with a curt turn of his wrist. "You're military?"

"That's in my file," replied Baker, still stone-faced.

"When I worked for the sheriff's office," Buck said, "I made it a point not to hire military. I found most of them to be a little too gung-ho, and they had trouble remembering that civilians are not the enemy. Would you say that description fits you, Officer Baker?"

"No, sir." There was not a flicker of emotion in his eyes.

"On the other hand," Buck added, "one of the finest law

officers I ever worked with was ex-military. Smartest, too. The only problem I ever had with her was that she was a little too by-the-book. Would you say *that* description fits you, Officer Baker?"

Baker replied flatly, "I swore an oath to uphold the law, sir, and that's what I mean to do."

Buck regarded him steadily. "Do you think the men you work with feel the same way?"

"I don't know how any of them feel. Sir."

"I'm asking your opinion. I need to know if there are any problems in the ranks I should be aware of."

Baker said steadily, "Chief Aikens ran a fair operation. He paid good wages. Promoted equally. If a person had a problem, you could go to him. And he understood..." Now there was a slight bite to his voice, "that when a Black police officer goes to arrest a White male suspect, he may have to use more force than ordinary to subdue him. He also understood that in cases like that, the Black officer is about ten times more likely to have a complaint filed against him than a White one would be. Also," he added pointedly, "there hasn't been an officer-involved shooting in Mercy in over five years."

Buck nodded, watching him. "Are you aware of any officers on the force taking money from business owners or Mercy citizens in exchange for favors or extra protection?"

Everyone else Buck had questioned had vehemently denied the mere possibility of such a thing, but Baker surprised him. "If you're referring to Miss Corinne's tax-collecting incentives, that's a voluntary program that I've never participated in."

"Why not?"

He replied carefully, "It seemed to me that there were too

many opportunities for a person of my particular skin color to be misunderstood."

Buck said, "It seems to me there are a lot of opportunities for an officer of any skin color to take advantage of the program, with or without being misunderstood. For example, taking his cut off the top. Or falsifying the amount that's legitimately owed so as to line his own pockets."

Baker replied stiffly, "I have no personal knowledge of anything like that ever happening, sir." But there was a flicker of something in his eyes that suggested to Buck that if he'd pressed a little harder, he might have gotten a different answer.

So, he pressed harder. "You know, Officer Baker, I have a lot of respect for loyalty, especially when it comes to the people you work with. But remember that oath you took? The law applies the same to members of this department as it does to people outside it. And my policy regarding officers who refuse to report malfeasance by another officer is to fire them both. So let me rephrase my question. Have you heard talk about anyone in this department using the mayor's incentive program to help himself to cash at the citizen's expense? I'm not looking for names. Just an answer."

He saw Baker's jaw tighten, and he thought for a minute he'd misjudged the man. Then Baker said, "I've heard talk. I don't know anybody personally. But the word is, sometimes an officer will stop a driver with an out-of-state tag for a moving violation and offer to save the person a court appearance by allowing him to pay his fine right then. The officer takes the cash and writes up the stop as a warning. Or he writes the citation and adds a couple of hundred to the fine, off the books. That way he can turn in the cash, keep the extra, and still get his bonus from the mayor."

Buck's back teeth were clamped down so hard that they hurt. He took a couple of deep breaths through flared nostrils and stretched out his fingers to keep them from tightening into fists. He said after a moment, as levelly as he could, "Thank you, Officer."

He took another moment to gather himself, glancing over his notes. "What about your partner?" He turned a page. "Torrance. Are you happy with him?"

Baker gave him a mildly disdainful look. "We ride alone. Torrance isn't my partner. He works nights. He's just some guy that happened to get to the crime scene the same time I did the other morning."

Buck should have known that. He had far too much on his mind.

Buck opened the personnel folder again. "You live in Mercy," he observed. "Do you like it here?"

The other man replied cautiously, "Well enough."

"Good neighbors?"

A hint of suspicion joined the hesitancy in his voice. "I guess."

"You've got three children."

He didn't answer, and when Buck glanced up at him, he replied reluctantly, "That's right."

"How old?"

This time he hesitated longer before replying, "Seven, ten, and thirteen."

Buck asked, "Boys or girls?"

"Two boys and a girl," he answered, a little sharply. "But if you'll excuse me, sir, I don't see what that has to do with my job performance."

"Absolutely nothing," Buck answered. "The youngest one, the seven-year-old, where does he go to school?"

Baker frowned. "Why?"

"I just wondered what you thought of the school system here."

Baker looked uncomfortable. "I'm sure you can find better people to ask about that than me."

"I'm asking you."

Baker replied briefly, "It's fine." He shifted in his chair. "Sir, if there's nothing else…"

Buck said, "What about church? Does your family go to church?"

Baker stiffened. "Chief Lawson, I don't know what you're getting at, and I'm no expert, but I'm pretty sure you're not allowed to ask me anything about my religion in the workplace."

Buck frowned impatiently and made a dismissing motion with his hand. "That's not…" He stopped abruptly when he caught a glimpse of his watch. "Crap, is that the time?" He closed the personnel file and stood abruptly, gathering up his phones and another set of folders from his desk. "How long does it take to get from here to the county jail?"

Baker stood more hesitantly. "About twenty minutes," he replied. "In good traffic."

Buck said softly, "Shit." Now he *knew* Lydia was mad at him, if she had neglected to inform him of when it was time to leave for his appointment. "Better use lights and sirens then," he told Baker. "You're driving." And at the other man's confused look, he added impatiently, "I'm paying overtime. Let's go!"

Among the things Buck disliked about being the new guy in town, relying on other people to drive him where he wanted to go ranked toward the top of the list. If Billy had lived, Buck would have had a month to learn his way around, to memorize street names and county roads, to find shortcuts and learn traffic patterns. He would have known the bad parts of town and the working-class neighborhoods, the school zones and the traffic circles and the narrow bridges as well as he did the ones in his own county. As it was, he was chief of police of a town four square miles wide and he couldn't have even found the fire station without GPS.

To say Baker drove aggressively would have been an understatement; he started pushing 90 mph as soon as they left the city limits. Buck didn't try to make conversation. The other man was pissed and Buck didn't blame him. He would have been, too, if he'd been dragged into work on his day off to drive around a big shot who couldn't even find his way to the county jail.

Buck checked his texts. Sully reported that the coroner's preliminary call was death by accidental overdose of narcotics mixed with alcohol, a thorough search of the house had turned up no ammunition of any kind, and the Chevy truck belonging to Tucker was inoperable due to what appeared to be a faulty alternator. Buck then spent some time trying to access the transcript of the post-arrest interviews with Tucker —all seventeen consecutive hours of them—conducted by arresting officer Don Sullivan and Detective Craig Teller. He scanned the last several pages, the ones that had eventually led to a confession.

Det. Teller: So you were already mad at Chief Aikens when he found you crabbing by the pier.

Tucker: I never liked the son of a bitch.
Sullivan: Yeah, he could try a man's patience all right. So, what did he say to you when he came up?
Tucker: Don't recall.
Det. Teller: Probably something like, "Let me see your fishing license, boy." Man, it used to tick me off when he called me "boy." Didn't it you, Sully? I guess that got under your skin too, didn't it, Carl?
Tucker: I reckon.
Sullivan: So, you told him you didn't have a license, right? And he started to write you a ticket.
Tucker: That bastard was all the time trying to throw me in jail. All the time.
Det. Teller: So you'd had it with him. Your gun was right there on the cooler...
Tucker: What gun?
Sullivan: The gun you brought for snakes, remember? You told us that this morning.
Tucker: I didn't have no gun.
Det. Teller: Now, you know better than that. What kind of fool would go crabbing at Lost Creek without a snake gun? You're no fool, Carl.
Tucker: Damn right, I'm not.
Sullivan: We found your gun in the weeds right next to the chief's car. How do you suppose it got there all the way from your house if you didn't bring it with you?
Tucker: Of course I brought it with me. I'm no fool.

The police officers were building the narrative, painting the picture and virtually putting words into the suspect's mouth. It was, in Buck's opinion, a lazy interrogation method that could be shot full of holes in front of a jury by any half-competent defense attorney, but that didn't matter if your goal was a plea bargain. And it worked. Buck fast-scrolled to the end of the transcript.

> *Sullivan: So we talked to the prosecutor and he's agreed to the deal. Your lawyer, here, Mr. Jones, has approved everything we talked about. Thirty years, all the medical, everything.*
> *Atty. Jones: That's right, Mr. Tucker. You and I have talked about what your chances would be in front of a jury. This is a good deal. I'm going to recommend you take it.*
> *Det. Teller: All of us here in this room, we just want to help you out. Nobody wants Death Row to get any more crowded than it already is. But we can't do anything for you until you tell us, in your own words, exactly how you came to kill Billy Aikens that Sunday at Lost Creek Pier.*
> *Tucker: State pen, not federal?*
> *Atty. Jones: That's right. I've got it all written down for you here. Take your time looking it over.*

Baker said, "Do you want me to wait for you here, or park the unit?"

Buck looked up to see they were stopped in front of the visitor's entrance to the county correctional facility. He exited the program on his phone and gathered up his folders. "Go get a cup of coffee. I don't know how long this will take. I'll text you when I get ready to leave."

"Yes, sir." The reply was a little too crisp, trying a little too hard to hide resentment.

Buck put his hand on the door handle and then turned back. He took out his personal phone and brought up a photograph. He showed it to Baker. "This is why I was asking those questions, by the way," he said, "not to be personal. Sorry if you were offended."

Baker looked confused. "What am I looking at?"

Buck replied, "My family."

He put the phone away and went into the jail.

CHAPTER EIGHTEEN

Dobie Jones was a tall, thin man in his mid-thirties with the whitest skin and blackest hair Buck had ever seen. His handshake was firm when he introduced himself, and his grip ice-cold. His voice was welcoming, though, and his manner confident as he gestured Buck toward a seat at the wooden table that bisected the room.

"I'm sorry to keep you waiting," Buck said. "I'm afraid I haven't quite gotten used to how long it takes to get from place to place here, yet."

"Not a problem," Jones assured him. "I was running a little late, myself. To tell the truth, though, I'm not entirely sure why you wanted to be here. I could have handled this myself."

"I know." Buck pulled out a chair and sat down. "But I'm the one who found Mr. Tucker's wife, and it seemed only right. Besides, I have a few things I wanted to ask him."

The other man looked puzzled. "I don't understand. The plea deal is practically in place. We have a confession. Is there something I should know?"

Before Buck could answer, the metal door to the interview

room buzzed open and a deputy entered with Carl Tucker. The minute Buck saw him, he knew that Tucker had not killed Billy Aikens.

Tucker was probably in his fifties, although he looked older, with a gray stubble on his sagging cheeks, meth-blackened teeth, and a few strands of greasy hair clinging to his mostly bald skull. His left eye was opaque with some kind of cataract, his right eye narrowed with suspicion when he looked at Buck. His hands were cuffed before him, and his gait was so awkward that at first Buck thought his feet were also shackled. After a moment he realized that the man's right leg was a prosthetic, the foot encased in a badly fitting boot.

The deputy cuffed Tucker to the ring embedded in the table across from them and started to take his place outside the door. Buck stopped him with a raised finger. "Deputy, would you send somebody to find a laser pointer and bring it back to us here? There's got to be one somewhere in the building. Try the training room."

Both the deputy and the lawyer gave Buck a puzzled look, but the deputy said, "Yes, sir. I'll see what I can do."

When he was gone, Dobie Jones turned his attention to his client. "How are you doing, Carl? Are they treating you okay?"

Tucker kept his one good eye narrowed on Buck. "Yeah, okay, I guess." He turned to Jones. "When am I gonna get my new leg?"

Buck glanced at the lawyer curiously.

Jones said, "Carl, this is the new chief of police, Buck Lawson. We wanted to talk to you for a minute. I'm afraid I have some bad news."

Tucker growled, "What'd you mean, bad news?"

Buck said, "Mr. Tucker, your wife suffered an overdose. It

looks like narcotics mixed with alcohol. We found her this morning. She was dead. I'm sorry."

Tucker stared at him with his one good eye. "What do you mean, dead?" He looked to his lawyer for confirmation. "What's he talking about, dead?"

"I'm sorry, Carl," said Jones.

"But she can't be dead!" Tucker seemed more outraged than grieved. "Who's gonna run the place? Who's gonna collect the rents?" He turned angrily to his lawyer. "I can't go to the pen without nobody to send me money! That wasn't the damn deal!"

"Carl," Dobie Jones explained patiently, "what happened to your wife was no one's fault. She was an addict, you know that. As for the trailer park, I'll look into getting someone to manage it while you're away…"

"And rob me blind!" declared Tucker furiously. "No sirree, not a chance in hell! No, I tell you!"

He brought his cuffed hands down on the table with a clatter that caused the deputy who was standing outside to look in through the mesh-reinforced window in the door. Tucker leaned toward his lawyer and shouted again, "No! The deal's off!"

Jones said calmly, "You signed a confession, Carl. You agreed to the plea bargain."

"Then tear it up," returned Tucker. "Tear it all up! I ain't agreeing to nothing!"

Buck said, "Did you shoot Chief Aikens, Carl?"

Carl Tucker glared at him resentfully for a silent moment, then said, "I never shot nobody."

"Then why did you say you did?"

He stewed over his answer for a moment. "Because them damn detectives, they kept telling me nobody would believe me if I did it or not." He shot a dark look at his lawyer. "You sat right here and heard 'em say it. Said if I signed their damn confession they'd see to it I went to state prison, not fed, and be up for parole in ten, twenty years. Meantime, they was gonna get me a new leg..." He thumped the floor with his ill-fitting foot and both men saw him grimace in pain. "One I could walk with. And they was gonna fix my eye, too, and my teeth. Hell, I'd be better off in prison than I am now and not have to work for it, neither. But..." he turned his glare on his lawyer. "I ain't going upstate without nobody to put money in my commissary, so the damn deal is off."

Jones said, "I can see about getting money sent to your commissary account, Carl. You need to think carefully before you say any more."

Tucker said fiercely, "I want a trial, goddammit. I didn't shoot nobody! I wasn't nowhere near Lost Creek that day and I done told you, I didn't even have a gun!"

Buck frowned. "What do you mean, you didn't have a gun?"

"Damn po-lice confiscated it when they took me in the first time," he replied sullenly. "Didn't even have no bullets in it, but they took it anyhow."

"Carl, we've already been through that," Dobie Jones reminded him patiently. "The evidence shows that Billy returned your gun that day, the day he was killed."

"Can't afford no bullets," Carl went on angrily. "How the hell am I've supposed to shot somebody when I can't even afford bullets?"

The door buzzed and the deputy entered, a small laser pointer in his hand. "Will this do for you, Chief Lawson?"

Buck thanked the deputy and asked him to stay another minute. To Carl he said, "Are you right or left-handed?"

Carl scowled at him. "What the hell has that got to do with…"

"Just answer the question, Carl," his lawyer said, sounding weary. "It's not a secret."

"Right," replied the other man grudgingly.

Buck said, "Deputy, will you uncuff Mr. Tucker's right hand? And stand by, please."

When he had done that, Buck passed the laser pointer across the table to Carl and then stood up, walking from the table to stand against the wall a few feet away. "The medical examiner's report said that Billy was shot from a distance of about twenty feet away," he said. "This is more like ten feet from the prisoner, wouldn't you say? Now Carl, I want you to aim that flashlight right here at the center of my head." Buck pointed to his forehead.

Carl looked skeptically from the device in his hand to the deputy and then to his lawyer. "This some kind of trick?"

"It's okay, Carl," Jones said. His expression was almost as confused as Carl's. "Go ahead."

Carl Tucker lifted the laser pointer, aiming it at Buck's forehead.

"Have you got it centered?" Buck said. "Take your time." When Tucker nodded, he added, "There's a button on the side. Push it."

A red beam of light appeared about six inches away from Buck's right shoulder.

Buck came back to the table. "His focus is off," he told the lawyer. "And so is his peripheral vision. He couldn't site a target even if he did have bullets. And I was standing a lot closer than Billy was when he was killed."

Tight-lipped, Jones nodded. He opened his briefcase, took out a legal pad, and began scribbling notes. "Okay, Carl," he said. "You go back to your cell now. We'll talk about this later."

The deputy retrieved the laser pointer, repositioned the cuffs, and marched Carl out of the room. When the door clanged shut, Jones said, "The judge will never allow a demonstration like that in court." He did not look up from his notes.

Buck said, "I can't believe you—or anybody else—ever actually thought Carl Tucker could take down an experienced lawman like Billy Aikens, much less hike home over a mile through the woods carrying a cooler. He could barely walk across the room."

Still writing, Jones said, "The first thing they teach you in trial law is that it doesn't matter what you think. It matters what you can convince a jury to think. And you know Billy was shot in the back of the head, not the front."

"While he walked back to his car to get a ticket book," Buck replied. "A ticket book that was never found, and for good reason. He was in his personal vehicle. He was chief of police. He probably didn't even carry a citation book when he was on duty."

Jones nodded, still writing.

"We didn't find any ammo in Tucker's house," Buck went on, "either on the original search or this morning. And we've got a trailer park full of witnesses, including a trigger-happy dog, to testify that Carl never left his house that day. And what's this about him not having a gun?"

Jones continued to make notes. "He was talking about the gun he had the day Billy arrested him for domestic violence. They confiscated his weapon, of course, and there was some mistake about giving it back to him when he was released the next day. Turns out it was Billy himself who checked it out of evidence that morning before he was killed."

Buck frowned. "So the theory is Billy returned Tucker's gun to him at the pier, and Tucker shot him with it?"

"That's the case the prosecutor is trying to make."

"That would explain what Billy was doing out there," Buck said. "But there was nothing about that in Carl's confession. He talked like he had brought the gun from home."

"My client," said Jones carefully, "is easily confused. But you can be sure we will be looking into that."

Buck frowned. "He said the gun was empty when it was confiscated. Even if it wasn't, Billy wouldn't have given it back to him loaded."

Jones finished writing and closed his legal pad, sliding it into his briefcase. "You're a peculiar kind of cop, Chief Lawson," he said. "Whose side are you on, anyway?"

"Believe it or not," returned Buck, a little impatiently, "and as corny as it sounds, I'm on the side of justice."

Jones stood. "I'll discuss this with Mr. Jeffries," he said. "The judge will probably refuse the plea, even if he doesn't withdraw it. I'll file to exclude the confession, but the motion will probably be denied. They usually are." He shook his head sadly. "That plea deal was the best chance Carl Tucker had of staying out of the electric chair. I sure hope you don't think you did him any favors."

Buck said, "He didn't kill Billy Aikens."

Jones replied, "It doesn't matter." He extended his hand. "Good to meet you, Chief Lawson."

When the door buzzed open, they walked out together, but didn't speak again until they reached the wide double doors that opened onto the exit of the building. There Dobie Jones paused and remarked, "If we do go to court, I guess you'll be my star witness." He gave a wry shake of his head. "That'll be a first. The chief of police testifying in defense of the man accused of murdering his predecessor. I don't imagine that will do a lot to increase your popularity." He pushed open the door. "Well. Good luck to you, Chief. I'll be in touch."

"He's still out there," Buck said.

Jones paused halfway through the door and looked back.

"If Carl Tucker didn't kill Billy," Buck said, "the man who did is still out there. *That*'s why it matters."

Dobie Jones did not reply, but his expression had lost a little of its swagger as he stepped out into the sun.

CHAPTER NINETEEN

Buck spent the ride home absorbed in his phone. There was a text from the prosecutor's office, requesting a meeting. There was another from Ken Jeffries, Dobie Jones's boss. There were also a couple of more texts from Sully, which he didn't bother replying to. Mostly he spent his time reading back over the jailhouse interviews, looking for something he had missed. There was nothing.

He didn't even look up until they reached town, and only then because he couldn't help noticing that Baker had slowed to the speed limit. Buck put his phone away and Baker glanced at him.

"I wasn't going to bring this up," Baker said, "but you did ask if there were any problems you should know about, and I didn't want it to look like I was holding anything back."

Buck looked at him with interest. "Go on."

Baker's eyes were focused on the road. "Every now and then," he said, "you hear talk about the way some officers treat females on traffic stops, especially at night, and especially women of color. Never anything verifiable, and never anything a person would want to take too seriously, especially when you're talking about a fellow officer."

He glanced at Buck again, and Buck nodded his understanding. Baker made the turn onto Main Street and stopped at the traffic light. He went on, "Not long ago my cousin Cheryl said she knew somebody personally who'd had a bad experience driving home from work one night. She clammed up when I started asking her for details, but I could tell there was something there. I brought it to Chief Aikens's attention, and he seemed real interested. Said he was going to look into it. I wonder if he said anything to you about it."

Buck wondered if there was anything else that could possibly go wrong today. He said, "When did you speak to him?"

"Last month. A couple of weeks before he died."

"I haven't had a chance to go through all the open cases," Buck admitted, "but I'll check into it."

Baker pulled up to the police station and put the car in park. "Yes, sir. Just thought you should know."

Buck opened the door and looked around carefully for Hobo before he got out. No sign of the town mascot. He left the vehicle. "Thanks for your time today, Officer Baker."

Baker replied, "Calvary Baptist."

Buck bent down to look at him.

"Calvary Baptist on Union Road," Baker repeated. "That's where we go to church. Nice folks."

Buck nodded and closed the door. He even allowed himself a small smile as he went up the steps, but it didn't last long.

Lydia said, "The mayor's office called several times. Mayor Watts wants to speak with you right away."

"I'll just bet she does," Buck muttered, barely pausing on his way past her office. "Is Sully in?"

"I believe so, but…"

He didn't slow his stride.

Sully must have heard him approaching, because he was at the door when Buck arrived. "Yo, Chief," he said pleasantly, but his smile faded when Buck stepped inside the small room and closed the door behind him.

"Carl Tucker is innocent," Buck said.

Sully said nothing, but all expression faded from his face.

"Any law officer with half a brain would have known he couldn't have fired the shot that killed Billy, much less have dragged his body to the water and then hiked a mile through the woods to get home with only one good leg," Buck said. His voice was tight. "I don't know a lot about you, Sully, but you don't strike me as stupid. You railroaded Tucker into a confession and you couldn't even come up with a plausible story. You rehearsed every word he said and then made him memorize a confession that had about as much resemblance to the truth as I do to a drag queen. You bribed him with a reduced sentence and medical care into admitting that he was at a place he wasn't at a time he couldn't possibly have been there. You conspired to hoodwink justice and convict an innocent man. Have I got that about right?"

Sully said stiffly, "We had physical evidence. The gun with Carl's fingerprints on it and the same serial number as the one the chief had confiscated from him three days earlier. Ballistics made a perfect match for the bullet they took out the chief's skull. Work gloves with Chief Aikens's blood on them. Witnesses, including several police officers, who heard Tucker threaten to kill Chief Aikens. That was documented in a police report. He had a known history of erratic behavior and drug use. Last summer we found him shooting at the sky and claiming aliens were attacking his trailer with laser beams. The next day he didn't remember a thing about it." He drew a breath and stated firmly, "We had motive and opportunity. Tucker was a likely suspect from the beginning."

Buck said coolly, "He was likely suspect to be brainwashed into believing he did whatever you told him he did."

Now anger flared in Sully's eyes. "That's not the way it happened."

"How many bullets were in the gun?" Buck demanded. "When you found the murder weapon, how many bullets were in it?"

Sully swallowed. "None. It was empty."

"And did you find any discharged rounds when you searched the area? In the trees, the ground, maybe a few even ricocheted off Billy's car?"

Sully's nostrils flared with a breath. "You know we didn't."

"So your theory is that a man who's blind in one eye and likely drunk or high at the time managed to hit a moving target the size of a cantaloupe from twenty feet away with one shot? Hell, if *you* can do that stone-cold sober I'll give you a week's salary. Mine, not yours."

Sully's jaw set, but he did not reply.

Buck said, "When you all picked up Carl on Thursday on the domestic charge, was his gun loaded?"

"No," Sully said, "but brandishing a weapon is…"

"So if Billy returned his gun to him on the pier in the middle of nowhere that Sunday afternoon, how do you suppose he got the ammunition to shoot Billy a few minutes later?"

Sully released a tight breath. "If you're asking me, I don't think that's the way it happened. I think Billy dropped the gun off at the house, probably before church that morning, and Tucker loaded it and took it with him to the pier. When Billy came back that afternoon, for whatever reason, they got into an argument and Tucker shot him."

"I need to talk to the officer in charge of the evidence room last Sunday."

Sully shook his head. "That's not the way it works. You sign in with the time and date, then access the evidence room with your key card. There's a computer record," he assured him, "and a security camera. It's not like we take in that much evidence here."

Buck was sure that if it had been any other town of this size, those measures would have been enough. In Mercy, he was not so sure.

Sully said, "The mayor asked you to investigate, didn't she? She pushed us to make a quick arrest, but she couldn't live with her decision. I figured that would happen."

"Well then, for the love of God, why did you...?" He broke off, pushing a hand through his hair. "*Damn* it," he said tightly. Then, his temper under control, he looked back at Sully. "Just so you know," he said, "the case is officially reopened."

"Yes, sir," replied Sully briskly. "Who do you want on it?"

Buck stared at him for a moment in simple incredulity. It was a rational question, but he had no answer. Who did he want on it? The same people who had screwed up the first time? Or maybe the ones who were fleecing the public and lying to him about it, or the ones who were on the mayor's payroll instead of his own, or…

He held up a hand, as much to stop the rat's maze of his

own thoughts as to silence Sully. Then he turned and walked away without answering.

Buck returned to his office, glanced over the papers Lydia had left for him to sign, and scowled when he noticed the mounted alligator head still glaring down at him from behind the desk.

Lydia said from the doorway. "Shall I get the mayor on the phone for you?"

"No," Buck said. "I'll walk over there. I thought somebody was coming to get rid of that thing." He nodded toward the alligator.

"We had to reschedule." No one could have pinpointed even the slightest note of accusation in her tone, but it was there, nonetheless.

Buck said, as patiently as he could, "Look, Lydia. I know you're used to doing things a certain way, and I respect that. But this is a police station. Emergencies come up. You can't expect everything to stay on schedule every minute of the day. There's got to be some room for flexibility."

Lydia replied calmly, "I've managed this police station for twelve years and I'm perfectly aware of the nature of emergencies. We had a rather large one here a last week, you may recall, but the police department continued to function without interruption because we have a structure in place. It's my job to maintain that structure, but I can't do it without your cooperation. Sir."

Buck was chagrined, and tried not to show it. "You're right. I don't mean to make your job harder. But I'm in the business of catching criminals, and they're not always predictable."

"Actually," she corrected gently, "you're not. You're not a street cop anymore, or an investigator. You run a branch of government. That's your job now. And it's very, very important that government be predictable. Wouldn't you agree?"

He had absolutely no reply for that.

She nodded toward his desk. "Please don't leave without signing those. And…" She handed him a sheet of paper. "This is your schedule for tomorrow. You have a breakfast with Lyle Brighton, the prosecutor on the Carl Tucker case, at 8:00 in the morning. You'll be meeting at the Copper Kettle, which is across the street from here and two doors west. It's the white storefront with the red awning. Lunch is at 1:30 with Ken Jefferies at the Roundtree Country Club. Roland will pick you up at 1:00. Coat and tie for gentlemen, no jeans."

"Doesn't sound like a place I'll be going to very often, then," Buck tried to joke, but she didn't respond.

He took the paper and looked it over, then smiled in what he hoped was an apologetic fashion as he folded the schedule and put it carefully in his pocket. "Better day tomorrow," he promised.

"It could hardly help but be," she replied and turned to leave the room. "Have a good evening, sir."

Corinne removed a pair of oversized fashion glasses and stood when Buck came in, smiling warmly as she declared, "There you are! And just in time to take me to dinner." She pushed a button on the phone. "Wendy, have Roland bring the chief's car around. We're going to The Bait Shop for dinner.

Best seafood in town," she assured Buck as she came around the desk. "You're going to love it."

She was wearing a sleeveless white blouse with the collar turned up high, a flared black-and-white polka dot skirt, and a chunky necklace of oversized black and white beads along with the perennial red spike heels. On any other woman her age the outfit would have looked ridiculous, but she had the legs for it.

Buck said, "Thank you, Miss Corinne, but I didn't come here for dinner."

"Maybe not, but that's what you're going to get." She took a red patent leather clutch from the credenza and tucked her phone inside, removing a pair of sunglasses at the same time. She threaded her arm through his and gestured him toward the door. "Now, sweetheart, let's talk about this new directive of yours."

Buck resigned himself to dinner, which probably wasn't the worst thing that could happen, given the day he'd had. "I'm not sure there's much to discuss." He opened the door for her, and they moved out into the hallway.

"Then we're in agreement. Because, my dear, it's simply not going to happen."

Buck replied amiably, "I think the department manual gives the police chief the authority to make policy."

"But the council has oversight, and, well..." She smiled sweetly. "I *am* the council."

"Understood," Buck replied, nodding somberly. "That means I'll know exactly where to send the special agents when the DOJ opens an investigation into policies and procedures. Because, Miss Corinne, what you appear to have going here is a racketeering scheme that would put Bugsy Malone to shame. Now, you can take your chances with whatever scam you've got going behind the scenes, but you are not..." He looked down at her, his tone going hard as they paused at the outer door. "Let me repeat, you are *not* going to use my officers as your enforcement agents."

Buck did not know her well enough to determine whether the brief flare in her eyes was from anger, surprise, or outrage —or perhaps none of the above. But it was gone in an instant, and she laughed lightly, squeezing his arm. "Darling, you *are* fun. Oh, look." She slipped on her sunglasses and pushed open the outer door. "There's Roland."

They stepped out onto the sidewalk as a Mercy police cruiser rounded the corner and pulled up in front of the building. It was a sedan, white instead of black, with the city logo and "Chief of Police" emblazoned in gold on the side panels. The driver got out and trotted around the car quickly to open the back door for them. Buck remembered being mildly impressed by the car and driver when Billy had taken him on a tour of the town back in February, but it hadn't occurred to him that he would now be ferried around in the same fashion.

"Buck," said Corinne, "have you met my son, Roland? Roland, this is Chief Lawson."

Roland was a big, slope-shouldered man with curly brown hair who bore absolutely no resemblance to his dainty, sharp-eyed mother. He wore a rumpled khaki brown work uniform with "City of Mercy" embroidered on the pocket, and his expression was sullen as he shook Buck's hand. "Chief," he muttered.

The prisoner cage had been removed from the backseat to make it more passenger friendly, and when the two of them were settled into the creamy leather interior the mayor proceeded to ignore her son and turned to Buck chattily. "So," she said, "how do you like the house? Are you finding everything you need?"

One of Buck's most valuable assets was an ability to make conversation with just about anyone, and he could instantly tell Corinne was not about to discuss business in front of her son. He followed her lead effortlessly, and in the ten-minute drive from her office to the riverfront restaurant they touched on a variety of subjects, not a single one of them of any import at all.

The Bait Shop was a rambling cedar-plank structure shrouded by more of those moss-laden live oaks and decorated with so many bayou-reminiscent relics that the atmosphere hovered just this side of creepy. Inside, however, the tables were covered with white cloths and wildflowers displayed in cut crystal vases, and the vista provided by the bank of windows that overlooked the sun-sparked river was all the decoration that was needed. The hostess ushered them to one of those tables, and Roland muttered, "I'll be in the bar."

At Buck's concerned look, Corinne laughed. "Don't worry, honey, he's a teetotaler. He's always safe to drive." She slid into her chair and told the hostess, "Be a sweetheart and send me over one of those luscious strawberry margaritas, will you, honey? And one for the new chief of police, here."

Buck quickly held up a cautionary finger and shook his head in the negative, and Corinne's eyes danced. "All right then, sugar, I'll have his, too. You'll be sorry," she confided in Buck. "They really are scrumptious. And the bartender knows better than to skimp on the tequila."

The hostess smiled. "Right away, Mayor." She turned inquiringly to Buck and he absently ordered a draft beer.

When she was gone, Corinne smiled at him and leaned

back in her chair. "Now, Buck," she said, "we're not going to spoil our lovely evening by arguing. The best thing about being the boss is that you get to make the rules. I'm the boss, and I make the rules. Because I make the rules, do you know how much the average resident pays for city water? Twelve dollars a month. We have one of the most reliable, lowest-cost, high-speed internet systems in the state, and we make enough profit selling excess broadband to surrounding communities to fully fund a state-of-the-art fire department. Why? Because Mercy manages the utility and I know what I'm doing. Look at your police department. We pay the highest salaries outside of Atlanta, and we have one of the most efficient rates of enforcement, too. If the community wants to reward those boys for keeping them safe with free meals and other little goodies from time to time, I say let them do it. Because I make the rules, and just about everybody who lives here would agree that they're good rules."

A waiter in a red vest and bow tie set two giant, salt-rimmed glasses of pink-tinged tequila in front of Corinne, and a beer in a frosted mug before Buck. He left a basket of bread and two menus on the table and discreetly disappeared. Buck suspected that something about the way Corinne's and his eyes were locked suggested to the young man this might not be a good time to recite the specials.

When he was gone, Buck said quietly, "Well, at least I understand now why you didn't call in the GBI on Billy's homicide. Because when they start turning over rocks, there's no telling what they're going to find. And you have a lot of things in Mercy you didn't want them to find."

Corinne sipped her margarita, licking salt from the rim with a quick flick of the tongue.

Buck was getting so used to that down-the-rabbit-hole

feeling that it barely even registered any more. He wasn't at all sure that was a good thing. He said, "Carl Tucker is innocent, by the way. He's so blind in one eye that he couldn't have hit a barn with an elephant gun, but you knew that, didn't you? Now we've got witnesses who say Tucker never left his house on Sunday, and a trail of evidence to back that up. Again, I think you knew that, or at least suspected it. Hell, any halfway competent investigation would have already turned up everything I found today and more. So just tell me: why did you let Tucker take the fall?"

By the time he finished speaking, the margarita glass was half-empty. She finished the other half while forming her reply. He waited patiently.

At length she said, "You have no idea what it was like then, Buck. A Georgia chief of police had been murdered, execution-style, and dumped in the river. There were camera crews down here from all over the state. No, all over the south. People were talking crazy—drug gangs, organized crime, political revenge—and some of those people were law enforcement. The governor himself was on the phone to me the next day, and it wasn't just a condolence call, either. All kinds of crazy stuff was flying all over the internet, our people were so scared they were afraid to leave their homes... we had to put a stop to it. We had to."

Buck said flatly, "By framing an innocent man."

She gave a short, dismissing turn of her wrist and picked up the second margarita. "Oh, he wasn't that innocent. The prosecutor made a case against him, didn't he? And the deal he got was more than fair."

Buck had to take a minute. He picked up his beer, took a sip. He put the mug down and turned for a moment to look out over the water. Then he looked back at her. "Well," he said, "that deal is off the table. We can probably hold him while the prosecutor reviews the charges, but I don't see how he's going to be able to make anything stick."

Corinne said, "What are you going to tell the press?"

"Nothing, if I can help it," Buck admitted, "aside from the fact that we're holding a person of interest but the case is ongoing."

He saw her shoulders relax fractionally, and she picked up her glass again. "I knew Billy picked the right man," she said. "What's the next step?"

"The next step," said Buck, "is to find out who killed Billy. And I don't have the first idea where to start."

Corinne smiled and reached across the table to pat his hand. "You'll be fine, sweetie. I'm counting on you. Billy's counting on you."

Then she sat back and picked up a menu. "You really should try the pecan-crusted catfish, honey. It's out of this world."

———

Over the next hour Buck finished his catfish, which really was good, and his beer while watching Corinne pick at a salmon salad and consume three more drinks. Her eyes grew glassier and her demeanor more withdrawn as the evening went on, but she never once slurred her words or relaxed her drawing-room posture. Buck was enormously relieved when, just as the waiter brought her another drink and was asking about dessert, a fellow diner came over and introduced himself as the head of the Chamber of Commerce. He was a jovial man who seemed fond of Corinne, so Buck felt comfortable about leaving her in his hands when, after a few more minutes of conversation, he told them he had to leave, using work as an excuse. He found Roland in the bar, eyes glued to the television set while he finished up a grouper sandwich. As far as Buck could tell, he'd had nothing to drink but the Coke that was in front of him.

"Just run me back to the station," he said, "and then make sure your mother gets home okay."

"No problem." Roland got to his feet and wiped his mouth with a napkin. "That's what I do."

Buck felt ridiculous sitting in the back of the police car by himself, but Roland beat him to the car and opened the back door, clearly indicating that was Buck's place. It was probably just as well, since the other man did not appear to be much of a conversationalist. As he was climbing in, Buck's foot dislodged the back floor mat and he caught a glimpse of something shiny. He picked it up as Roland closed the door. It was a delicate silver chain with some kind of medallion on it, and he thought at first Corinne might have dropped it. But then he remembered the big black-and-white beaded necklace she'd been wearing, and knew it wasn't hers. Did Roland use the car for dates? That would be against department policy in a major way, but what else was new? He dropped the chain into his pocket and was about to start questioning Roland when, to his surprise, the other man spoke first.

He said, glancing at Buck in the rearview mirror, "She wasn't always this way, you know."

Buck replied, "Your mother?"

"She's a smart woman," Roland said. "Has a law degree from William and Mary. Everybody thought she had her sights set on Washington, or maybe even the Supreme Court. I'm just telling you what folks say."

Buck waited until he saw Roland's eyes in the mirror again, and then he nodded.

"I had a brother," Roland said, making the turn onto the highway. "He drowned in the river when he was three. Nobody knew if he'd been pulled in by a gator, or just fell in. But I guess it was pretty bad when they, you know, found his remains. Again, I'm just telling you what folks say. I wasn't but five months old at the time."

Buck nodded mutely, and this time his throat was too constricted to speak as he tried very hard not to picture what Roland described.

"A couple of years later," Roland went on, "my daddy killed himself. He'd been a captain in the army, and I guess he got all dressed up in his uniform one day, put a pistol in his mouth, and fired it. Mama came home to find him all laid out on the foyer floor, blood and brains everywhere. Again, I'm just telling you what I hear. I was two when it happened, and spending the weekend with my grandma. But there's a rug in the foyer now that nobody ever takes up."

He didn't say anything for another mile or two, and then he added, "I just thought you should know."

"Thank you," Buck managed in a moment, "for telling me."

They didn't speak again until they reached the police station. Buck thanked him for the ride, but before he could add anything else Roland put the car in gear and was gone.

CHAPTER TWENTY

When Buck got home, he texted Jolene to set a time for a video chat, then found himself wandering back into Billy's study. To be fair, it was the only fully furnished room in the house, and also the only one with a television set. He poured himself a bourbon and spent a few minutes looking for the remote control. He found it on one of the bookshelves, but did not turn on the television. He was thinking about the dream he'd had, and how Billy had wandered around the room, finally taking a green leather-bound volume off the middle shelf. Buck counted down and over until he found the book Billy had chosen. *The Poems of Sidney Lanier*.

Buck opened the book and a yellow sticky note, folded in half, fluttered to the floor. He picked it up, noting the ten-digit number that was scribbled on the paper. It looked like a phone number. Just because he was curious, Buck took out his phone and dialed the number. All he got was a recorded, *We're sorry, your party cannot be reached. Please check the number and try again.* He tucked the paper back into the book with a shrug and started to close the volume when his eyes fell on the passage the paper had marked. It was the last stanza of "The Marshes of Glynn." Wasn't that the poem Miss Corinne had quoted to him yesterday?

> *How still the plains of the waters be!*
> *The tide is in his ecstasy.*
> *The tide is at his highest height:*
> *And it is night.*
> *And now from the Vast of the Lord will the waters of*
> *   sleep*
> *Roll in on the souls of men,*
> *But who will reveal to our waking ken*
> *The forms that swim and the shapes that creep*
> *Under the waters of sleep?*
> *And I would I could know what swimmeth below*
> *   when the tide comes in*
> *On the length and the breadth of the marvelous*
> *   marshes of Glynn.*

A gust of artificially cooled air caused the back of Buck's neck to prickle as the AC unit kicked on. *And I would I could know what swimmeth below when the tide comes in...* Jesus, this whole place was starting to creep him out.

But the man did have a way with words.

He closed the book and returned it to its shelf when his phone chimed with an incoming video call. The darkness that threatened to suck up his soul exploded into a bright cacophony of familiar faces and happy voices and suddenly all was right with the world.

Willis howled with laughter when Buck told the story about almost shooting Hobo, the town mascot, and Eloise oohed and ahhed over the roses out front when Buck took them on a tour of the house and grounds. He heard about Willis's day and Eloise caught him up on the neighborhood gossip. He hated to say goodnight to them, but was glad, too, when it was just Jo and him, spending a twilight evening together like they used to do.

"So," Jolene asked, "are you really going to stay in that haunted house?"

"It's not haunted," he objected. "Well, not much. Don't you like it?"

"It's fine, I guess. Awfully big. I'll bet it costs a fortune to heat."

"I think down here they worry more about cooling," he pointed out. "But Miss Corrine has probably got some scam going on with the power company to take care of that too."

"The yard is nice," she allowed.

"I was thinking about putting a swing set in back for Willis," Buck said. "Do you think he's too old for that?"

She smiled. "No, he's not too old. How far away is the elementary school?"

"Two miles. The school bus goes right by here."

"It stops right in front of the house here," she pointed out. "Willis doesn't even have to walk."

"What do you want to bet the school bus driver could be persuaded to stop in front of the police chief's house here, too?" he said.

"You're on a real power trip, aren't you?"

"It comes with the job," he admitted modestly.

Buck propped himself up on his unmade bed with the bourbon on the night table beside him, and she asked about the rest of his day. When he got to his interview with Baker, she chuckled.

"Baby, he probably thought you were planning to stalk him," she said. "Poor guy."

"Shut up," he replied affectionately. "I was just trying to be helpful."

"Well next time, just ask him where his wife gets her hair done," Jolene said. "That's all Mama and I care about anyway."

"Yeah, not going to do that." He rubbed the knot between his brows. "And get this. Baker seems to think there's something going on with the patrol officers mistreating female citizens at traffic stops. He said his own cousin knew somebody it had happened to. Didn't you read something about that on the internet? You know, that night you were trying to tell me all the things that were wrong with this place?"

Something flickered across her face that was almost like uneasiness, but it was gone as quickly as it had appeared. "Yeah," she said. "I think I did. I can look it up and send you the link if you want."

"Thanks."

She was wearing a peach-colored tracksuit that hugged her curves in a way that elevated athletic wear to new levels, with the zipper undone just to that point on her cleavage that made it almost—but not quite—impossible to concentrate. She lay on her stomach on her own bed with her ankles crossed in the air and her hair in a thick braid over her shoulder. He had to stop himself from reaching out to caress the screen, he missed her so much.

He said heavily, "It doesn't look like I'm going to be able to make it home this weekend. They've planned this inauguration ceremony for me on Sunday, and next weekend is Memorial Day…"

She was laughing. "Installation," she corrected. "It's an

installation ceremony. Unless they've decided to elect you president down there."

He frowned a little and sighed. "Who the hell knows what these people might do?" He felt compelled to add, "Honey, I'm real sorry about the cruise next weekend. Maybe we can change the dates?"

She gave a dismissing wave of her hand. "I already canceled the tickets. And let's talk about something else. I'm tired of being mad at you about it."

"Glad to hear that. There's nothing worse than a woman who holds a grudge."

She returned mildly, "Oh baby, you haven't seen grudges like the ones I can hold. And you *will* be making this up to me, you can count on that."

He smiled. "I sure do miss you."

"Good. So, what else did you do today?"

He went on to tell her about the shake-down ring the mayor was running with small businesses and how Miss Corinne—in complicity with his own police department—had railroaded an innocent man on a murder charge just to avoid the scrutiny of the press.

"Lovely," said Jo, not looking pleased at all. "And the best part is when this whole thing unravels, guess who's going to be left holding the bag? The chief of police. That'd be you, by the way. It looks like your good friend Billy really screwed you over, baby."

Buck rubbed the knot between his eyes. "Well, one thing's for sure. I can't walk away now. If I do, I'll look as guilty as the rest of them."

She nodded thoughtfully. "And that explains why the mayor waited until they had a suspect behind bars to call you in. She knew she wouldn't be able to stop you from turning over the investigation to GBI."

"And she was right. Now it's too late. Once the GBI opens an investigation they won't limit their scope, and there's no telling what they'll find now that I'll have to explain. Which I can't. So looks like I'm on my own."

She looked worried. "Is there anything I can do?"

He tried to smile. "Yeah. Go back in time and try harder to talk me out of this."

"Wish I could."

He was quiet for a moment. "I run a branch of government now," he said. The words sounded as heavy when spoken as they had when he'd heard them. "Me."

"You ran a branch of government when you were sheriff," she reminded him. "And you'd still be doing it if you hadn't dropped out of the election."

He shook his head. "That was different. I was working. I mean, yeah, I was in charge, but mostly I was enforcing the law like I've always done. Here it's all meetings and speeches and lunches and dinners and negotiations and compromises. Not what I'm good at."

"Well, you're the boss," she pointed out. "Seems to me you're the one who ought to decide what the job is."

"Yeah, you'd think so, wouldn't you?" Then he smiled at her, sadly and tenderly. "I just miss you, Jo," he said softly. "Without you everything seems off-kilter, broken. It's like trying to play the guitar with one hand. I didn't think it would be like this."

"Yeah," she said. "Me, either." And then she sighed. "But unless this conversation is going to end in phone sex…"

"Wait," he said, "I didn't know that was an option."

She smiled and finished, "I have to go. I promised Willis a story before bedtime, and he's waiting."

"What are we reading?"

"Something about a dog, a cat, and a canary on a spaceship."

He grimaced. "That can't end well."

"I think the point is they all have to learn to get along."

"Yeah, well, let me know how that works out."

She chuckled and touched her fingers to her lips, blowing a tender kiss. "Good night, Buck."

His attention was caught by a glow from the window and he sat up. "Hold on, baby. You've got to see this."

Buck walked out onto the balcony, where the whole world was bathed in red. "Check this out." He turned the camera view to take in the crimson sky and the river below that looked like it was on fire with dancing red and gold flames. It was amazing. "Have you ever seen anything like that?" he said.

———

"Gorgeous," she agreed. "Like a painting or something." Then, "Where are the mountains?"

Buck walked down the pier into the blood-red sunset. Billy sat on the bench at the end of the pier, his arm stretched over the back. The gnats had gone in for the night, and the temperature wasn't bad at all. The river shimmered with fiery light as far as the eye could see. Buck thought it was like being on the surface of Mars, or at least what he'd always imagined Mars would be like.

He sat down beside Billy. "Now this," he said, "was almost worth waiting for."

"Yep," agreed Billy. "Every single time. It's like God's way of saying, 'Hang in there. It gets better.'"

"Maybe." But Buck was far from convinced.

Billy glanced at him with a grin. "So," he said. "You pissed off Lydia, blew up the prosecution's case, declared war on Miss Corinne, and tried to shoot the town mascot. I can't wait to see what you do on Day Three."

"I feel like a country dog in the city," Buck admitted. "You stand still, they screw you; you run away, they bite you in the ass."

Billy chuckled. "That's about the size of it, all right."

"Things would be a lot easier," Buck said, "if you'd just tell me who killed you."

Billy's smile was only slightly tinged with regret. "Actually, I can't. You'd be surprised how little that kind of thing matters to me now. But I can tell you who didn't."

Buck said, "Carl Tucker."

Billy cocked a finger at him and winked. "Right."

Buck said, "Did you know about all the crap that's going on in the mayor's office?"

Billy slanted him a glance. "Do I look like an idiot to you?"

"So Jo was right. You set me up. You picked me for this job because I looked like the perfect patsy. The outsider who could blunder into a criminal enterprise and take the fall."

"Nah," Billy said easily. "I picked you for the job because I knew you could do it. Keeping the law in this town is like driving a team of spirited horses. You've got to know when to pull in on the reins and when to give them their strides. That takes instinct. You've got the instincts. You just need to learn to pick your battles."

"From what I can tell so far, I don't have a lot to work with. Half my men are corrupt, the other half incompetent, and they're all lying to me. Except maybe Baker." He was thoughtful for a minute. "I was supposed to ask you something about him. I can't remember what it was."

"Well, you've had a long day."

"You got that right."

They sat there in silence for a while, watching the night grow richer and redder. Then Billy quoted softly, "'And now from the Vast of the Lord will the waters of sleep roll in on the souls of men, but who will reveal to our waking ken the forms that swim and the shapes that creep under the waters of sleep?'" He looked at Buck, his face, as though covered with a scrim of blood, bathed in red light. "There's a lot of truth in that, son. It's all about what we can't see beneath the deep, the dark in the souls of men."

Buck said, "I'm not much for poems." He frowned a little, remembering. "Say, what's in that field notebook you left in your desk? You got some kind of numbers racket going on the side?"

Billy chuckled. "You already know the answer to that. You've seen those numbers before. Besides, you've got bigger problems to figure out."

"Oh yeah? Like what?"

Billy glanced down at Buck's hand. "What's that you've got there?"

Buck opened his fingers and saw that he'd been clutching the silver necklace he'd found in Billy's car. He turned it over, looking at the pendant. But the light was fading, and before he could make out what it was, he woke up.

Buck lay in bed for a moment, staring at the dark, reliving the dream. Then he turned on the bedside lamp and went into the bathroom where he'd left his clothes on the floor. Squinting in the overhead light, he searched his pocket until he felt the silver necklace he'd stored there. He pulled it out and turned it over, looking at the pendant.

It was a silver half-heart with the word "Friend" written on it. It took him a moment to understand what he was looking at. Peyton McGilroy, the girl from the convenience store whose car had been found on the side of the road, had been wearing a necklace just like this one, only her half of the heart had "Best" engraved on it. This was the match for Peyton's necklace.

What had it been doing in the back of Billy's car?

From the Diary of The Marsh Dragon
May 8, 2021

Damn it, Billy. Damn it, damn it, damn it, and damn *you* to hell! Why did you have to keep looking, keeping poking around, keep asking questions? There are lines, damn it. There are *lines*!!!

But okay. What's done is done. Back into dragon mode, the wily kind, the kind who knows how to cover his tracks, to make himself invisible, a part of the landscape. No problem. You taught me well, old man. I got this.

CHAPTER TWENTY-ONE

Back home in Hanover County there was a place on Main Street called Meg's Diner where all the men of the town would gather before work for breakfast—construction workers, bankers, lawyers, county commissioners, business owners, cops. They'd discuss the state of the world and come up with solutions for every problem, often at the top of their lungs and punctuated with loud, good-natured guffaws of laughter. They would then move on to catching up on the news around town, the latest about their neighbors, their wives, their kids. Anyone who thought women had a patent on gossip had never been to breakfast at Meg's Diner. Buck had solved a lot of cases just by eating breakfast and paying attention.

The Copper Kettle was not like that.

There was a hostess stand and piped in music, blue checked cloths on the tables, and copper kitchen accoutrements hanging from the exposed beams overhead. Buck figured the blue-collar workers were all breakfasting at the Huddle House, because the diners here were dressed in business attire and spoke in quiet, cordial tones across the table to each other. Buck was glad he'd put on a sports jacket and tie in anticipation of his lunch at the country club; otherwise, he would have felt out of place.

Lyle Brighton was a genial, pleasantly obese man with thinning gray hair who rose to greet him with a firm handshake, and then got right to business.

"So," he said, "I've been talking to the judge and he's agreed to postpone the hearing another two weeks while we review the evidence." He gave Buck a penetrating look across the table. "I don't suppose you've got any, do you?"

"Nothing that will help your case," Buck replied. "And probably nothing you don't already know."

Brighton gave a sanguine nod and picked up his menu. "I hear the spinach frittata is good here if you like that kind of crap. I'm a ham and eggs man, myself."

"Then we have something in common." Buck waited until the waitress had poured his coffee into a porcelain cup to add, "Did you really think you could win a case against Tucker in court?"

"Me? Nah." He gave a single shake of his head and put down his menu. "They would have appointed a special prosecutor if we'd gone to trial, and making the case would've been his problem. But it was in the best interest of the people to dispose of this case as quickly as we could, so that's what I did."

Buck said, "Do you think they got the right man?"

Brighton picked up his coffee cup, regarding Buck thoughtfully. "I only know what your office tells me. I build my case off what they give me. But if you're asking a personal opinion, I don't see how it could've been anybody else."

"Why's that?"

"Folks liked Billy, for one thing," the other man said. "He had a way of dealing with people that, even if he was telling you no, made it sound like he was saying yes. A real diplomat, you might say. For another thing, he just didn't get involved in day-to-day law enforcement, you know, the kind that might piss somebody off. Ever since that time fifteen, twenty years ago, he shot that fellow in front of his kids. Shook him up real bad, almost left policing on account of it, I heard. But here's the kind of man Billy was. He made sure those kids had Christmas every year, took care of their mama while she lived, even sent the oldest one to college. Never said a word about it to anybody, but we all knew."

He drank from his coffee cup. "So what I'm saying is raiding a drug house, slapping somebody in cuffs and hauling them off to jail, the kind of thing some lowlife might spend time plotting revenge for… that wasn't the kind of police officer Billy was. Except for that one time, with Tucker. Tucker threatened to kill him, and not even a week later, Billy is shot in the head and Tucker's gun is found at the crime scene." He shook his head sadly. "Seems open and shut to me."

"I have some questions about how the gun got to the scene."

"So did we all, at first. But the scenario Sully came up with—that Billy had driven out there to return confiscated property—seemed the most likely."

"Carl never confessed to that."

The waitress arrived with her pen at the ready and Brighton said, "Bring me three eggs, scrambled, with that country ham of yours and a couple of biscuits and honey."

The waitress turned to Buck and he said, "Sounds good. Same here."

Brighton went on, "Carl Tucker's brain is so scrambled it's

a wonder he can remember his own name, much less what happened a week ago. But I don't see any other way it could have happened."

Buck said frankly, "And I don't see any way Carl could have killed Billy. I think it's time we started looking elsewhere. Everybody has enemies, and it's hardly ever the ones you know about that are the most dangerous."

Brighton regarded him thoughtfully for a moment. "Miss Corinne told me to work with you," he said, "give you whatever support you need, and I'm fine with that. I know she's pretty broke up about this and wants to make damn sure that, when all is said and done, she can look back and say she did the best she could for Billy. But here's the thing, Buck."

He took a sip of his coffee and put the cup down before continuing. "You seem like a nice fellow, and I know Billy was mighty excited when he got you to sign on. He said he'd found somebody who thought like him, reminded him of himself in his younger days. Said you were the perfect fit for the job. He got everybody on your side before you even showed up, and folks here are ready to welcome you with open arms, almost like they're honoring Billy's last wish by doing it. But I want you to know if we let Carl Tucker get away with this, it'll tear this town apart, and it'll be the end of your career, at least in this part of the country. Mine, too." He picked up his coffee cup, sat back in his chair, and took a sip, holding Buck with his eyes all the while. "So let's try not to let that happen, what d'you say?"

Buck smiled, though barely, and picked up his own cup. "So," he said politely, "how long have you lived here?"

Buck stopped by Lydia's office on the way to his own to let her know he was in. He was scrolling through his phone, trying to remember the name of the state trooper who had called him the other night and hoping caller ID had captured it, but he stopped when he saw the flowers on her desk. It was a big, showy bouquet of pink and red roses, white hydrangeas, deep magenta lilies, and a bunch of other things he couldn't identify.

"Good morning, Chief," she said pleasantly. "How was your breakfast?"

"Good," he said. He gestured uncertainly to the bouquet. "Nice flowers," he said. "Is it your birthday?" Even as he said it, he felt guilty because he should have known, but how could he? The person responsible for telling him things like that was, well, Lydia.

"No, sir," she replied, and handed him a card. "They're from your wife."

Buck looked in surprise from her to the small card in his hand. He could barely repress a grin as he read, *Thanks for taking care of him. I know he can be a handful.* It was signed, *Mrs. Buck Lawson.*

"She seems nice," Lydia observed as he returned the card to her.

"Believe me, she's not," he muttered dryly.

"Yes, sir," she replied, unfazed. "But please thank her for me."

Buck let the grin break through when he reached his office and punched Jolene's number.

"I'm calling for Mrs. Buck Lawson," he said when she answered.

"I'm sorry, there's no one here by that name."

"Well, thanks for the laugh anyway." He sat down behind

his desk and booted up his computer. "Lydia says thank you for the flowers."

"Any little thing I can do."

"Whose idea was it, anyway? Your mother's?"

"I resent that. I can be nice, you know." She added, "Your problem is you don't know how to deal with a strong, powerful woman."

"You got that right. You scare the hell out of me."

"Well, aren't you lucky you get a chance to up your game? Between me, Lydia, and that mayor, we'll have you in fighting shape in no time."

"Oh, boy. Can't wait."

Her tone sobered. "Buck, I hoped you'd call." She hesitated a moment, just long enough for Buck to stop what he was doing and pay attention. "Last night when you brought it up, I wasn't sure whether I should say anything. It seemed kind of silly at the time…"

He took his hand off the computer mouse and sat back, his focus fully on the phone. Lydia entered silently and set a cup of coffee on his desk, but he barely noticed. "What?"

He heard her draw a breath. "I need to tell you something."

CHAPTER TWENTY-TWO

February
Outside of Mercy, Georgia

The original plan had been for Jolene to drive down on Saturday and meet Buck at their beachfront hotel that afternoon. But it had seemed foolish, since they both had Friday off, to waste the day, so she'd decided to drive down after her shift on Thursday, arriving in Mercy shortly after midnight. Buck had checked in a few hours earlier, and had texted her their room number at the Comfort Inn. It was now 1:30 a.m. and, according to the GPS on Jolene's phone, she was still twenty minutes away from her destination. According to her own gut, she was completely lost.

It had started to rain about halfway through the drive, and she'd missed her exit off the expressway. She took the next exit and started to backtrack, but the GPS insisted she could make it to Mercy via the county road she was on. Thus began an endless journey down empty roads through the blackest night she had ever seen with nothing but the squeak of the windshield wipers for company. The rain was the annoying kind that congealed on the glass like grease but never got thick enough to justify leaving the wipers on, so she divided her attention between looking for street signs—of which there were none—and manually operating the wipers while trying to figure out, from the tiny screen of her phone, just where the hell she was. No streetlights, no building lights, no headlights from other vehicles. Just flat, narrow blacktop crowded with thick black trees on either side of the road, like something out of a very scary fairy tale. She actually considered calling Buck, just to hear the sound of another voice. She had never felt so alone. And then she wasn't.

She saw the blue lights strobing in her rearview mirror and instinctively glanced down at the speedometer. She wasn't sure what the speed limit was, but out here on a deserted country road it couldn't be less than the forty-two miles per hour she was currently traveling. She slowed even further, just to indicate to her pursuer that she saw him, and the blue lights drew closer at an alarming speed. The siren whooped. Jolene slowed and pulled to the side of the road, more relieved than alarmed. At least now maybe she could find out where she was.

Jolene waited interminably while the officer ran her plates and the blue lights strobed a colorful pattern across the crystals of rain on her windshield. The bright white glare of a flashlight searched her backseat, cargo area, and passenger area.

When the sharp tap on the window finally came it startled her so much that she jumped, and the blinding glare of the flashlight caused her to fling up an arm to shade her eyes as she rolled down her window. A mist of rain dampened her hand and the inside of the car door. She squinted past the light, trying to make out the face beneath the hood of the blue rain jacket. He said, "Do you have a gun on you?"

"Yes, I do," she replied. "I'm an off-duty law officer."

"Where is it?"

"In the glove box," she informed him, but she did not reach for it because she could see now that while one hand held the flashlight, the other was on the grip of his service weapon. For the first time she felt a twinge of apprehension.

"Are you aware that you need a permit to carry a concealed weapon in Georgia?"

"I didn't know that," she replied with all the politeness she could muster, "but I do know that carry permits between North Carolina, Georgia, and Florida are reciprocal, and that a gun that's transported in the glove box of a car isn't considered concealed." Which, she thought but didn't add, even a bone-head patrol officer should know. No wonder Buck called the Georgia cops stupid.

He commanded sharply, "Open the glove box with one hand and give me your weapon, grip first. Keep your other hand on the steering wheel."

Jolene had made dozens, if not hundreds, of traffic stops during her time with the Hanover County Sheriff's Office. She was known to be firm, humorless, and efficient. When she made an arrest, she used exactly as much force as necessary—or, at least, that was what she assured herself every single time. She had never, before tonight, considered what it must be like for the person behind the wheel. The next time she made a stop, she knew she wouldn't be able to think about anything else.

She cursed herself for not knowing the laws in Georgia even as she handed over the gun. Maybe they were allowed to hold a weapon during a traffic stop here. More likely, she had just pissed him off. "That's an eight-hundred-dollar piece of equipment," she informed him.

"And how would you know that?" She still couldn't see his face, but there was no mistaking the trace of a sneer in his voice.

"Because I'm still paying for it."

"Is that right?" He ejected the magazine and pocketed it, then did the same with the bullet in the chamber. "Are you sure you didn't steal it? Maybe lifted it off some perp somewhere? Maybe I should run the serial number just to be sure. *Officer.*" He practically spat the last word, but he returned the gun to her, grip first.

For the first time in a very long time—perhaps in her life—Jolene Smith was too flabbergasted to speak.

"Let me see your license and registration," he commanded.

Jolene had the documents ready, along with her badge and gun permit. She passed them through the window to him. Her heart was pounding in her chest, loud and hard, from rage, she thought, not fear. But if she was honest, it was both.

He turned the flashlight briefly on her ID. At this point he had two options. He could return her credentials with a polite warning as a professional courtesy and send her on her way, or he could be an asshole and keep her waiting twenty minutes while he ran her paperwork through the system and plugged her name into every database available to him. Jolene got the impression that this guy wasn't big on professional courtesy.

He surprised her by passing the paperwork back to her.

"Seems to be in order," he remarked. He did not sound happy about it.

Jolene returned the documents to her wallet and he danced the flashlight beam over the interior of the car again, then fixed it for a moment on her lap. On her crotch, to be exact. She was wearing jeans and a V-neck tee shirt, comfortable and appropriate for driving. Both of them fit her well. She watched in incredulity as the flashlight beam moved slowly up her torso and stopped, unwavering, on her cleavage. "They sure do grow 'em big up in North Carolina, don't they?" he remarked.

Jolene stared at him, trying to make out his face in the dark. "You have got to be freakin' kidding me," she said.

He took an abrupt step back. "Get out of the car," he ordered.

Jolene said, "No." She reached to turn the key in the ignition.

He moved suddenly to reach inside the car, unlocking the door. Jolene snatched up the phone on the seat beside her. "Okay, cowboy, that's it. I'm calling 911 and getting a supervisor out here. What's your damn badge number?"

She had dialed the first two digits before the flashlight swung into her eyes, blinding her again. She raised her forearm to block the light, and he said, "No need for that. We don't have a problem here."

Jolene said, very calmly, "Are you sure about that? Because if you put your hand inside this vehicle again, you're going to have a very big problem."

She could hear his heavy breathing even above the sound of hissing rain. Even above the roar of blood in her ears. Then he said, "It's against the law in Georgia to drive with a phone in your hand. But seeing as how you're from out of state, I'll let you go with a warning this time."

She had not been driving with the phone in her hand. She did not say so. Instead, she said coldly, "Give me back my magazine."

A long time passed while the bright light burned her eyes, and then his hand appeared in the window, holding her ammunition magazine. She took it from him, then extended her hand again, her face absolutely expressionless. "And the bullet in your pocket."

She thought for a moment that would trigger the showdown. But after a deliberately drawn-out hesitation, he reached into his jacket pocket and dropped the bullet into her open palm. "Now," he said in something resembling a low growl, "get the fuck out of here before I change my mind."

She rolled up the window, started the engine, and put the car in gear. She did not take a deep breath until, some ten miles later, she saw the glow of security lights from a service station, and she knew civilization was near.

CHAPTER TWENTY-THREE

Buck said quietly, with ultimate control, "And you didn't tell me this because?"

"I told you," she snapped back. "I told you I was late because I'd been pulled over."

His silence throbbed across the miles between them.

"Oh, for God's sake, Buck," she said shortly, after the silence had gone on a beat too long. "We'd just had a huge fight about you taking that job, and then I'm supposed to come to you right before your interview with a story about some cop being mean to me? How self-serving would that look? Besides, it was nothing. Literally. No ticket, barely even a warning. Nothing."

He was silent for a moment. "This is why you were looking up all those cases from Mercy when we got home. Missing persons, misconduct complaints, sexual assault…"

Her own silence was confirmation.

He said brusquely, "Could you identify him from a photo?"

"I told you, I never got a look at his face. White guy, undetermined age. Mercy Police Department insignia and badge on his coat. And in that bulky raincoat with the hood pulled up, bent over the way he was, he could've have been 180 or 280, five-six or six-five. I've got nothing."

"Okay," he said calmly, "can you retrace your steps to figure out what road you were on? You said you took the next exit after the one you were supposed to take for Mercy. Did you turn right or left?"

"Buck." Her voice was tense. "It's over, okay? I only brought it up because I thought it might be some kind of pattern, after what your officer told you yesterday. I've told you what I know. There's no point in going overboard."

Buck's tone was low and carefully controlled. He said, "I have been here less than forty-eight hours and I've already made more compromises than I have in my entire career. But this one doesn't slide. Whoever this jerk was, he works for me now and I am going to make it my personal mission to find him and hang him up by his balls. Is that okay with you?"

"Oh, sure." Her tone was so deadpan it could not possibly convey anything but sarcasm. "As long as you don't go overboard."

Buck blew out a breath. "Jolene, you know as well as I do the average woman wouldn't be able to handle herself the way you did when she's pulled over on a deserted road. And if this is how he treats a law officer…"

"There was nothing about that stop that was actionable," she pointed out.

"Except that he had no reason to pull you over in the first place," Buck returned sharply. "You have a hands-free phone and he couldn't have seen inside your vehicle in the dark anyway."

Jolene agreed heavily, "Right." Then, "Do you have an internal affairs department?"

"Yeah," Buck said grimly. "Me. I'll call you tonight, baby. Take care of yourself."

"You, too. I mean it, Buck," she added sternly. "Don't do anything stupid."

"Two days ago," he answered flatly, "I put my hand on the Bible and swore to uphold the laws and ordinances of Mercy, Georgia. Stupid is already in the rearview mirror."

As soon as he disconnected, he brought up Google Maps and tried to find I-75. He remembered the exit for Mercy, since he'd just driven the route two nights ago, and went one exit past it, which led to Highway 124. He lost patience trying to trace Highway 124 on the tiny screen after only a couple of minutes, and he called, "Lydia!"

He was surprised to find her standing in front of his desk when he looked up. "Your ten o'clock is here, sir." She stepped back to allow him a glimpse of the young officer hovering uncertainly at his door. "Officer Jim Torrance."

Buck stood up. "With you in a minute," he told the officer. To Lydia he said, "I need a map. A big one that shows all the county roads and the surrounding areas."

"Do you mean like that one?" She pointed over his left shoulder to the framed county map hanging on the wall.

Buck frowned to hide his embarrassment. "Right. As soon as we're done here, will you get me the commander of the local state patrol post on the phone? Major…" He had no idea who was in charge there, any more than he knew where the local state patrol office was located.

"Hollister," Lydia supplied. "And Captain Sullivan needs fifteen minutes to review the Memorial Day details."

"Thank you, Lydia." He was determined to be on his best behavior today, otherwise Jolene—or, more likely, her mother—would be sending flowers for the rest of the month.

He beckoned Torrance inside as he walked over to look at the map. "Just give me another minute."

Torrance came inside the room. "Can I help you find something, sir?" he offered uncertainly.

It took Buck only a minute to realize that the map did not cover the area as far as the expressway, so he was no better off than he had been on Google. "Yeah, maybe you can," he admitted. "It sucks to be the new guy in town. Which one of these roads leads back to 1-75?"

Torrance stepped forward eagerly. "A few of them do," he said. He pointed on the map. "There's 215, that'd be the road you came in on."

He shot a quick uncomfortable glance at Buck, and that was when Buck put the name and face together with the officer who had taken his weapons after Baker had shoved him to the floor in the convenience store. Lydia was clearly wasting no time getting the difficult personnel interviews out of the way.

Torrance cleared his throat and looked back at the map, moving his finger. "And here, County Road 62, it joins up with Highway 319, which will get you to the Tifton exit for 75. A lot out people like that route. Pretty drive."

Buck said impatiently, "What about Highway 124? That's one exit south of 215. Where does it come out?"

Torrance looked thoughtful. "That'd be a good bit out of your way if you're trying to get back to the expressway. But if you take 215 to Post Road out of town, it will eventually hook up with 62, and then 319." He traced the route with his finger on the glass-covered map until the highway fell off into the frame. Buck studied that section of the map for a moment, then turned back to the business at hand.

"Have a seat, Torrance," he said, walking back to his desk. "Thanks for coming in on your day off."

"No problem, sir."

Jim Torrance was a fresh-faced, eager-looking young man in his twenties—twenty-seven to be exact, Buck noted as he opened the personnel file Lydia had efficiently placed at the top of the stack on his desk. Torrance smoothed his hands on his trousers in a nervous gesture as he sat down, and he blurted, "Sir... Chief Lawson, I just wanted to formally apologize for the misunderstanding the other night at the convenience store. I wanted to uncuff you when you identified yourself, but Officer Baker is my superior and he said we should wait for Captain Sullivan. I just... well, I wanted to say I'm sorry, sir."

Buck replied without looking up, "Officer Baker was right. You both followed protocol and that's not what this is about. I just wanted to introduce myself and see if there was anything I could do to make your job easier going forward." The words were starting to sound dry at this point, even to his own ears. "I see you have a degree in criminal justice." Now he glanced up. "So do I."

Torrance seemed to relax a little. "Yes, sir. I had my sights set on the FBI, but Billy—I mean, Chief Aikens—thought I needed boots on the ground experience first, so I went to work for the sheriff's department out of college, hoping something would open up on the police department here. I liked it a lot, but when the chief offered me this job, I snapped it up."

"So is that how you ended up in Mercy?"

"No, sir. I was born here. Mercy's always been home."

Buck turned a page. "You've been on the force, what? Three and a half years? Nights all that time?"

"Yes, sir," Torrance replied, and smiled. "I asked for the night shift. It's quieter, and being a single man, I can keep my own schedule."

Buck closed the file. Except for a minor reprimand for using social media during work hours—which was a fairly common problem among young recruits—the kid's record was spotless. He sat back. "So how are the guys you work with? Pretty good men?"

Torrance shrugged. "To tell the truth, we're not that close. A few of them tried to haze me at first, being a newbie and all…" He gave a sideways grin and another lift of his shoulder. "But it was all in good fun. They seem like straight-up guys, but you know, we ride alone and I can't say I've gotten to know anybody that well."

Buck nodded. "Is there anything about the department you'd like to see changed? Anything we can improve on? You can speak freely here. We're starting a new chapter, and now's the time."

The young officer pretended to consider this, but Buck could tell he wasn't the type to make waves. After a thoughtful moment he gave the expected answer. "No, sir, I can't think of anything. This is a good place to work, and I'm learning a lot."

"Good to hear."

Torrance looked at him expectantly, but Buck made no move to end the interview. "Officer Torrance," he said at length, "you don't have to answer this if you don't want to, but I want you to know whatever you say stays between you and me. Do you know of anybody on your shift who has a particular problem with women?"

Torrance looked monumentally confused. "Do you mean, like, gay? Because…"

"No." Buck made a sharp dismissing gesture with his hand.

"No, not gay, that's not what I meant. I'm looking for someone who's disrespectful, contemptuous, maybe feels threatened by females in general."

Torrance thought about it for a moment, still looking confused, and then gave an uncertain half-laugh. "Heck, Chief, you just described half the cops I know."

In a moment, Buck smiled wryly. "Yeah, me, too, sad to say. Okay, thanks for your time. I just want you to know if you ever need to talk about anything, I'm here to listen. I won't claim to run the department like Billy did, but I'm going to do my best to run it well."

Torrance smiled as he stood. "Yes, sir. It's a pleasure to have you here, sir. You can count on me."

Buck barely had time to pull up the duty roster on his computer before Lydia buzzed him on the intercom. "Chief, do you have a minute for Detective Moreno?"

It took him a beat to remember who Detective Moreno was. "Frankie? Send her in. What about Major…"

"Hollister," she supplied. "Yes, sir. I'll have him for you as soon as you're finished."

Frankie appeared, somewhat hesitantly, at his doorway. She had made an effort to look presentable in a tan straight skirt and checked shirt that was belted at the waist, but managed somehow to look even more frumpy and rumpled than she had yesterday. Buck gestured her in, trying to arrange his face in pleasant lines.

"Good morning, Frankie. Have a seat. What can I do for you?"

She sat on the edge of the chair in front of his desk. "Chief Lawson, I followed up on the convenience store robbery like you asked me too. I interviewed the suspect, Farhan Singh, personally in jail. He told a fairly extraordinary story. I thought I'd better bring it to your attention personally."

She placed a file folder on his desk. Buck opened it and saw it was a copy of her jailhouse interview with the suspect, formatted and ready to go into the official case file. *Good for you, Frankie*, he thought. At least one person on his force knew how to take a note. He glanced over the report as she went on.

"According to Singh's statement, the robbery was a setup, like we thought," she said. "But he added a few details he left out of his initial interview. He seemed upset that he was still in jail and wanted to talk to the police officer he had made the deal with."

Buck glanced up curiously. Her fingers were clasped in her lap, her expression dead earnest.

"Go on," he said.

"According to Singh," she said, "he was contacted by a Mercy police officer on Sunday evening who said he knew Singh and his uncle had conspired to rob the store and split the money on several occasions before. This police officer proposed that he repeat the operation at 5:00 the next morning. He was to wait until he received a text before entering the store, and he was very specifically instructed to hold all customers hostage until the police arrived. He was assured he would not be arrested, and that the security camera would be turned off before he even got there. He was told that he could keep all the money, and that his uncle's tax debt would be erased." She hesitated, looking uncertain. "I'm not sure if you know…"

Buck made a curt gesture with his wrist, frowning over the report. "About the mayor's protection racket? I heard."

"Well, it's not really…"

"Frankie," he interrupted sternly. "Go on."

She twisted her fingers together. A fine line appeared between her brows. "He said he couldn't identify the officer he spoke to, who approached him from behind in the alley next to the Denny's where he works, but that he saw him get into a Mercy police car and drive away. Not before, however..." She held Buck's eyes. "Giving him a gun."

She took a breath. "Suspects make up wild stories all the time," she said, "as I'm sure you know. They especially like to target cops. But there's no record of Singh ever having purchased a gun, and I checked Singh's phone—he gave us permission, begged us, in fact—and there was a text at 4:50 on Sunday morning. It said 'Go.' I wasn't able to trace the number it came from. I suspect a burner phone."

Buck turned over the last page of the transcribed interview and closed the folder. He looked at her. "Where're you from, Frankie?"

She seemed unsurprised at the change of subject. "Miami-Dade County," she replied. "I was on the investigative team there for three years."

"And how did you end up in Mercy?"

"I wanted a quieter pace," she said. Then she gave a shy half smile and lifted one shoulder, adding, "And I fell in love."

This interested him. Buck said, "Any regrets?"

"About following my heart? Not a one. But if I'm being honest..." She glanced at him, almost as though for permission, and the encouraging nod he gave her was barely perceptible. "I don't think I entirely understood the challenges of being a big-city Latina woman on a small-town police force filled with hometown boys. So if you found my performance lacking yesterday when you reviewed my case files..." She lifted her chin slightly and finished, "It's not an excuse, but I need this job, and most days I like it. So I learned to adapt. To keep my head down and not attract attention. The chief—the former chief—seemed okay with that."

"You're right," said Buck, "that's not an excuse." He passed the folder across the desk to her. "But I appreciate your honesty, and thanks for bringing this to my attention. Make sure this finds its way to the proper file."

Two red stripes appeared across her cheekbones, and she inclined her head as she took the file and stood. "Yes, sir."

"And Frankie," he added, "good work."

The flush on her cheeks began to recede. "Yes, sir."

Lydia buzzed him twenty seconds after Frankie left the office. "Major Hollister on line one," she said.

Buck pushed the button for line one.

"Chief Lawson," the man on the other end of the phone said. "I was going to give you a call but figured I'd let you get settled in first. I was real sorry to hear what happened down in Mercy. Billy Aikens was a good man."

"Yes, he was," Buck said. He allowed a solemn moment before going on, "I don't mean to keep you. I'm just doing a quick follow-up on a report I got from one of your troopers night before last about an abandoned vehicle outside of Mercy. The registered owner was Peyton McGilroy. I wondered if she ever claimed her car."

He could hear computer keys clacking on the other end. "Okay, here we go. Red Acura, eight hundred feet past mile marker 18 on Highway 62... Tagged and notified. Not every day the police chief takes an interest in... Oh." There was both surprise and understanding in his tone. "I see her folks filed a missing persons' report. Just came in this morning. Are your boys involved in the search? It's about twenty miles outside your jurisdiction."

Buck clicked the sheriff's department's alerts and scrolled

down until he found the bulletin. A familiar face looked back at him: blond hair, blue eyes, 115 pounds. *Wearing a silver half-heart necklace with the word "Best" engraved on it,* Buck thought, and made a note to call the sheriff's office and have that detail added. Out loud he said, "Looks like Mercy might've been one of the last places she was seen."

"Right. Well, I wouldn't read too much into it, if I were you. We get two or three reports about these college girls gone missing every spring. Usually they turn up safe and sound and tanned from the trip to Mexico they forgot to tell their folks about."

Buck tried to put a smile in his voice. It wasn't easy. "You're probably right. Anyway, thanks for your help."

"Good talking to you. I'll see you at the LLE meeting next week?"

"Looking forward to it."

Buck hung up the phone and went back to the map, frowning over it. If Jo had taken the exit for Highway 124, her GPS would have led her south to 62, and then to Post Road, where the Mercy Police Department would have picked up jurisdiction. Buck thought it likely that Jo had been stopped on Post Road, since she'd said it had taken another twenty minutes to get to the motel. Peyton, on the other hand, had started out on 215, seven miles outside of Mercy. She had come from the Comfort Inn, and had most likely taken Post Road to get there. Frightened and upset when she left the convenience store, she'd gotten back on Post Road instead of staying on 215, and had eventually ended up on Highway 62 where, twenty miles outside of town, where something had happened.

There was a tap on his doorframe, and Buck looked

around to see Sully standing there, an electronic tablet in his hand. "Is this a good time?"

Buck waved him in. "What's the update on the Tucker death?"

"The toxicology came in," Sully said, taking the chair Frankie had just vacated. "Blood alcohol was 1.86, which is enough to put a full-sized man in a coma, and the narcotics read like a pharmacy inventory. Not to mention heroin. She might not have meant to kill herself, but there was no way she was getting out alive from that combo. We canvassed the neighborhood, such as it is, and no one saw anybody coming or going in the twenty-four hours before her death. I'd say it's exactly what it looked like—an overdose, intentional or otherwise."

Buck said, "Okay, keep me updated."

Sully hesitated. "Chief, you kind of left it open yesterday, and I was wondering if you've got any leads on Billy's homicide you want us to follow up on, or something we should be working on…"

He let it trail off, and Buck realized how uninspiring his actions had been so far. He had reopened a case they thought they'd solved but had given them absolutely no direction in which to go, no leads to investigate, not even an idea of what the truth might be. And the worst of it was that while he knew talking it through with Sully would help, he wasn't quite ready to do that. He said, "I need to check some things out. I'll get back to you later today."

"You got it."

Sully turned his attention to the maps and graphs in his hand, and Buck spent the next ten minutes listening to him describe the traffic patterns, crowd control, and mitigation efforts associated with the upcoming holiday weekend. Buck paid only the vaguest attention. Sully knew more about what was needed for the holiday than Buck did, and he would study the details once they were uploaded to his computer.

"Now, we usually get a lot of parking violations," Sully was saying, "especially on River Road and in the historic district. Not as bad as the Fourth of July weekend, when we've got cars parked on both shoulders of the highway for two miles out of town, but it can get rough. We've got kind of an informal agreement with the business owners not to ticket unless a vehicle is blocking an entrance or creating a traffic hazard. Is that good with you?"

Buck nodded vaguely. "Makes sense. What about traffic lights in town?"

"We'll increase the stoplight time at the main intersections by thirty seconds to give pedestrians time to cross. We found any more than that causes too much of a traffic backup. Do you want to go over the schedule of events?"

Buck said, "Just send me the file. I'm sure you've got everything in hand." He hesitated, then said, "Tell me about Highway 62."

Sully looked confused. "We don't really cover that far out."

Buck gave an impatient shake of his head. "No, I mean in general. What kind of road is it? Well traveled? Populated?"

Sully shrugged. "Two lane, not much out there but farm land until you get to Middleton—that's a little town about thirty miles north. Most of it's out of county, in state patrol territory."

"And Post Road? That's in our jurisdiction, right?"

"In a manner of speaking. It kind of wanders in and out of Mercy's official border, but we patrol it by agreement with the sheriff's department."

"Do you keep a man on it all the time?"

Sully gave a dismissing shake of his head. "No need. No houses or businesses out there, and it's pretty far down on the list of highly trafficked roads. Usually we make one patrol pass a shift down Post Road, but it's not a priority."

"Okay, Sully, thanks." As Sully started to rise, Buck added, "By the way, that girl from the convenience store, Peyton McGilroy? Her parents filed a missing person report."

A quick flicker of concern, or maybe it was alarm, crossed Sully's eyes and was gone. "Yes, sir," he said. "I'll make sure her picture goes out. Where'd you say her car was found?"

"About twenty miles outside of town, on Highway 62. But the report will be amended to read 'last seen in Mercy, Georgia' before the end of the day."

Sully's lips tightened briefly. "Right. I'll let the men know." He stood, but hesitated before leaving. "Hell of a first week for you, Chief."

Buck released a slow breath. "I'm hoping this isn't typical."

Sully just smiled and left the room.

From the Diary of the Marsh Dragon
May 18, 2021

Today I added two more ornaments to the tree. That brings my number up to eight, which was twice as many—by my count, at least—than my daddy had done at my age. 'Cause here's the thing: the dragon has to sleep sometimes, otherwise he gets tired, he gets careless, he gets caught. This will be the last for a while. Truth be told, the other one should have been the last, but what was I to do? I had a plan, a nice, clean wrap up: GIRL DIES TRAGICALLY IN POLICE SHOOT-OUT. But hey, you know what they say about plans.

It worked out okay anyway. Maybe it's even better this way, almost like it was meant to be. Two ornaments hanging on the tree, two halves of a whole. Symmetry, I like that. It's a nice way to finish up this round.

Because I'm getting tired. Time for the dragon to sleep awhile.

CHAPTER TWENTY-FOUR

The minute Buck identified himself on the phone to Peyton McGilroy's mother, he heard her call, "John! John, it's the police!" Then, "Did you find her? Is Peyton okay? I'm putting you on speaker."

Buck said, "Mrs. McGilroy, I don't have any new information about your daughter. I'm sorry. I'm just calling to ask you some questions that might help us find her, if that's okay."

A man's voice demanded, "Where did you say you're from?"

"I'm Police Chief Buck Lawson," Buck repeated patiently, "from Mercy, Georgia. I actually met your daughter here Sunday night—well, I should say, Monday morning. She was a witness to a robbery at a convenience store and I interviewed her."

He heard the woman gasp, "Oh my God!" and the father said at the same time, "What do you mean, robbery? We didn't know anything about that!"

The mother said tremulously, "Do you think that's what happened to her? Was it the criminal she saw…"

Buck said quickly, "We apprehended the perpetrator almost immediately and he's still in custody. Peyton's statement was just routine. I don't think the two cases are related. In fact, we don't have any reason to suspect foul play in Peyton's disappearance at all."

"Oh, thank God," breathed her mother.

The man said, "I don't understand. First you say she was involved in a robbery—"

"Not *involved*," snapped the mother. "*Witnessed*."

Buck spoke up before the conversation could go on without him. "What I'm trying to find out," he said firmly, "is what brought Peyton to Mercy in the first place. Did she know anybody here?"

"Oh, God." The words, coming from the mother, were barely a moan. "I told her not to go. I had a feeling, a bad one…"

It was the father who answered the question. "Peyton was concerned about her roommate, Mandy. Amanda Jane Wolford. She'd gone down to interview for a summer job at the country club there as a waitress… saw some ad on Facebook or something. What was the name of the place again, honey?"

"Roundtree," supplied his wife immediately. "The Roundtree Golf and Country Club. I remember because Peyton said if it worked out for Mandy she was going to apply for the summer there too, and I looked it up. It's actually the only country club in town. Seemed like a nice place."

"Anyway," the father continued, "Peyton got worried when she didn't hear from Mandy over the weekend…"

"When was this?" Buck started taking notes. "Last weekend?"

"No," replied the woman, "two weeks ago. Mandy's interview was on Saturday, May first."

The man went on, "Peyton said the last she heard from Mandy was some kind of weird text on Saturday, nothing but a picture of some kind of building covered in vines. It worried her. She started calling and texting but never got an answer."

Buck frowned. "Mandy hasn't been heard from in two weeks and nobody was concerned?"

"Of course we were concerned!" This from the mother. "Mandy didn't have any family," she added, "just Peyton. They'd been best friends since freshman year. She spent holidays with us and even one summer at the lake, so of course we were worried. We contacted the school; they said Mandy had finished all her exams and wasn't even expected back until fall. I even called the country club, but of course they couldn't give a perfect stranger information about an applicant. Peyton said she talked to the chief of police in Mercy, and even texted him that weird picture, but that was before he… well, you know. That was a terrible thing. All over the news for a while."

"Yes, ma'am," replied Buck. "Do you know when she talked to him?"

"Wednesday, I think," said the mother. "He said he was going to see what he could find out and call her back, and he did, the next day. She called me right after she talked to him and I remember I was in the grocery store… Thursday is my shopping day, so it must have been Thursday. She said he asked her some more questions, but she was a little annoyed because he didn't tell her anything except he was looking into the matter personally and he'd get back to her. But then I guess he died that weekend..." She trailed off.

The father went on, "Anyway, we tried calling the police down in Mercy ourselves, but the man we talked to said he couldn't find any report of Mandy ever having been reported missing. That made Peyton mad. She could be headstrong. She finally decided the only thing to do was to go down there herself…"

"A terrible idea," interrupted the mother, her voice tight. "I told her."

The father went on, "She texted us on Saturday that she'd talked to the police there…"

"Did she give you the name of the officer?"

"No." He sounded distressed. "It was a text, for God's sake. How much can you say in a text? She said she was going to stay over Sunday night and drive back to school early Monday morning. She had a ten o'clock class Monday but said she'd call us that afternoon. When we didn't hear from her and she didn't answer her phone, we called the school, then the police. But she's an adult, and they wouldn't put out a missing person report for forty-eight hours. We just heard last night that they'd found her car."

"First Mandy," the mother said in a choked voice, "now Peyton."

Buck said, "When I met her, your daughter was wearing a necklace that looked like a broken heart with the word 'Best' engraved on it. It looked like part of a set. Do you know who had the other necklace?"

"Of course," replied Peyton's mother. "Mandy gave her the necklace for Christmas two years ago. It was a set, like you said, and Mandy wore the one that said 'Friend.' Neither girl ever took hers off that I know of."

The father said urgently, "Do we need to come down there? Do you think…"

Buck found exactly the right tone of compassionate reassurance and firm authority. "I don't think that's necessary just yet. We have no reason to believe that anything untoward happened to your daughter, and it's entirely possible that she'll show up completely unharmed. Give me a little time to check out some things. In the meantime, you can help by sending us an updated photo of Peyton. The only ones we have are from her driver's license and student ID."

"We're coming down there," Peyton's mother said firmly. "We're going to that state patrol post that found Mandy's car and we're getting her backpack, and we're doing it today. As soon as we do that we're coming straight to Mercy. We'll bring the pictures."

The father said, "Yes, of course. That's exactly what we're doing. We'll be there late this afternoon."

Buck said, "I understand. But I want you to know we probably won't have any new information for you."

"We'll stay as long as it takes," Peyton's mother said firmly.

Buck said, resigned, "I'll make sure my detectives know to expect you."

"Thank you," replied the mother fervently. "Officer, um…"

"Lawson," Buck replied. "Chief Lawson."

She murmured, "Yes, of course."

The father added, "You're the first person who's taken this seriously."

"Well, I hope it turns out there's nothing *to* take seriously," Buck replied, but he knew in his gut that was not the case. "I'll be in touch."

CHAPTER TWENTY-FIVE

Hanover County, North Carolina
May 8
Eleven Days Earlier

"In the first place," Jolene informed him, her dark eyes filled with defiance and outrage, "Black people don't camp."

"Oh yeah?" Buck tossed a rolled-up tarp, secured with several extra bungees, into the back of the pickup. "How come?"

She frowned in frustration. "I don't know, they just don't."

"All the more reason for Willis to learn."

"In the second place," she continued, gathering steam, "if I wanted to spend a week sleeping on the ground, fighting bugs and snakes and cold, I'd reenlist. Like I didn't get enough of that in 'Stan."

"Too early for snakes," he replied, "and not that cold." He

added a coil of rope and a collapsible butane stove to the small pile of supplies in the back of the truck. They would divide it all between the backpacks when they got to Jolene's house to pick up Willis.

"And in the third place," she went on indignantly, "*this* is what you call a honeymoon?"

The debate over their wedding had gone on for weeks. He wanted her to have a big wedding, with an elaborate gown and lots of flowers, because she'd never been married before, and he knew—or thought he knew—that was every woman's secret dream. Eloise wanted it to be in a church, with a real preacher sanctioned by God. Jolene insisted a big wedding would embarrass her. She didn't know anyone in town outside the sheriff's office and a big church wedding would be stupid. The only people she wanted in attendance were the ones who mattered—her mother, Willis, and Buck.

In the end they'd been married in a little white clapboard church halfway up a mountain by a unitarian minister whose wife played the dulcimer in the background and whose son charged them $100 for a thumb drive filled with professional quality digital photos. Jolene wore a pink lace sheath that took Buck's breath away and carried a bouquet of white roses. Willis wore a matching pink bow tie with his suit and solemnly bore the wedding rings on a blue satin pillow. Eloise, in blue silk, dabbed at her eyes all the way through the ceremony with an embroidered handkerchief. Buck's own eyes got more than a little misty when the minister asked if he freely accepted before God the responsibility for the family this union would create. That mistiness spilled over when the minister asked Willis if he freely accepted Buck as his stepfather and Willis replied in a loud clear voice, "Yes, sir. I freely do."

They laughed when the gold band Jo had bought him wouldn't fit on his ring finger and had to be placed on his pinkie instead. Their kiss tasted of salty tears of joy and sentiment and wonder. They spent their wedding night in a Holiday Inn on the highway, drinking cheap champagne from the liquor store and making love until they were exhausted. Then they had driven home to pack for the camping trip.

That had been yesterday.

Buck smiled tenderly at her and rested his hands on her shoulders. "This," he told her, "is not our honeymoon." He brought his forehead slowly down to rest against hers. "Our honeymoon begins one week from next Saturday when we get on that plane in Atlanta and fly to Miami for a seven-day, six-night cruise aboard the *Caribbean Star*. None of which," he reminded her with a light kiss on the tip of her nose, "would be possible without that generous signing bonus from the City of Mercy. So maybe be a little nicer when you speak of them in the future."

"Right." A corner of her lips turned down sourly. "I just don't know why we can't do the *Caribbean Star* now, and camping later. We just got married, for heaven's sake."

"Because I've been promising Willis this trip since Christmas," Buck replied, "and he's only got a week left of spring break. You don't have to come," he added innocently, turning to secure the items in the back of the truck. "We'll be fine by ourselves."

"Oh sure, like I'm going to let my baby go off into the wilderness for a week without me," she shot back. "I'm coming." In the background, there was a muted chiming sound. "Is that your phone?"

"Oh crap, I left it on the porch."

He started toward it, but she said impatiently, "I'll get it. You left the cooler there too."

She returned in a moment with his phone and a neoprene mini-cooler packed with flash-frozen, vacuum-packed steaks, hot dogs, and hamburgers. Buck liked MREs as much as the next fellow, but he knew from experience there was nothing like a real steak cooked over an open fire, and long about Day Three they'd all be ready to kill for one. He tucked the cooler inside a pocket of his backpack and zipped it closed.

"You missed a call from your boyfriend," Jolene said, her lips turning down dryly as she handed him his phone.

Since Buck had accepted the job, he'd talked to Billy, either on the phone or via video conference, just about every day. Billy kept him up to date on what was going on in the office and any new changes in policy or procedures he needed to be aware of, occasionally throwing in a pop-quiz like, "Say, Buck. I just picked a fellow up on a 701. What do you think I should do with him?" To which Buck would reply, "Well, I'd hang him if I were you. Urinating in the fountain is a damn serious offense." Then they'd laugh and talk about more interesting things—life and people and things they'd done or planned to do. They'd grown to be friends over the weeks, and Buck looked forward to their chats. He dialed voice mail.

"Hey, Buck," the familiar voice said. "I was hoping to catch you before you went off the grid, but I guess I didn't. How does it feel to be a married man? I wish you a long and happy life together, and kiss that pretty lady for me, will you?" His tone changed slightly. "Listen, a little something has come up I thought you ought to know about. Probably it won't amount to anything, and it's nothing to spoil your honeymoon over. I'm going to be looking into it, but wanted to keep you in loop. Call me when you get out of the woods and we'll get caught up."

Buck automatically started to punch Billy's number, and then he caught a glimpse of Jolene's face, watching him. She didn't look annoyed or impatient. She simply looked resigned, and maybe a little forlorn. Without her saying a word, he knew what she was thinking. Was this the way it was going to be now? Would he always put Billy first?

Buck dropped his phone into his pocket and walked over to her. Taking her face in his hands, he smiled and placed a kiss firmly on her forehead. "This," he told her, "is from Billy."

He did not return the call.

Mercy
The Present

Buck ran Amanda Wolford's name through their internal system and came up with nothing. Billy had not opened a case file when Peyton reported her friend missing, and, knowing how Billy worked, there could be a couple of reasons for that. He might have wanted to check it out before filing an official report; he might have turned it over to another officer to investigate. He might have actually opened a case, but had not had time to file it before he was killed. It was frustrating, though. Like Lydia said, there were systems in place for a purpose. Now Buck had to start from the beginning.

Two young girls had come to Mercy. Two young girls had gone missing.

Peyton had talked to Billy first on Wednesday. By Thursday, Billy was investigating. On Saturday, he had called Buck, worried about something that had come up. On Sunday, he was dead.

Buck got up and left his office.

Lydia called, "Chief, your ten thirty…"

"Five minutes," he replied without looking back.

He walked down the hall to Frankie's office. She half rose from behind her desk when he came in, and sank back down again, a kind of muted alarm in her eyes, when he closed the door behind him.

"You said you were a good detective," he said. "This is your chance to prove it."

CHAPTER TWENTY-SIX

Another white tablecloth-covered room, another bow-tied waiter escorting him to another table with a magnificent view—this one of an emerald green fairway—where another dignitary was waiting to greet him. Ken Jeffries was a robust, fifty-ish looking man with an ample gut hanging over his belt and a firm, welcoming handshake.

"Chief Lawson," he said. His voice was commanding but not booming. "Good to put a face with the name. Sit down, sit down. Miss Corinne said you weren't a drinking man so I ordered you a lemonade. They make it fresh here."

"Thanks," Buck said, although if truth be told he wouldn't have turned down a beer. They sat down and a solicitous waiter filled their glasses with ice water.

Jeffries folded his stubby fingers atop the table and got right to it. "I must say, you've caused quite a stir for somebody who's only been here a couple of days. I like a man who gets right to work and gets things done. We've got a couple of issues here. The first one is that I represent the City of Mercy and its interests, which means I represent you in your capacity as police chief, and I represent Miss Corinne in her capacity as mayor. When the two of you come to loggerheads about anything, it's my job to advise you both and get the thing settled. My advice to you, Chief Lawson, is don't go up against the mayor on this tax collection issue. You won't win and she won't back down, so it's just going to end up being one of those immovable-object-meets-the-irresistible-force scenarios. A big waste of time and energy for you both."

"You're not telling me that you think what she's doing is legal."

Jefferies seemed to gather his thoughts. "Every year," he said after a moment, "I do a little talk down at the high school about government and the law and how they work together to build a society. What I tell those kids is basically this. Government is nothing but a bunch of people coming together and agreeing, for the most part, on how they want to live. They decide what their priorities are, and what they're willing to give up to accomplish those priorities. Schools, police and fire protection, good roads—these are things people want, and they're willing to give up a portion of their income in the form of taxes, for example, to get them. Now, on the federal, state, and county level this gets a lot more complicated, but in a small town it really is just a matter of a bunch of people agreeing on how they want to live and what they're willing to sacrifice—or overlook—for that lifestyle. We have a lot of wealth here, I'm not going to lie about that, most of it inherited, a good bit from tourism and agriculture. But our standard of living is higher and our cost of living is lower than any in the state across the board, mostly because of what people have agreed to overlook. Do you understand?"

Buck said, very carefully, "I absolutely do not."

Jefferies smiled. "To answer your question, it's perfectly legal according to city ordinance. As to whether it might skate the edge of any higher laws…" he shrugged. "That would have to be tested in court. The person to bring those charges would be the state attorney general, and you know who that is, don't you?" When Buck did not answer, he supplied, "George Aikens. The mayor's nephew."

Buck gave a small grunt of smothered laughter and a shake of his head just as the waiter returned with their drinks and menus. "Of course."

"And just so you know," the lawyer went on pleasantly, "and this is notwithstanding anything I said earlier, if you ever get a notion to cause the mayor any hurt, I will take a bite out of you like a great white shark coming after a surfboard, and I can do it, too. Nothing personal, but my first loyalty is to the city. Just don't want any misunderstandings."

The two men locked eyes for a long moment. Then Buck lifted his lemonade to Jefferies in a salute. "To Miss Corinne, then," he said.

Jefferies inclined his head and returned the toast with what looked to Buck like a whiskey sour. He took a sip. "Now," he said, his expression sobering, "in the matter of Carl Tucker. I know it was the mayor who asked you to review the case, and you've done a hell of a job. But, Chief…"

"Buck," he corrected. "Just call me Buck." He didn't feel like chief of anything today.

"All right, Buck. The thing is, we need a suspect. I don't want to see poor old Carl go to prison for this thing any more than you do, but somebody killed Billy Aikens, and so far the only evidence—circumstantial as it is—points to Carl. The prosecutor pulled the deal, I guess you heard, so we're going to court. We can mount a defense, and Dobie is pushing for a change of venue, but even with that..." Again he shrugged. "It doesn't look good. So if you've got anything..." He paused hopefully. "It's going to come out in discovery anyway. Anything at all."

Buck shook his head. "Sorry. We're working the case. That's all I can tell you."

"Well, I had to try." He picked up the menu. "Say, if you like lobster roll, they know how to do it right here."

They placed their orders, and as the waiter was turning to go, Buck stopped him. "Could you ask the manager to stop by when he gets a minute?"

A flicker of concern passed the boy's face, but it didn't shadow his smile. "Yes, sir. No problem."

When he was gone, Jefferies asked, "Something wrong?"

"Business," Buck replied.

Jefferies waited for him to explain, then managed to look both offended and curious while never crossing the boundaries of polite behavior when Buck did not. "Well, then," he said, "since we have a minute, let's get to the last matter." Jefferies picked up the briefcase that had been resting at his feet, and opened it on his knees, removing a legal-sized manila folder. "I could have sent these over to your office, but thought we might as well get it over with here. That way I can answer any questions you might have."

He put the briefcase on the floor again and opened the folder. He took out another set of papers bound in a pale blue folder and passed it across the table to Buck. "Never a pleasant chore, I know, but this is your will. The City of Mercy provides for the preparation of a will as part of your compensation package. It's an exact copy of the one you had with the sheriff's office in North Carolina, so all you really have to do is sign it."

It was a ghoulish subject, particularly in light of the fact that the last police chief who had required this service had needed it much sooner than planned. Buck said, "There've been some changes in my personal information since then. It will have to be updated."

"No problem." He retrieved the folder. "Just get the particulars to my office as soon as you can, and we'll messenger over the final draft."

Jeffries took another set of papers from the folder, these bound together with an alligator clip. "This is the lease agreement on your house. Looks complicated, I know, but most of it has to do with the historic property aspect and the city's custodianship. Basically, you can use it as a residence, not business, as long as you're police chief. Should you leave that job for any reason, you have thirty days to vacate the premises. Lawn maintenance and repairs amounting to over $1000 are covered by the city."

Buck glanced up from the paper. "I like to mow my own lawn."

The other man chuckled. "In the mountains, maybe. In this heat it gets old fast. We've got a guy on a tractor mower who can knock it out in half an hour."

Buck turned a page. "Can I put up a swing set in the backyard?"

"No problem. Any permanent structures have to be approved by the city. Any alterations to the external façade of the house or the property as viewed from the street have to be approved by the historic commission. Beyond that, you're good to go."

"What if I decide to move? Buy my own house?"

"Nobody can force you to live there, of course. But as long as you're chief of police, the house will be yours. You can't sublet it or use it for a business, but maybe you'd like to use it for when guests come into town or let your kids live there when they're grown." Again he shrugged. "It's a little strange, I know, but we're just trying to preserve a historic property, and there's really not much of a downside for you. The rent is $100 a year. I usually pay it to the city in January and bill you later." He handed Buck a pen. "Three copies. Return two copies to me and keep one for yourself. Just sign where the yellow tabs are."

Buck would have felt better about it if Jolene had been there, but she'd said last night she liked the house fine and he really didn't have time to look for anything else. Maybe they'd try it for a year. Like the man said, no downside.

Buck signed. "So," he said flipping over copies, "if Billy hadn't died, what would the housing arrangement have been?"

"We were talking about that," Jefferies admitted. "Billy wanted to keep a place in town, but he wasn't sure he wanted anything that big. My impression was he was going to talk it over with you after you got settled, see what you wanted to do."

Buck handed over the two signed copies of the lease thoughtfully. "It's just that we talked almost every day and he never mentioned anything. Then, in those last few days before he died, when he knew he wouldn't be able to reach me for a week, he started making changes. Mentioning me in his will, making sure I'd move into the house."

"That was in place long before you came into the picture," Jefferies reminded him, tucking the folder back into his briefcase. "But I know what you mean. Like I say,

I've seen this happen before, especially when a person is about to make a major life change, like retiring or taking a new job or getting married. He updates his will, and like that he's gone." He smiled grimly. "It's enough to make you superstitious."

"Yeah," Buck murmured, and the sip of lemonade he took didn't taste nearly as good as it had before.

"Mr. Jefferies."

Both men looked up to see a tall, dark-haired man in an expensive-looking suit standing at the table. Jefferies introduced Buck to Harold Katz, the restaurant manager, and they shook hands. "Is everything all right?" Katz asked after the formalities had been covered. "Cody said you wanted to see me."

"Thanks for coming over," Buck said. "I don't want to take up your time, just wondered if you could look something up for me. A job application from an Amanda Wolford, college student, looking to waitress here this summer?"

But before he even finished speaking, the other man was shaking his head. "I don't have to look it up. You're the third person who's asked. Billy called me not long before he died, and some young girl was by here only this weekend, and before that my secretary said some woman had called looking for her."

Buck thought that must have been Peyton's mother.

"Like I told them all," Katz went on, "I never saw the child. We fill summer jobs here in March and we have *never* advertised on Facebook."

"Huh," Buck said thoughtfully.

Katz leaned closer. "If you ask me," he said, lowering his tone confidentially, "that girl was trying to pull something over on her parents. You know, pretending to be holding down a job at a reputable place like this for the summer while she was really off in Baja doing whatever kids do these days."

He stepped aside as the waiter arrived with their dishes. "Let me know if there's anything else I can do for you, Chief. I hope you'll take advantage of our one-year free membership. There's lots to enjoy here for the whole family, not just golf. Be sure to pick up a brochure."

Buck smiled and thanked him, and for the rest of the meal, which thankfully did not last through dessert, he listened to Ken Jefferies talk about the club and golf and the social life around town, and did not argue when Jefferies picked up the tab. He had rarely been so glad to see anyone as he was Roland, standing beside the police chief's car when Buck exited through the front door.

Buck had been busy texting back and forth with Frankie on the way over and, aside from asking Roland if his mother had gotten home okay last night, Buck hadn't spoken to him. But this time when Roland opened the back door of the police chief's car, Buck said, "I'll sit up front with you, if you don't mind. I feel weird being chauffeured around like a celebrity."

Roland looked surprised, and not all that pleased, but all he said was, "Yes, sir."

Buck opened his own door before Roland could do it and got in the passenger seat. He made a few minutes of small talk while they got underway, asking how long Roland had worked in the motor pool, what he had done before, whether he had a girlfriend, and what he liked to do on weekends. Mostly he got monosyllabic replies, so he pushed it a little.

"That first day I got here," Buck said, "I walked in on some kind of argument between you and your mother. I got the feeling it was about work."

Roland shrugged one shoulder. "It was nothing."

Buck studied his profiled face. "Because if you're not happy in your job, I need to know about it. Maybe I can help."

Roland's brows drew together briefly. "The job is fine."

Buck waited, watching him. Eventually Roland said, "I've been thinking about opening my own place, that's all. A garage. Mama thinks it's stupid." A quick angry shrug of one shoulder. "So that's that."

Buck said, "Well, we'd hate to lose you. But I've always believed a man should follow his dream. So just let me know what your plans are."

Roland shot him a quick, mildly puzzled look, and, in a moment, seemed to relax a fraction. "Yes, sir," he said. "I'll do that."

Buck moved on to what he really wanted to know. "So do you clean the units after every shift when they're turned in?"

"Yes, sir," Roland replied.

"What do you do if you find something—like, you know, drugs or a knife that a suspect tried to hide?"

Roland replied immediately, "We document and report it, and turn the evidence over to the watch commander. It's an officer's responsibility to search and clear his vehicle thoroughly before turning it back in to the motor pool." His tone was as precise as though he was taking an oral exam.

"But not this car, I guess," Buck observed.

"Prisoners are never transported in the chief's car," Roland replied, and darted a quick glance toward Buck, as though wondering why that wasn't already obvious. "There's no prisoner cage."

"Right," Buck murmured. "Did Chief Aikens ever drive this car himself? Or did you take him everywhere?"

"Depends," Roland said. "Usually he'd check the car out in the morning, but if it was a long trip when he needed to get some work done, or if he had somebody riding with him he wanted to talk to, I'd drive."

"I don't suppose anybody but you and the chief ever drove this car."

Again, Roland gave him an odd look. "No, sir. It's not equipped for patrol. And it has 'Chief of Police' written on the doors."

Buck was thoughtful as they reached the station. "Would you happen to know when this car was last driven?"

"Do you mean before last night?" Roland pulled up in front of the employee entrance and put the car in park. He tapped the screen of a computer set into the console. "That would be Thursday, May 6." He looked up at Buck and added unnecessarily, "While Chief Aikens was still alive."

Buck nodded. "And nobody has been in it since? Not even to service or clean it?"

"No, sir." His expression was equal parts confusion and curiosity. "I mean, it was serviced and cleaned that Monday, the third, and it was only driven that once, and it's been in the garage ever since, but I can get one of the guys to wash and detail it for you this afternoon if you want."

"No, that's okay," Buck said. "Tell you what, Roland. I'd like to take the car home tonight. Check it out to me the rest of the day and tomorrow."

Roland looked at Buck uncertainly. "Um, that's not usually…"

"Didn't Chief Aikens ever drive the car home?"

"No, sir," said Roland. "Not that I recall. He had his own vehicle, and unless it was raining, he walked to work. He liked to stay fit."

"Well, I like to drive," Buck replied pleasantly. He held out his hand for the key.

Roland still looked a little reluctant, but he handed over the key.

"Thanks, Roland. You have a good rest of the day." And, always keeping a wary eye out for alligators, Buck mounted the steps and went back to work.

CHAPTER TWENTY-SEVEN

Buck's office was awash in mayhem when he returned. There were men with step ladders and women with measuring tapes and sample books. A bolt of what looked like blue velvet was unfurled across the sofa, and his desk had been pushed aside to accommodate a six-foot stepladder and a young man with a long, blond ponytail. Another man on another ladder was measuring the window, and two women were holding what appeared to be paint chips—or perhaps fabric swatches—against the wall.

One of them turned when she saw him and came forward with her hand extended. "Chief Lawson!" She was a young woman with a bouncy blond haircut and square-framed eyeglasses, wearing a linen suit that Buck could almost guarantee had come from one of the trendy, overpriced shops downtown. "I'm Deanna Lowry and this is my assistant Marge..." Another young woman, this one a brunette, smiled and waved at him. "And Tom."

She indicated the man on the window ladder, who said, "Out of your hair in a minute, Chief."

Buck turned to call for Lydia and found her at his shoulder. "The decorating team from Aikens Furniture," she explained. "And Amos Solby, the taxidermist."

The ponytailed man on the ladder behind his desk waved a screwdriver at him. "Sorry about the mess, Chief. I'll put it all back. Shouldn't take much longer."

Lydia retreated and the bouncy blonde went on, "We hoped we could put together a plan before you got back from lunch, but let me just tell you what we're thinking so far. I understand you like the colors of the marsh. I thought a deep gray carpet with a teal accent wall there behind your desk…" she held up two paint chips to illustrate. "And deep blue draperies. I like this fabric for the sofa…" She gestured to the velvet. "And this"—she went over to the coffee table, which was scattered with sample books, and rummaged around until she came up with a scrap of fabric that seemed to be printed all over with ducks—"for the guest chairs. It's a silk tapestry called 'Duck Blind'; isn't that cute? Now for the dominant walls, we can go with a neutral violet gray that will really make the art pop—I'll e-mail you photographs of the paintings we're considering—and I thought we'd install a closed hutch in a nice, burled walnut instead of the open shelves, with a matching console and desk. Your thoughts?"

Buck pretended to give the matter his most deliberate consideration. "Deanna," he said, placing a hand on her shoulder, "I think you are brilliant at your job. No velvet on the sofa."

"Oh, it's not velvet," she assured him. "It's a deep-pile suede. Very up-to-the-minute."

"Like the ducks," he continued, gently guiding her toward the door. "Like the teal." He wasn't entirely sure what teal was. "What I think you should do is sit down with Lydia and hammer out the details." By this time they had reached Lydia's office. The other woman, Marge, was scrambling to gather up the sample books and follow. To Lydia he said, "I trust your judgment. No velvet."

He left the two women and most, if not all, their paraphernalia in Lydia's office and closed the door. The man who'd been measuring the window edged past him with the folded stepladder. That left only the ponytailed man on the ladder behind his desk, loosening the screws that held the mounted alligator head in place.

"Man, I can't believe you're getting rid of old Oscar," the young man—who Buck now recalled was named Amos—said. "He's been hanging here, what? Ten, fifteen years?"

"I guess." Buck rubbed the back of his neck. "Do all the amphibians have names around here?"

"Actually, he's a reptile," corrected Amos good-naturedly. "Alligators have scales, makes them reptiles. I remember back when Billy shot him. My dad did all the work, mounted him up pretty."

"Billy shot him?" Buck repeated, alarmed. "Here? In his yard?"

Amos chuckled. "Naw, down in Florida somewhere on one of those big gator hunts. We don't have anything like this around here. Anyway, old Oscar only hung in Billy's house four or five years when he snagged that marlin, so he decided to move him down here to the office and mount the marlin at the house. Boy, was that ever a job."

"Did your dad work on the marlin too?"

"Yep," he replied proudly. "Of course, by then I was old enough to help. Have you seen her? She's a beaut."

"Actually," replied Buck, "I own it."

Amos glanced over his shoulder, impressed. "Cool." He

turned back to his work. "Took three men half a day to get her up there, though."

"Yeah, I guess." Buck's phone buzzed and he took it out of his pocket. "Something that heavy."

"Oh, once they're done, they're not that heavy," replied Amos. "After the guts are out and all. No, the problem was the mounting plate and the hinges, getting her to swing right for the clearance and all."

"Uh-huh," said Buck.

The text was from Jo. It read: *Here are the links you wanted.* This was followed by a list of highlighted web addresses.

"Had to order the hinges from London, if you can believe that," Amos was saying. "Hydraulic hinges. Never even knew there was such a thing. Guess those folks over there have a lot of things they want to hide."

"I guess," replied Buck.

He typed back, *Like I said, you need to work for me.*

I do, she replied. *I'm just not getting paid.*

Buck smiled and put the phone back in his pocket. He looked up at Amos. "You okay here? Need any help?"

"Almost done," Amos replied. He looked around at Buck. "Say, what do you want to do with him? Because we can sure box him up and deliver him to your house if you want. Small fee."

Buck said quickly, "No." He had a flash of the expression on Jo's face, not to mention Eloise's, if they walked in the house to find an alligator head on the wall. Willis would love it, though. "Is there, like, a museum or something?"

The young man looked baffled for a moment, then his expression cleared. "I'll ask Lydia," he decided.

"Good plan."

Buck left and walked down the hall to Frankie's office.

"Chief." She got up from her desk when he came in, looking even more rumpled than he had left her that morning. "I was just about to text you."

He closed the door and pulled up the hard, black, Naugahyde visitor's chair. "What have you got?"

She sat back down. "I pulled the security footage from the evidence room for last Sunday, like you asked." She typed a few keys on her computer and turned the screen so they both could see. "The manual log and the release form says Billy checked out the weapon belonging to Carl Tucker at 7:45 a.m. But as you can see"—she indicated the screen, which showed a grainy black and white image of an empty corridor and a closed door marked *Evidence Room. Authorized Entry Only*—"there was no activity until 4:30." She fast-forwarded the video. "There were no arrests that day, so it fits. Then, at time stamp 4:33 p.m.…" She slowed the video to normal speed and showed a man in a Mercy PD windbreaker and cap, face carefully averted from the camera, walk into the frame. He picked up the log ledger and spent a few minutes signing in and filling out the evidence release form. Then he swiped his card in the door and went in. "Billy's key card was used to open the door," she said.

Buck looked at her. "Billy was dead by then."

She merely nodded, and they both returned their attention to the screen, watching as the man emerged from the room with an evidence bag containing a handgun. His head was down, not even his profile visible. Just before he moved off screen, he tucked the handgun inside his jacket.

Frankie stopped the video.

Buck said, "Do you know where Billy kept his key card?"

"Policy is that we keep our security cards on our persons

at all times, not in our desks or vehicles. Every time I saw the chief use his card, he took it from his ID wallet."

Buck nodded. That was exactly where he kept his. "No copies?"

"No, sir. And I checked the inventory of belongings after Chief Aikens… after he was found. His key card wasn't among them."

Buck said, "So whoever entered the evidence room and removed Carl Tucker's gun on Sunday took Billy's key card from his body. A body that wasn't officially discovered until twenty-four hours later."

He could see her swallow. "Yes, sir. That would be my conclusion."

"Would it also be your conclusion that whoever is on that video killed Billy?"

She managed a single nod. "But just because he's wearing a Mercy PD uniform doesn't mean he's one of us."

Buck looked at the frozen, empty screen for long moment. "I don't suppose there's anything about him you could identify."

"I watched it over and over again for almost an hour," she replied. "There's never even a glimpse of his face, and the jacket disguises his body shape. There's the handwriting on the log entry, but if I were him, I'd disguise my writing."

Buck said, "We're sending the security footage and the log to the FBI. Also the release form for a handwriting analysis. They've got ways of identifying things we haven't even thought of."

"Yes, sir."

But both of them knew it would be weeks, if not months, before they received results.

She said, "I checked the cameras at the front and back

entrance for Sunday, too. The only people who entered the building that day who weren't officially on duty were Ron Beeker and Jim Torrance from night shift. Both of them came in about 3:00. Beeker left at 4:00 and Torrance left at 5:30. There was supposed to be an audit Monday morning—Billy used to do them once a month—and some of the guys leave their paperwork until the last minute. Beeker confirms that's what he was doing here, but I haven't been able to reach Torrance yet. The janitorial staff comes in at four on Sundays, and the laundry service got here at 4:30, left at 4:50. Also, the vending machine stockers were here from 3:30 until 5:00."

At Buck's raised eyebrows, she explained, "They park their truck here and stock all the businesses on the block at the same time. It keeps from blocking traffic." She handed him a printed list. "This is everyone who entered and left the building that day."

Buck frowned over the list. For a Sunday afternoon in a small town, the police station had been busier than a New York subway at rush hour. He said, "Okay, we're going to have to talk to everybody who had access to the building before 4:30. I'd start with the officers we know were in the building, and then the laundry service. They would've had easy access to a uniform."

"Yes, sir, that's what I thought too."

Buck glanced up. "What was Captain Sullivan doing here on a Sunday?"

"He had the duty," she said. "He doesn't usually work Sundays, but I think he's trying to pile on some extra vacation days so he switched with somebody."

Buck took a breath and sat back. "Okay. Next item."

She turned the screen back toward her and brought up another page. "There's no official record of the traffic stop on

February 13 you mentioned," she said, "which just means the officer didn't file a report. Sometimes they don't when they just issue a warning. And in this particular case, he didn't run her credentials so there's nothing in the system."

Buck scowled.

"However," she went on quickly, "I did follow up on your information from Officer Baker's cousin. I interviewed…" She checked a page of her notes. "Tarina Johnson, age twenty-three, who claims she was stopped for speeding on November 2 of last year at 2:30 in the morning as she was coming home from work at the Blue Lion Bar. She said the officer offered to tear up her ticket if she would perform oral sex on him. She did."

Buck's jaw tightened in fury and disgust. "Description?"

"White male, brown or black hair, between 5'10" and 6 feet tall, medium build. It was dark and she didn't get a look at his face." Frankie hesitated before adding, "She said he smelled like cinnamon."

Buck tried very hard to keep a dark stab of rage from showing in his eyes, and he took a moment before speaking. "Where did this happen?"

She replied, "On Post Road, just past the city limits sign. She also said she'd heard about similar incidents with other young girls driving alone at night along that section of road. She couldn't give me any names. But she did say she had talked to Chief Aikens about it the week before he died."

"Any paperwork on that?"

Frankie shook her head. "The chief could be a little informal about things like that." She seemed to debate with herself before adding, "And he was protective of the department. He wouldn't have opened an official investigation."

"Or he was doing the same thing we are," Buck said

thoughtfully. "Keeping this on the down-low until he had enough evidence for charges."

Frankie was noncommittal.

Buck said, "So who was working night shift on February 13 and November 2?"

Frankie slid a paper across the desk to him. "We had five units on patrol on November 2 and four on February 13. I also checked the weekend of May first, when Mandy Wolford disappeared, and this past weekend, as you suggested."

Buck glanced at the paper, then at her. "It's not the same guys."

"No, sir. Every six weeks half the day shift rotates to a weekend of nights. Aside from the watch commander at the desk, none of the same men worked all four nights."

Buck frowned over the roster. "If there's an incident—like the one at the convenience store, for example—don't they call in a detective to start the investigation? Detective Teller was conducting interviews before 8:00 the other morning."

She nodded slowly. "Craig is on call for things like that."

He held her gaze, waiting.

She went on, "On February 13, Craig was called in on a burglary investigation at 12:15 a.m. His interviews lasted less than an hour."

Jolene had been stopped on Post Road at 1:30 a.m.

"On November 2 of last year," Frankie went on quietly, "Craig questioned a stalking suspect and ended up making an arrest. He turned the suspect over to booking at 2:00 a.m. At 2:30, Tarina Johnson was stopped for speeding and was subsequently molested. However, on the weekend of May first, when Mandy Wolford disappeared, Craig was in the hospital, getting over pneumonia. He didn't come back to work until the next Monday."

Buck got up and walked over to Craig Teller's empty desk. It was a mess of unfiled papers and half-completed reports. He slid open the top drawer and found, atop the other clutter, an open pack of cinnamon gum.

He returned to Frankie and resumed his seat. "Does Craig ever make traffic stops?" he asked.

Frankie hesitated only a moment. "Sometimes, when he's called out late at night or has to work overtime on a case, he'll check out a patrol car and troll for what the guys call high-value violations. For the, um…"

She looked uncertain, so Buck supplied flatly, "For the mayor's incentive bonus."

She nodded. "I guess he feels it compensates him for the inconvenience of being called out on a case in the middle of the night."

Buck looked at her, brooding, for a long time. "Do you think Craig Teller is a sexual predator?"

The succinctness of her reply let him know this was not the first time she had considered the question. "I think he is a bully, a smart-ass, and an opportunist. He's one of those cops who thinks the law only applies to him when it's convenient. If you want to know whether I think he's a capable of doing what Tarina Johnson described, the answer is yes. But then I may be prejudiced by my extreme dislike of him."

Buck was quiet for a moment. Then he said, "All right, Frankie, I'll take it from here." He folded both lists she had given him and put them in his jacket pocket. "I want you to open a missing person case on Amanda Wolford. The manager at the country club said they never interviewed her for a job and they didn't place a Facebook ad. Talk to her friends at school, her teachers, see if anybody else saw this ad or knew anything more about her plans than we do. Track her steps down here as far as you can." He drew a breath. "Also, open a file on Peyton McGilroy. I'll assign a couple of men to work with you on that. Her parents are on their way here and it would be good if we could tell them something besides what we don't know."

He glanced over at the empty desk on the other side of the room. "Where is Teller, anyway?"

She looked up from making notes. "He's off today."

"Probably just as well."

Frankie lowered her gaze back to her notepad. "Yes, sir."

He said, "Start at the Comfort Inn where Peyton stayed this weekend. See if anyone saw her meeting anybody, or if she placed any calls from her room phone. Her parents said she had talked to someone here at the station about her missing roommate, once last week and again while she was in town this weekend. Any idea who that would have been?"

She glanced up from jotting notes. "It should have been referred to Craig or me, but last week we were in the middle of a homicide investigation. Captain Sullivan was in charge, but I doubt he took the call. Same reason. It could have been anyone who happened to be at the station."

"Find out."

"Yes, sir."

He was silent while she finished making notes, his expression thoughtful. Frankie said, "Chief, I know you think there's a connection here, between the two girls and the misconduct complaints on Post Road. But McGilroy's car was found twenty miles outside our jurisdiction and Amanda Wolford's car hasn't yet been located at all. It would help if you could give me a theory."

Buck said, "Let me ask you something. What would cause

you to abandon a perfectly operational vehicle on the side of a deserted road?"

She thought a moment. "I don't know. If a friend came to get me?"

"And would you leave your phone and your backpack behind?"

She shook her head. "Backpack, maybe, if we were coming back for it. Phone, never."

He said, "My business card was found on the floor of Peyton McGilroy's car. I saw her put it in her purse next to her driver's license. What's the first thing you do if you're pulled over?"

Frankie said on a breath, "Take out your driver's license."

He nodded. "Which might cause a card to drop on the floor."

"And if you're arrested," Frankie went on, "you don't take your personal belongings. Only if she'd been arrested, her name would be in the system. It would have come up as soon as the missing person report went out."

"If it was a legal arrest," he agreed.

She swallowed hard. "So your theory…"

He said, "Peyton told me that she was meeting someone that morning at the convenience store. I assumed it was someone she knew, but she thought it was me at first. A cop." He frowned. "What if whoever she talked to here called her back and told her he had some information about Mandy, and arranged to meet her at that store at, say, 5:00 that morning?"

Frankie drew a short breath. "When, according to Singh, a very precisely timed armed robbery was scheduled to happen."

His gaze was fixed on the opposite wall as his thoughts

unfolded. "In which a civilian might very easily be accidentally killed."

She said softly, "But you interrupted the robbery."

Buck nodded slowly. "And he had to make another plan."

Frankie's nostrils flared as she took a deep breath. "If whoever has been molesting women at traffic stops lured Mandy Wolford here for something more than a quickie on the side of the road, he must have been pretty confident no one would come looking for her. At least not right away. So when Peyton started asking questions, he had to stop her."

Buck stood and started to leave the room, then paused. "Who was the watch commander?" he asked. "You said the only officer who worked all four nights in question was the watch commander."

She replied, "That would be Captain Sullivan, sir. He always takes the desk when the day shift rotates to nights."

Buck frowned a little, nodding. "Finding Peyton McGilroy is a priority," he said. "Any resources you need you let me know."

"Yes, sir." She looked up at him, her eyes filled with dread. "This is bad, isn't it, Chief?"

Buck replied simply, "I think it's what got Billy killed."

―――――

Buck stopped at Sully's office but did not go in. Sully looked up from his computer and tossed the toothpick he'd been chewing in the trash. "Yes, sir, boss," he said genially.

Buck looked at him for a moment. Then he said, "Pull Baker in off patrol and tell him to report to Frankie. He's going to be assisting with the Peyton McGilroy investigation until further notice."

"You got it."

Buck added, "Peyton's parents are on their way down. Do we have a victim's liaison? I don't want them interfering in the investigation, but they are to be treated with every courtesy."

"I'll assign somebody."

Buck hesitated, then said, "Make it a female."

Sully looked mildly surprised, but replied only, "Yes, sir."

There was more he should have related to his second-in-command, starting with the video from the evidence room taken the day Billy was killed. He was probably breaking a regulation by not doing so. But given everything else that had been broken in this department already, that seemed like a minor infraction. For the time being, silence was his best option.

So he said simply, "Keep me informed." He turned to go.

"Chief?" Sully said. "Everything okay?"

At least on that point, Buck could be completely honest. "No," he said, and turned back toward his office.

He passed Amos in the hall as he turned the corner. The young man carried a wooden crate with the head of Oscar the alligator inside, which he juggled to give Buck a thumbs-up. "All set, sir," he said cheerfully. "We found him a new home down at the sulfur springs welcome center. Gonna do up a nice plaque and everything."

"Sounds good." Buck turned toward his office door when something occurred to him. He looked back. "Say, Amos."

The young man turned.

"A minute ago," Buck said, "you were talking about the marlin. What did you mean, hinges?"

CHAPTER TWENTY-EIGHT

Buck drove Billy's car home, planning to walk back to the station for his truck once the sun went down and things cooled off. When he went inside the house, the first thing he noticed was that the boxes he'd stacked in the kitchen were gone. Everything smelled like lemon polish and pine cleaner. There was a note on the refrigerator, held in place by a sunflower magnet. In a precise, almost childlike cursive script, it read:

Dear Mr. Buck Lawson,

This is Betsy Freedman, your housekeeper. I left a casserole in the fridge, please reheat at 350 for 30 minutes. Also a salad. I put your things away and did your laundry. I ironed your shirts and hung them in the master. The charge is $100. I will be back on Monday. Please leave a check.

Yours truly,
  Betsy Freedman

Buck texted Jo: *We have a housekeeper.*

She replied: *Is she pretty?*

He answered: *She ironed my shirts.*

Jo replied: *Keep her!*

Buck found a stepstool in the broom closet off the kitchen and carried it to the study. He used it to locate two latches on the underside of the giant marlin and release them. The walnut plate on which the fish was mounted swung upward toward the ceiling on the hiss of hydraulic spring hinges, just as Amos had described. Behind it was a small door, so well crafted to blend in with the surrounding paneling that it took Buck a moment to even find it. He slid the door to the left to reveal a safe with a digital keypad.

"Okay then," he said out loud, staring at it. "So, this is why you left me the fish. Do you think you might have bothered to leave me the combination to the safe, too?"

Buck thought about it for a minute. If Billy really *had* meant for Buck to find—and presumably open—the safe, he would have changed the combination to something Buck knew or could find out. He tried his own social security number, then his phone number and his birthday. He even looked up his employee ID and his badge number. After twenty minutes of frustration, he stepped down from the ladder and poured himself a bourbon. He sat down at the desk, staring at the fish, which was now floating at a 45-degree angle in the air with one glassy eye pointed toward the ceiling, the other gazing sightlessly at the floor.

He took a thoughtful sip of the bourbon. On the other hand, Billy had no idea he was going to die before he had a chance to change the combination to the safe. He wanted to make sure that no one removed the fish—or, presumably, the contents of the safe—before Buck got here, just in case. But would he really have changed the combination?

Buck had no way of knowing which numbers might be significant to Billy—his children's birthdays, his anniversary, or his social security number—and it was highly unlikely that someone who'd worked in law enforcement as long as Billy had would choose something so obvious. And then it hit him. *Numbers.*

Buck opened the top drawer of the desk and took out the field notebook in which Billy had scribbled rows of numbers. Six digits in one column, three or four in the second, and what looked like dates in the third. He got up quickly, taking the notebook with him, and returned to the safe. He spent another fifteen minutes punching in numbers from the notebook, first as they were written, then in various combinations, to no avail.

He tossed the notebook on the desk and resumed his seat, glaring at the fish and the safe it had once concealed. He took a sip of bourbon. *If you get a chance to go after the big one,* Billy had said, *promise me you'll take it.*

"Man, you really set me up with that one," Buck muttered, thinking about Miss Corinne, and Ken Jefferies, and cops who were pulling over young girls after midnight and assaulting them. And Peyton McGilroy, whose disappearance would have brought it all circling back to land on Billy's head… if he had lived. "Why didn't you clean up your own damn town?"

And that was when something occurred to him. *You've seen these numbers before*, Billy had said. He pulled the notebook closer with one finger and spun it around so that he could see the numbers. And Billy was right. He *had* seen them before.

"You wily old fox," Buck muttered.

The numbers in the first column were Mercy Police Department badge numbers. The third column contained dates, as he'd first thought. And the middle column was a list of sections and paragraphs from the police department policy and procedures manual, as well as the occasional entry from the Georgia criminal code. Buck didn't recognize them all, but one section was eminently familiar to him. He had practically memorized it yesterday in preparation for the inevitable call from Miss Corinne.

Mercy Police Department Policy and Procedures Manual, Section 132.5.1: No police officer shall accept a monetary gift or a bribe from any citizen...

They had gotten around that by having the mayor issue "bonuses" to the police officers who brought in the most revenue. But if what Baker had reported as rumor was fact and officers were accepting cash from citizens who were stopped for moving violations and then pocketing that cash... That was more than accepting a bribe. That was theft by taking, as Buck could just about guarantee that the criminal code number following each entry would confirm.

There were eight badge numbers, and between them approximately fifty violations. One of the badge numbers, which appeared numerous times on the list, was starred on the date November 2—the date on which Tarina Johnson claimed to have traded sexual favors for a dismissed traffic ticket on Post Road. Buck used his phone to access the week's duty roster, which listed personnel assignments by name and badge number. A grim smile tightened his lips. The badge number corresponding with repeated policy and criminal violations belonged to Craig Teller.

"Gotcha, you bastard," he muttered.

He started to call Frankie—or better yet, go out to Teller's house and haul him in himself—but gave it a second thought. This would have to be handled carefully, and he didn't want to lose this fish by jerking the line. He needed paperwork, in the form of citations or warnings issued, and he needed witness statements. That was how Billy had come up with this list, so they should be easy to find. Clearly, Billy had been preparing to clean house before Buck got there. He just hadn't had time to finish the job.

Buck sank back in the chair, letting relief wash over him. "Son of a bitch, Billy," he said, shaking his head in wonder. "I don't know what's in that safe, but it can't be as good as this."

He lifted his glass in a salute to the departed chief who had not, after all, left the department in quite the shambles Buck had imagined. That was when his eyes fell on the bookshelf, and he thought with a wry smile it would be just like Billy to inscribe the combination to the safe on the inside cover of a copy of *Moby Dick*.

Buck sat up suddenly, set the glass down on the desk with a thunk, and strode over to the bookcase. He scanned until he found the green leather volume of *The Poems of Sidney Lanier* and opened it to "The Marshes of Glynn," the passage marked by the yellow sticky note. He snatched up the note, went back to the safe and entered the digits that were written there.

The door clicked open.

There were the usual things a man might keep in his safe: file folders marked "insurance forms" or "legal papers," an envelope with a couple of thousand dollars emergency cash which Buck would have to remember to turn over to Ken Jefferies. Toward the back was a larger, heavier clasp envelope with "Police Chief" scrawled on the outside in bold black marker. Buck had to assume this was what Billy meant for him to find.

He opened the clasp of the envelope and emptied the contents onto the desk. He stood looking at the items scattered across the desk surface for a long time, baffled. Billy had arranged the papers into stacks held together with paper clips. Old newspaper clippings. Copies of police reports from as far back as 1962. Black and white photographs that looked as though they'd been printed from the internet. Each one was his own version of a case file. Additionally, there was a collection of small zip lock plastic bags, each marked with initials, that contained various trinkets—pieces of costume jewelry, a faded hair ribbon, a rusted-out Timex watch, a ring with a red stone, a charm bracelet...

Buck left the room and returned in a moment with the half-heart necklace he was now certain had belonged to Mandy Wolford. He unwrapped it from the white handkerchief in which he had stored it and laid it down on the desk beside the other trinkets. He could not take his eyes off the picture that was beginning to form.

"Jesus, Billy," he whispered. "What did you do?"

CHAPTER TWENTY-NINE

Hanover County, North Carolina
May 16
Three days earlier

Buck stared at the phone in his hand with eyes that were still and stunned, then slowly raised them to Jolene, who had overheard part of his side of the conversation and stood by curiously. "That was the mayor of Mercy," he said. "Billy's dead."

"Oh, Buck!" She came to him swiftly, her expression awash in compassion, and wrapped her arms around him. "Oh, baby, no. I'm so sorry!"

They were standing in her driveway, backpacks and coolers and folded tents scattered around them. They both smelled like camp smoke and a week of bathing in the lake. In the background, they could hear Willis excitedly relating all his adventures to his grandmother. "And it was *this big*!" he exclaimed. "I'm not even joking! But Buck said we shouldn't bother it because it was important to the… to the eco-some-thing. You should have seen it!"

And Eloise, laughing, replied, "Sweetheart, I can tell you right now I'm glad I didn't. Now, let's see if we can get you cleaned up."

"But I didn't tell you about…"

Eight days and seven nights immersed in the tranquil rhythms of nature had not been, after all, such a bad way to start a marriage. They learned each other's silences and quiet looks, the ease of a smile, the warmth of a brushing touch. They hiked and swam and foraged; they discovered a natural reciprocity in parenting Willis, teaching him the ways of nature and keeping him safe. They laughed, they talked, they lay wrapped in each other's arms gazing at the stars and listening to the soft breathing of the little boy they both loved. Buck knew it would be a shock, returning to civilization. He hadn't expected this.

Jolene stepped away from him, her troubled gaze searching is face. "What happened?"

It took a moment for him to even gather his senses enough to shake his head. "She didn't say. Said we'd talk when I got there. He had a heart condition." It was hard to say "had." Hard to speak of Billy in the past tense, hard to believe he'd never hear his voice again, hard to imagine a world without him. Harder still to rearrange in his own head how different the days and weeks and months before him would be now. He had counted on Billy. He had never intended to do any of this alone. But Billy was gone.

Jolene caressed his arm, laid her cheek briefly against his bicep. "My God," she said softly. "Just like that." Then she looked up at him. "You said when you got there. You mean for the funeral, right?"

He compressed his lips, gathering himself with an effort. "They want me to start right away. I have a meeting with the mayor tomorrow morning."

She stepped away, shocked. "Tomorrow? They want you to start *tomorrow*?"

He looked around distractedly at the camping supplies scattered around the truck. "I'll carry these things up to the house for you, then I have to go. Lots to do if I'm going to leave out of here today."

She caught his arm. "Today? How can you leave today? Stop it," she insisted. "Just stop for one minute and let's talk about this!"

"Nothing to talk about," he said. He swung the strap of her backpack over one shoulder, picked up Willis's tent bag with his other hand. "I told Mayor Watts I'd be there in the morning, and I will."

"But that's crazy!" She followed him up the walk to the porch. "You can't just pack up and move to another state overnight."

He said, "I'll just pack as much as I can get in the truck for now, the things I'll need. I'll come back next weekend and make arrangements for everything else."

"What about me?" she demanded. "Am I one of the things you need?"

He gave her a pained look. "Baby, I can't do this now. You know Willis has another month of school. You have to work out your notice at the sheriff's office. I don't expect you to come with me."

"What about our honeymoon? Have you forgotten we're supposed to be taking a cruise next week?"

He had forgotten, and it showed on his face. "I don't know." He pushed a hand through his hair. "I don't know if I'll be able to take the time off now. We might have to postpone. I'll let you know when I see how things go."

"You'll let me *know*?" She spun away from him in disgust. "Thanks for that!"

"For God's sake, Jolene, I don't have time to argue with you now. I'll let you know. It's the best I can do." He moved around her to the porch.

"So you just leave?" Her voice was strident as she stalked up behind him. "We've barely been married a week, and you just pick up and *leave*?"

He placed the backpack and tent on the porch and turned to her, taking her shoulders between his hands. He tried to smile. "'Loved I not honor more,'" he quoted.

She stared at him. "What?"

"The stupid poem, remember? 'I could not love thee, dear, so much, loved I not honor more.' The guy's name was Richard Lovelace, by the way, not Wordsworth. I looked it up."

When she remained stone-faced, he abandoned the attempt to soften her. Jo," he said simply, "the town is without a police chief. I took the job. I made a commitment. I don't have a choice."

"You most certainly do! You pick up the phone and you call that woman back and tell her your start date is July seventh. That's what you agreed to, that's what the contract says, that was the plan!"

He dropped her shoulders. "I can't," he said flatly. He walked past her to the truck to pick up another load.

"*Damn* it, Buck!" She grabbed his arm again. "You can't do this! We were going to take the summer—you promised me the summer! We were going to take our time finding a house, finding a school, seeing if we even liked it there! Willis is already signed up for Bible School up here in June, just so you and I could take the time to look around... we've got two houses to pack up, four people... you can't just *do* this!"

The move to Mercy had, not surprisingly, been the biggest bone of contention between them since they'd decided to get married. Though he wasn't officially scheduled to take over as police chief until July, Billy had wanted him to come down the first of June and start learning the ropes. Buck had finally convinced Jolene they could use that first month getting to know the town and finding a place to settle in, going back and forth between Georgia and North Carolina to pack up. She could have the summer to look for a job. Their official moving date would be in August, just before Willis started school. He had always suspected that the reason she had wanted to postpone the move until the end of summer was because she hoped something might happen in the interim to make him change his mind about the job. Now he was sure of it.

"We can still do that, Jo," he said. His tone was a little clipped. "I'm just going down two weeks early, that's all. You'll come down the first of June like we planned."

"Maybe I will," she retorted, "and maybe I won't."

"Well, thanks a lot for the support."

He pushed past her, carrying two sleeping bags, and dumped them on the porch. He turned on her. "You know something?" he said. His eyes were angry, his words tight. "You do what you want. You always do anyway. Come to Georgia, don't come to Georgia. At this point I just don't care."

She returned spitefully, "I expected more from you. God knows why, but I did."

"Yeah, well, I expected more from you too."

They stood there, tempers churning, glaring at each other for another minute. It wasn't their first fight, and it certainly wouldn't be their last. But this one hurt more because they both were right. He knew he wasn't being fair to her. And she knew he had no choice. They both knew he was leaving.

He said gruffly, "I'm going to say goodbye to Willis." And he went inside.

He hugged Willis and explained that he had to go out of town for work, but that he'd talk to him soon. Willis took it a lot better than Jolene had. When Buck came back outside Jolene was not waiting for him. He got in his truck and drove away without saying goodbye.

When he was almost ready to leave late that night after twelve hours of packing, six runs to the dump, and two trips to the store for travel supplies; after turning off the well pump and draining the house, shutting off the power and cleaning out the refrigerator; after another run into town to visit the ATM and after making some calls to people who would be hurt if he didn't say goodbye, after loading his truck and tying down the tarp and, in fact, putting it off as long as he could, she texted. The truth was, Buck could have packed a duffle bag and been out of there in an hour; he would have arrived in Mercy in time for dinner, a little HBO on the motel television, and a good night's sleep. Instead, he had kept himself busy all day, waiting for her to call. And she texted.

Call me when you get there, was all she said.

He typed back, *OK.*

He waited, but she did not reply. So he left. And he didn't look back.

CHAPTER THIRTY

Jolene said, "What am I looking at?"

Buck had propped his phone up against a stack of books so that she could see what he was seeing. The jewelry, newspaper clippings, and police reports were arranged in sequence across Billy's desk, each one matched with its counterpart. Buck had studied them for over an hour before calling Jo.

He blew out a long slow breath. "Souvenirs. I think each one of these pieces of jewelry belonged to the victim of a serial killer—or kidnapper, but probably killer since none of these women was ever found. Jesus, Jo, Billy practically drew me a map. This was what he was working on when he was killed. No, what I mean is I think he must have been working on it off and on for years. All those unsolved cases you found, the ones that were in the links you sent me, they're here. Look." He moved one of the newspaper photographs closer to the camera. "Mary Elizabeth Purcel, age twenty-three. Last seen March 13, 1976, at the Sinclair Station outside Mercy, Georgia. Sully was just telling me about that place the other day. It's not even there anymore. According to the police report, she was wearing pink slacks, white sweater, ruby ring on her right third finger." He held up the envelope containing the ruby ring. The initials "MP" were written in careful black marker on the outside, matching the jewelry to its owner.

Jolene leaned in. "I can't see. I wish I was there. Hold up the picture."

He did. "I wish you were here too."

It was her day off, and he could see she was sitting at the kitchen counter, wearing jeans and a tee shirt, half-unpacked bags of groceries around her. This was how they worked, studying case files together, one of them peering over the other's shoulder, bouncing ideas off each other. Only they weren't usually four hundred miles apart.

She shook her head. "I don't get it. It could be anybody's ring, and the photo doesn't show her wearing it."

"Emily Park, 2000." He held up another photo. This one looked like a copy of a high school photo, professionally taken, perfectly posed, details clear. "Do you see the necklace she's wearing?"

"It looks like a flower. A gold rose."

Buck held up the envelope containing a gold chain necklace with a carved gold rose on it, turning it carefully so Jolene could see the contents. "Billy wrote on his copy of the police report, 'Parents state the necklace was a graduation gift. Love Mom and Dad inscribed on the back.'" Buck turned the pendant over and held it close to the camera.

"'Love, Mom and Dad,'" she read. She sat back thoughtfully.

"And this one." He held up another evidence bag, this one containing a silver ankle bracelet with the name "Tanya" engraved in script on an oval plate. "Tanya DeFoe, a student at Georgia Southern, went to Panama City on spring break in 1968 and never returned. And remember that couple you were telling me about? The one that wrote 'Mercy' in blood on the tree? Their names were Jarred and Amelia. There's a locket…" He shook it out of its bag and into his gloved hand, holding it up for her. "See the 'A&J' engraved on it? There's a photo of a man inside." He pried it open and showed her. "It's kind of beat up, but it sure as hell looks like the same guy to me." He held up an 8x10 printout of a clearer photo.

"There are about a dozen case files here," he said, returning the locket to its bag, "or parts of case files. He must've been collecting them for decades. Not all of them have physical evidence that matches, but there are enough to make a pattern."

Jolene looked troubled. "Where did he get the jewelry?"

Buck shook his head. "I don't know. It's all in kind of rough shape, dirty, rusted… maybe buried? Or stored outside or in a leaky shed somewhere?" As he spoke he picked up the half-heart necklace he had found in Billy's car, the only one that wasn't weather-beaten. The one he was certain belonged to Mandy Wolford. The chain was intact, indicating that it had not been torn off, but carefully removed. Perhaps from a corpse.

"Buck," Jolene said, worried. "You're talking about over a half century of disappearances, here. If they're all connected to the same perpetrator, you're looking for a really old man." She hesitated. "How old was Billy?"

Buck shook his head. "Sixty-eight. But if you're thinking it was him, not possible. He would have been nine years old when the first girl we have here disappeared, and he was dead by the time Peyton went missing."

She frowned. "Still, it would explain how he collected all that stuff."

Buck turned the half-heart necklace over and over in his hand, thinking. "He wanted me to find all this. He wanted me to find it badly enough to add a codicil to his will, but he could just have easily written me a letter or sent me an e-mail telling me what it all meant."

She said, "Maybe he didn't know. Maybe that's what he wanted you to find out."

"Yeah," Buck murmured. "Or maybe he did know—or thought he knew—and was trying to prove it. He must've also known that was going to be dangerous, which was why he wanted to make sure I could pick up the case if he couldn't."

"God, Buck. Why would Billy keep something like that a secret? If he had a suspect and he knew the man was dangerous, which he clearly was, why wouldn't he form a team, get some help?"

"Because," Buck said softly, thinking out loud, "it was somebody he knew. It was someone on the force."

He turned the phone so that he could look at her. "Think about it. Peyton called to report Mandy Wolford missing on May fifth. Billy investigated just like I did, found out she was lured here by a phony ad. He knew about the other women who had disappeared around here over the years. He'd been collecting the cold cases all this time, studying them. Hell, some of them happened when his dad was in charge here; he had a natural interest. He knew about the bad traffic stops, Baker had reported one to him just that week, and he was keeping a notebook filled with other infractions by his officers. He knew there was more than one bad actor on his force, and had started to suspect one of them was *really* bad. He probably narrowed down the suspects by going over the duty roster, which led him to find Mandy's necklace, and maybe the other souvenirs at the same time. He started putting together this whole profile…" He gestured to the case files spread out over the desk. "And realized he had a serial killer on his hands. He went to confront the guy, and he was shot."

She shook her head slowly. "And you're sure it was one of his officers?"

"We have video evidence of a police officer using Billy's key card to take Carl Tucker's gun from the evidence room—two hours after Billy died. Carl's gun was a 9-millimeter Glock, just like every cop in this department carries."

"So, if Billy was shot with the cop's weapon," Jolene said, following his train of thought, "all he had to do was to switch the barrel from his own gun—the murder weapon—with the one on Carl's gun so that the ballistics would match. Then he threw it in the weeds near the body for the cops to find, and Carl Tucker would be made for the murder."

Buck nodded. "There's something else. When Peyton came to town asking more questions about her missing friend, she talked to a police officer—no record of who—and apparently arranged to meet him early Monday morning at that convenience store. The suspect we have in custody for the robbery said it was a police officer who turned off the security camera and instructed him to hold hostages in the store until he got there. I think he was setting Peyton up to be killed in the cross fire. But when I called 911 I blew his plan."

"So he tracked Peyton out of town, pulled her over…"

"And that's the last anyone heard of her," Buck supplied.

"There are a couple of problems with your theory," she pointed out. "The first is that the person responsible for all those disappearances is way too old to be an active cop."

He sighed. "Right."

"What if it's not the same person?" she suggested. "What if it's, I don't know, some kind of copycat? Somebody who was inspired by some of those cases from the seventies."

"Maybe." Buck rubbed a hand over his face. "Or maybe I'm completely off track. Maybe none of this has anything to do with who killed Billy or why."

"Well, if it doesn't, it sure is a weird-ass coincidence," Jolene said.

"Yeah." He looked at her bleakly. "So what's the second thing? You said there were two things wrong with my theory."

She frowned a little. "It's just that… there are two different profiles here. One is an opportunistic sexual predator, the other an organized serial killer. Buck, I don't think they're the same man."

He tried to find a way to argue with her logic, but couldn't. And if it was Craig Teller who had been molesting women on Post Road, as he was almost certain it was, he had been hospitalized on the weekend Mandy Wolford disappeared. Buck had been working so hard trying to connect the two cases that he had overlooked the obvious. He wondered if Billy had made the same mistake.

Buck said heavily, "You tried to warn me about this place."

"Let that be a lesson to you." She mustered a weak smile. "Always listen to your wife."

For a while they just looked at each other, the ache of need stretching across the miles of electrons that both connected and separated them. He said, "Well, I've got a detective working on Peyton's case and I'm going to spend the night sifting through the back duty rosters and personnel files, seeing if any of the guys who were on duty on the nights of the traffic stops had complaints filed against them. Also, matching the badge numbers in Billy's notebook to names, and the code violations to criminal offenses. In other words, doing exactly what Billy did. I brought the chief's car home and thought I'd check the trip computer, see if I can retrace Billy's steps that last week."

Jo said solemnly, "Buck, you be careful. If you're right and it is someone on the force, you don't know who to trust. And that person might already be nervous about how much Billy told you. So, you just watch yourself, you hear?"

"Yes, ma'am." He gave her a tender smile. "Gotta go. I'll check in with you before work tomorrow."

"I love you, Buck."

"Love you too, babe."

When they disconnected, Buck started to stack all the papers and their corresponding evidence bags in order to return them to the safe. He rewrapped Mandy Wolford's necklace in his handkerchief, planning to turn it over to Frankie in the morning as part of the official missing person file. In the meantime, it, too, would go in the safe. He picked up the stack of papers, and as he did a newspaper clipping fluttered loose from the bottom of the stack. The headline read, *Local Man Killed in Police Shoot-Out.*

Buck put down the papers and read the article. It was brief and to the point.

> *Jimmy Raeford, age thirty-two, died of a gunshot wound during a confrontation with Police Chief Billy Aikens on Tuesday July 20, according to a spokesman for the police department. Police were called to the Raeford home on Long View Road at 1:30 in the afternoon, where they found Raeford holding a woman and two children hostage inside the house. Despite attempts to negotiate their safe release, Raeford refused to surrender and opened fire on police officers. Police Chief Aikens returned fire, striking Raeford in the torso four times. Raeford was pronounced dead at the scene.*
>
> *The hostages were released unharmed.*

That was it. No photographs, no mention of an investigation, no names of the survivors. But of course, a small-town newspaper would not glorify an incident like this, particularly if it in any way cast aspersions on their beloved police chief. Buck could understand why Billy had kept the article; it had clearly been a life-defining moment for him. But why was it here, in this file of missing girls?

But the oldest one, he turned out okay. He grew up to be a cop. The words came back to Buck as clearly as if Billy had spoken them out loud. Sitting on the bench beside the fountain, listening to Billy tell the story about the day he had killed a man in front of his two little boys. What else had he said, about things being passed down through generations? Buck couldn't remember, and just trying gave him a chill.

Raeford. Was there anybody on the force by that name? He started to go to his laptop to access the personnel files, then realized it wouldn't do any good. The paper said nothing about the woman who was held hostage being Raeford's wife, and Billy had referred to her as his girlfriend. The children probably didn't have Raeford's last name, and Buck didn't have the resources here to find out what their actual name was. He needed to go back to the office.

Or... he could just ask Lydia.

He checked the time on his phone: 6:40. Lydia left the office at 5:00, and by now would be peacefully engaged in preparing dinner or taking a Zumba class or walking her dog —did Lydia even have a dog?—or living whatever life she lived outside the office. The last thing she would welcome was a call from him.

Buck thumbed through his contacts until he found her listing: Lydia Browning, home. There was a notation, in all caps and highlighted in red, after the number: FOR EMERGENCY USE ONLY. Buck punched "dial," grimacing as he did so.

"Yes, Chief," she answered briskly on the second ring. "What can I do for you?"

He said quickly, "I'm sorry to bother you after hours, Lydia, but this will only take a minute. I need some information." He rushed on without giving her a chance to respond. "Billy told me that he killed a man in the line of duty some years back, and that one of the man's sons grew up to be a police officer. Do you know the case I'm talking about?"

She replied cautiously, "I do."

He said, "Is that officer on the Mercy police force now? Did Billy hire him?"

There was the briefest of pauses. "It's hardly a secret," Lydia replied. Buck suspected the annoyance in her voice reflected the fact that, not only was this not an emergency, but he could have easily looked up the information for himself. "The officer is Jim Torrance. You interviewed him this morning."

Buck didn't know what he had expected, but that wasn't it.

He had just hit another dead end. Torrance was twenty-seven years old, far too young to be the killer who had been operating since 1962. Even a copycat would have to be old enough to remember the murders, or to have read about them. And besides, where would he have gotten the souvenirs that Billy had found? Once again, he was trying to connect dots that weren't there.

Buck thanked Lydia, apologized profusely once again for disturbing her, and disconnected before she could get any more annoyed with him.

He returned everything to the safe, locked it, and restored the marlin to its original position. He went back out into the muggy late afternoon, where, in the hour or so that he'd been inside, the sun had heated the interior of the police cruiser to such a degree that the leather steering wheel burned his hands when he touched it. He started the engine and turned up the AC, leaving the door open to allow some of the heat to escape while the electronics came online.

While he waited for the vehicle to cool down, Buck brought up the trip computer on the console screen. Roland said that May 6 was the last day Billy had driven the car, and it was also the day that he had gone to Carl Tucker's house on the domestic abuse call. But Billy had not been at the office when that call came in. Buck hit the back arrow until May 6 showed up, and a map appeared with a green line showing everywhere Billy had been that day.

Buck followed the green line down Main Street out of town, west toward the water. He zoomed in and tapped the button for street labels, recognizing some of the roads he and Sully had taken the other day to get to Lost Creek, where Billy was killed. But that wasn't where Billy had gone on May 6. He had driven past the dirt road that led to the creek and moved deeper into the marsh. A mile or so later he'd taken a right turn onto a thin and twisty track that appeared to lead straight into a body of water. Buck moved the screen around until he found the label for the road name. *Long View Road*.

Long View Road. The place where, some fifteen years ago, Billy had shot a man to death in front of his children. A man who, according to Lydia, had been Jim Torrance's father.

It was not even seven o'clock. There was still plenty of daylight left. Buck pulled the car door shut, strapped on his seat belt, and pushed "Go" on the navigation screen map. He put the car in gear and followed the directions.

———

Four hundred miles away, Jolene sat at the kitchen counter, groceries still unpacked, her phone still in her hand. She was frowning, thinking, working things through, and she started a little when her mother poked her head around the corner. "You need any help getting supper on the table, honey? Willis will be home from Tommy's soon and…" Her expression changed to concern as she looked around and saw supper had not even been started. "Is everything okay?"

Jolene shook her head slowly, then she stood up. "I have to go," she said.

"Go? Where? Did something happen at work?"

Jolene paused briefly to kiss her mother on the cheek on her way out of the kitchen. "You're going to have to finish packing by yourself, Mama," she said. "Buck is in trouble."

CHAPTER THIRTY-ONE

Buck drove past corner where Sully had talked about his uncle using the Sinclair dinosaur sign for target practice, following the green line on the map. *And this road here*, Sully had said, *leads to the deepest part of the marsh. That's where they found that car you were talking about.* The sheriff's office car that contained the remains of the sheriff who had been missing twenty years. Buck didn't like the story that was spinning out in his head, so he tried not to listen to it. He made the turn, following the route Billy had taken. Long View Road.

From the map it looked as though the road led straight into the marsh, and the evidence of his own eyes didn't give Buck reason to believe otherwise. The path was narrow and weed-choked, lined so thickly with vine-covered trees that all but the sharpest rays of sunlight were blocked. Five hundred yards in, the automatic headlights came on, and the canopy overhead was like a tunnel. Dark-leafed branches squeaked against the side panels and pressed their greedy fingers against the windows. He could almost think no one had driven down this path in years, but he knew that wasn't true. He could see tire tracks in the compressed grass that unfolded beneath his headlights. Recent ones.

He stopped the car and switched the computer screen to satellite view. Six hundred fifty-two feet ahead, according to the legend, there was a clearing that melted into flat dark water and swamp grass as far as the eye could see. There were several structures in the clearing, but they were partially obscured by trees and his view wasn't clear enough to make out what they were. He didn't see any vehicles.

Buck switched the view back to the map route. This, according to the computer, had been the end of Trip One on May 6. Trip Two, which began when Billy started the car again, had taken him from this location back to the main road another mile to 34 Bob Cramer Road, Carl Tucker's house. Billy had been here, revisiting the site where once long ago he'd responded to a call for help that had turned deadly, when he received another call about another violent man. He had taken that call and begun the series of events that had led Buck here.

Buck turned off the engine and got out of the car.

Sweat congealed on his upper lip and his scalp before he'd walked fifty steps. The gnats began to swarm, landing on his eyelashes and in his nostrils, and he realized he had forgotten the insect repellent. He almost turned back, but a glint of sunlight through the trees told him he was closer to his destination than to the car. He protected his face with his forearm and moved forward. Thorny vines tugged at his slacks, and his dress shoes were not the best footwear for gripping the slippery surface of sandy grass. He should have changed before heading out, but who knew he'd end up here, on a dead-end trek to the middle of the swamp?

A column of late evening light broke through the green-blackness, and just as Buck stepped into the clearing an explosive whir of wings dropped him to one knee. His hand automatically whipped backwards for his gun even as he saw a wedge of blackbirds spread across the pale blue sky. But his heart was still thudding as he straightened up and moved cautiously into the clearing.

What once might have been yard was now a meadow of tall grasses and wild weeds. There was a house off-center, with a porch that had fallen off its pilings on the east and, oddly, the skeleton of a swing with most of its slats gone, hanging from a chain. A broken window grinned at him like a gap-toothed child. Across the yard from the house was a squat cinder block building, heavy with vines. And beyond it all was the marsh, all grass and colors and glinting mirrored water, as vast and unfathomable as any poem ever conceived, as any painting ever put on canvas.

Buck approached the house from behind, watching his step for hidden hazards, feeling as exposed as a polar bear on a black lake. The silence was intense, as heavy as the air he tried to draw into his lungs, as sharp as the glint of the western sun that blinded him. Sweat rolled down his sides and stung his eyes. He wiped his face with his sleeve and kept going.

He came around the side of the dilapidated house and found himself beneath one of those Medusa trees, the Spanish moss trailing like abandoned snakeskins toward the ground. Straight ahead was a wooden fish-cleaning station, its boards stained dark with years of blood and entrails. Buck touched the fish-cleaning table absently. It felt damp. When he looked at his fingers, they were red with blood.

Buck felt something brush his hair and he jerked away

sharply, ducking and throwing up his hand to swat away whatever it was. The movement caused the moss to sway and part a little, and that was when Buck caught the glimmer of something hanging in the tree, snagged in the moss. He moved closer, narrowing his eyes.

It was an earring, a gold hoop with its hook hung on one of the lower branches of the spreading oak tree like a Christmas ornament. Next to it, a few feet away, was a wedding band tied to a clump of moss with a green plastic garbage tie. Buck turned slowly around, his eyes picking out the glitter of a watch band, a jeweled hair barrette, the flash of a digital fitness tracker, a silver crucifix, pitted with age. This was what Billy had seen the day he had driven out here—an ancient tree decorated with trophies from crimes past and present. He had taken what he could, maybe at random, or maybe because he recognized them from his long study of the women who once had owned them. He knew if he had taken them all the killer would be alerted, so he gathered only enough to make his case. He must have planned to come back… and maybe he had.

Buck's throat was tight as he looked around the gruesomely ornamented, oddly beautiful old tree. A lifetime's work. Maybe several lifetimes. The jewelry looked down at him like knowing eyes, winking in the dying sunlight, each piece telling its own bleak tale. His gaze swung back to the fitness tracker. Its digital time display was still blinking, and those things had a battery life of less than a week. Next to it, on a lower branch half-concealed by moss, was Peyton McGilroy's silver pendant half-heart necklace with the word "Best" inscribed on it.

Buck reached for his phone, first to snap some photos, then to call Frankie out here. But he never got it out of his pocket. As he moved out of the shadow of the tree away from the fish-cleaning station, a sudden sharp sound pierced the thick silence. The warble of a bird, the creak of a hinge, the whimper of an animal. His eyes swept the landscape. There was a weather-beaten barn to his left, its plank doors closed, its rusted roof caved in on one side. About fifty feet to his right was a concrete block building that might once have been a garage. Parked behind it, only partially visible from this angle, was a City of Mercy police vehicle.

Buck drew his weapon, his heart pounding, and crossed the weedy expanse of yard as silently as he could, his eyes moving left and right, his breath dragging. As he approached the building, he could see that the part of the structure that had once held large garage bay doors had been sealed up with concrete blocks, the overhead doors replaced by a single walk-through metal door. That metal door was open a fraction, leaving a wedge just large enough for a man to edge through.

Buck slipped through the door and into darkness. There were no windows and the air was hot and fetid smelling. More than fetid. Dank, dusty, metallic. Blood. It smelled like old blood.

As his eyes slowly adjusted to the dimness of the light that came in through the door behind him, Buck could make out two things. The first was the black shadow of the oil pit in the middle of the floor in front of him. That was where the bloody smell was coming from. There were wet spatters around the rim that shone faintly in the dim light. The second thing he could make out was the shape of two people on the other side of the oil pit, on their knees.

Sully was wearing his uniform, and it was covered in blood. There were bloody streaks down one cheek and across his neck where flailing hands had struck him. He had one arm around Peyton McGilroy's shoulders, trying to drag her toward the pit, the other hand was clamped firmly over her mouth. She struggled, the glint of her eyes like a terrified animal's in the dark. She was naked except for her underwear, her hair matted with blood, her body torn with so many open wounds that it was hard to see them all at once. Her right foot was a blackened, crushed and swollen club. She was missing the small finger on one hand, and Buck had an awful intuition of what might have been carved on the fish cleaning station to leave it wet with blood. The sounds that came from her throat were like the peeping of a baby chick, frantic, manic.

Buck held the weapon steady on Sully but knew he would not be able to get off a shot unless he could convince the other man to let her go. "Sully," he said quietly, "I really hoped it wasn't you."

Sully looked up at him, his own eyes dark and desperate and filling slowly with apprehension. "It's not," he said.

That was when Buck realized that Sully was looking over his shoulder.

CHAPTER THIRTY-TWO

Buck saw Sully's eyes shift violently to the right just as he heard the snick of a footstep behind him. Buck spun right in a shooter's stance and saw the form of the man in the doorway, the glint of a knife. "Twenty-one steps," Jim Torrance said, smiling. "That's what they teach us in Academy, isn't it, Chief?" He sounded mildly amused. "Twenty-one steps is all it takes for a man armed with a knife to cross the room and cut your throat before you can pull the trigger. So, what do you say we give it a try?"

Jim Torrance, the eager, fresh-faced young officer Buck had interviewed in his office only that morning, did not look so young or so innocent now. He held a ten-inch skinning knife in his hand with the confidence of someone to whom using it was second nature and the certainty of a police officer who had been trained to assess and react.

Buck said steadily, "I don't shoot people in cold blood, no matter how much they deserve it. Neither did Billy. Your father fired on the police first all those years ago, and he would have killed you and your mother and brother if it hadn't been for Billy. You know that."

"Oh, I know," replied Torrance easily. "And it's not like I hated to see the bastard go. He was one crazy SOB. Billy's been real good to me since, making sure I got an education, even hiring on me on at the department. I hated to kill him, I really did. But he knew too much, and was getting ready to prove it. Isn't that always the way? People just get too smart for their own good."

Behind him, Buck could hear Peyton sobbing, whimpering for breath, as Sully removed his hand from her mouth. Buck shifted his position slightly to block Torrance's view of whatever Sully was doing.

"Careful there, Chief," said Torrance. "You don't want to fall into that oil pit. My daddy used to bleed deer there, kept the mess from getting all over the yard after a kill. Learned that trick from his grandaddy. Of course..." And now there was the trace of a complacent smile in his voice. "They weren't always deer, now, were they? And when my mama found out what he was really doing out here, she about went crazy. Of course, he kept her tied up most of the time, but he had to let her loose to fix his supper and whatnot, and that's when most of the beating happened." He was thoughtful for a moment. "You know the thing that always got me? After the shooting, this place was swarming with police, and not one of them thought to look in the oil pit. Or at the tree where Daddy and Grandpap hung all their trophies. It was right there for anybody to find, but the man was dead and they thought their job was done."

Buck could sense, rather than hear, Sully edging left behind him, planning to come up on Torrance's blind side. Buck kept him talking. "Your mother never said a word."

"Nah." He practically spat the word. "She was a worthless coward. Stuffing herself full of pills night and day, didn't even know where she was half the time. The world was well rid of her. But Billy, now. He was a fine man. I hated what I had to do."

Buck said, "Billy found some of your trophies."

"Did he now?" Torrance sounded interested. "I thought some of them were missing, but 'coons take them sometimes, you know. I wonder what brought him out here. Nobody's lived here in fifteen years. But I like it because it's private, and…" He tilted his head toward the door. Buck was certain he was smiling. "You can't beat the marsh for getting rid of things."

"I think Billy was looking for your last victim," Buck said. "Mandy Wolford. That's what brought him out here. You placed that phony Facebook ad, didn't you, looking for an applicant with no family to report her missing? A student who wouldn't be expected back until after spring break?"

"Well, I screwed the pooch on that one, didn't I?" replied Torrance cheerfully. "Didn't count on Miss Curiosity, over there." He jerked his head in Peyton's direction. "But it all worked out okay, right? Two for the price of one, as they say."

Sully had made it to this side of the oil pit, far on Buck's left. Buck could see with his peripheral vision that Sully's weapon was drawn and leveled at Torrance. Peyton wasn't even sobbing any more, just drawing in shaky, keening breaths. Buck had never heard sounds like that come from a human being.

Sully said, "It's time to give it up now, Jimmy. You've got two guns pointed at you, and all you've got is a knife. So, there are really only two ways you're leaving here: in cuffs, or a body bag. You choose."

"Or," suggested Torrance conversationally, "maybe I take one of you out and make a break for it. It's not as easy to hit a moving target in the dark as most people think. And you don't have any idea who I'll go for. Twenty-one steps."

The last syllable was barely out of his mouth before Torrance lunged toward Sully, the knife blade flashing. Sully fired. So did Buck. Both shots thudded into concrete. Buck heard Sully cry out and Buck spun around, trying to site a target, as the knife skittered across the floor. Buck couldn't tell which shadow was Sully and which was Craig. He heard the sound of scuffling, saw the barrel flash and heard the explosion, but the bullet went into the air. Then both men were on the ground; Sully's gun spun away into the bloody oil pit. Buck fired as Torrance ran past him toward the door. He couldn't tell whether he hit him or not.

"You okay?" Buck shouted to Sully.

"Go after him!" Sully replied hoarsely, gasping. "I'm okay."

"Get Peyton to the unit." Buck ran for the door. "Call for backup!"

Buck burst out the door into a spooky orange twilight in which shadows were elongated and trees were backlit with the blinding light of the setting sun. The marsh looked like a long black beast crouching in the foreground, and running toward it, zigzagging like a linebacker, was Jim Torrance. Buck raised his weapon, tried to get the man in his sites, but there was no point in wasting ammunition. He ran after him, dragging in hot air and invisible insects with every breath, brushing mosquitoes and sweat from his eyes with his free hand. "Torrance!" he shouted. His damaged lungs couldn't keep up this pace. He was wheezing already and his leg was throbbing, stiffening up. He was falling behind. "This is stupid! You've got nowhere to go and every cop in this county is on his way here!"

Jim Torrance didn't stop; he didn't slow down, and he didn't look back. Buck plunged forward into the waist-high grass and the blood-red sunset. He took a chance and fired a shot, hoping it would at least cause Torrance to look back, maybe even stop. It didn't.

The ground grew soggy beneath his feet. His slick-soled shoes slipped and skidded in mud, and water dragged at the cuffs of his pants. He scanned the surface of the water, looking for pointed snouts and sloping eyes even as he plunged forward. Mud splashed as high as his calves now, sucking at his shoes.

"Jim!" Buck shouted. "Stop! Don't make me shoot you! This is not what Billy wanted!"

Torrance kept going, plowing forward through the marsh toward the wide black ribbon of water that flowed into the Blood River. He was too far ahead for a clean shot, even though he, too, was slowing down.

"You've got nowhere to go!" Buck repeated, gasping. His lungs were on fire, and his leg felt like wood. "Stop!"

Jim Torrance turned around then and threw up his hands above his head in what Buck thought was a gesture of surrender. But it wasn't. Torrance waved his hands above his head, cried, "The marsh dragon lives forever!" He took off again, pushing through the marsh.

Buck thought if he could get another half-dozen yards on him, he could get off a disabling shot. He lunged forward, caught his foot on a root, and landed hard on his knees in two feet of brackish water. He managed to keep his gun dry, but when he went to push himself back up to his feet something hit his arm with the force of a hammer. Electric current shot up his arm to his jaw and he let out a cry, snatching his arm out of the weeds. His shirtsleeve was sodden and dark with mud, but already he could see a knot starting to swell beneath the fabric. Out of the corner of his eye he saw a sinuous shape parting the water, swimming away from him.

Buck staggered to his feet. Torrance was slowing down, wading in knee-deep water. Buck pushed forward grimly, his arm throbbing. The sludge was up to his calves now. He tried to get a double-handed grip on his pistol but the effort of raising his arm wrenched another cry from him. The fingers of his injured arm were tingling like bare wires were attached to each of them, and his hand was swelling so rapidly that he could no longer see the gleam of his wedding band on his small finger. Torrance was hardly moving at all, waist deep in black water, no more than twelve yards away, but with only one hand Buck couldn't steady the weapon enough to make the shot. Just a few yards more...

But when Buck tried to push himself forward, he found he couldn't lift his feet. The harder he tried, the higher the sucking mud around him rose. Up to his knees now.

"Chief!"

It was Sully, calling from the marsh a few dozen yards away, and when Buck turned to look at him, he sank several more inches into the mud. Sully held one hand protectively over a bloody gash in his side, and the other he threw up in a warning. He called, "Stay still! Don't move! It's quicksand."

Buck looked down at the black silt, slowly rising up to his thighs. He looked at Torrance, who had stopped moving too, but the marsh mud was now up to his chest.

Sully called, "I'm going for a rope! Stand still! Don't move!"

Buck's mouth was as dry as cotton and his breathing was labored. Salty sweat blurred his vision. Or at least he thought it was sweat. His focus moved in and out like the lenses on a cheap set of binoculars. He heard Sully splashing away from him, and he called out to Torrance, "Don't move! Sully is going for rope!"

Even the effort of shouting those instructions caused Buck to sink farther into the silt. It was up to his hips now. The skin on his injured hand felt as though it might burst. The fingers were turning dark, and his arm had swollen to fill his sleeve like a sausage in a casing. It was hard to breathe. He called out to Torrance again, "Just stay still!"

But Jim Torrance did not stay still. He twisted in the water until he was facing Buck, and he spread his arms out again. The muck was up to his shoulders now, but he was grinning. "Time to sleep now," he called back. The black water rose to his neck. "Just like the marsh dragon! But nobody sleeps forever! I'll be back for you!"

The sinking sun bled into the earth, turning the water crimson, and Buck watched helplessly as the marsh swallowed Jim Torrance alive.

CHAPTER THIRTY-THREE

Buck opened his eyes to a hospital room. He knew it was a hospital because of the softly bleeping monitors, the crisp, scratchy sheets, the bad art on the wall. And because he felt like shit.

Billy was sitting in a mustard-colored chair beside his bed, reading a magazine. Buck said thickly, "Am I dead?"

"Nah." Billy got up and walked around the bed, peering into the IV bag that was attached by a long tube to Buck's arm. His other arm was encased in a bandage and strapped to his chest. "You'll be fine. Four vials of antivenin, a shot of morphine, a ton of antibiotics. Looks like it was a cottonmouth that got you. Mean sons of bitches, but Sully got you to the hospital in time. They'll probably let you go in the morning."

Buck said, "Jim Torrance is dead."

Billy nodded solemnly. "It was what he wanted. That's why he ran. He wanted to die there in the marsh."

Buck looked at Billy. "So how did you figure out it was him?"

"I didn't," Billy said, "not really." His expression was sad. "Or maybe I did and just didn't want to believe it. There've always been some things about Jim that bothered me, some incidents in school, things he said... things I chose to overlook or not believe. But I felt responsible for him. I wanted to give him every chance."

He was silent for a moment. Buck waited.

"But to answer your question, you need to check with Darryl from IT. He brought it to my attention that one of the officers had used his work computer to place an ad on Facebook. You probably read it in one of the reports from the past couple of weeks. There were a lot of them."

Buck said, uncomprehending, "Torrance used his work computer? He had to know it was monitored."

Billy nodded. "Yeah, he knew. He tried to cover his tracks, of course. Took down the ad, tried to hide his profile, but I read somewhere that one of the symptoms of psychosis is a feeling of invulnerability. I think maybe he was taunting me, seeing if I could figure it out. And the truth is, I wouldn't have, except for Darryl."

Buck shook his head slowly against the pillow. "IT. I didn't even think to check there."

Billy said, "Come on, Buck. You've been here three days and you solved two cases it took the rest of the department weeks to crack—and in the case of Craig Teller, years. Give yourself a break."

Buck said, "So it was the Facebook ad? That's how you knew it was Jim Torrance?"

"Not entirely," Billy admitted. "It was my daddy who started studying those cold cases, you know, and he always did suspect Homer Torrance—that would be Jim's grandaddy—was involved in the killing of Sheriff Kissick back in the day. After all, they found the man's car in the marsh, when it finally surfaced, not a hundred yards from the Torrance's back door. Four women went missing that we know of in the ten years before Kissick himself disappeared, all of them last seen somewhere in the vicinity of that old gas station. Daddy always claimed the sheriff had found out something that connected old Homer to those cases. Then, of course, everybody knew Jim's daddy was off. He was strange before he even went in the army, came back just about loony. Moved out there into his daddy's old house on the swamp, lived all by himself until he got that woman to move in with him and they started having kids… and more young girls went missing."

Billy shook his head. "Jimmy was right about one thing. We should have figured it out about his daddy. We searched the place, of course we did. But we were looking for weapons, drugs, evidence of child abuse—of which there was plenty, let me tell you, on all counts. Nobody paid much attention to the oil pit in the garage, or the fish cleaning station, or the tree."

He paused, looking back. "So I guess all this was on my mind when Peyton called to report her friend missing. She told me about the Facebook ad, and of course I checked out at the country club, found out they never placed an ad. Then when she texted me that picture, the last one Mandy sent her… well, it took me a minute, a lot has changed in the past fifteen years and the photo was all blurry and turned sideways, but I couldn't help thinking how much it reminded me of the old Reardon garage." He shook his head solemnly. "How that girl got that shot we'll never know, but if she hadn't this whole thing would have gone down differently. Peyton would be dead, and Jim would still be out there. God only knows how many girls she saved, even if she couldn't save herself."

He held a solemn silence for a moment, until Buck said,

"Sully didn't mention finding any text from Peyton on your phone."

Billy said, "It was on my personal phone. I guess maybe I got a little lax about following procedure over the years. Don't tell Lydia."

He smiled faintly. Buck did not.

Billy went on in a moment, "Anyhow, I started thinking about that ad for a phony job, and Jim trying to erase his tracks on the computer, and eventually ended up looking at the trip computer in Jim's assigned car, just like you did mine. By the way, Buck, never skimp on state-of-the art technology. It pays for itself every time.

"I found the necklace that Peyton had told me her friend was wearing, hanging there on the tree in broad daylight, and all the other souvenirs with it. I took the ones I thought were familiar, but I really didn't believe what I was seeing. I just couldn't put it all together in my mind. I think I might've been in shock, a little. Then the call came in about Carl Tucker so I just stuffed everything in my pocket and responded."

"You dropped Mandy Wolford's necklace in the car," Buck said.

"Is that what happened to it?" Billy looked surprised. "I looked everywhere. Finally decided I must have lost it in the struggle with Carl, or dropped it in the grass out at the Torrance place. That was a problem, because without it I didn't really have any evidence of a recent crime and couldn't make an arrest. That's why I put everything in my personal safe, and called Ken the very next morning to put that codicil in my will, making sure that if I couldn't wind it up before you got here, you'd at least have what I knew. After a few days of studying, I had a pretty good picture of what was going on, but no real evidence, damn it. Nothing I could use to make an arrest or even the kind of accusation that would end a man's career…" He shook his head in slow frustration. "And of course I didn't want to believe it. That something like this could've been going on all these years right before my eyes… I even called you on Saturday to talk it over with you. I didn't want you to be blindsided."

"Yeah," Buck said wearily, "I appreciate the thought, anyway." He thought a moment. "So how did you end up at Lost Creek pier?"

He shook his head. "No idea. It bothered me that I hadn't done a better job searching the Torrance place when I was out there, and there was the matter of the Wolford girl's necklace. I didn't think she was still alive, but I thought I might be able to find some evidence of what happened to her. So I drove back out there Sunday afternoon, and Jimmy was there. Bad timing on my part. We talked." He shrugged. "I don't remember anything else, but it's pretty easy to piece together. I thought the place was deserted, left my gun in the car. Truth be told, I don't think I really believed Jim would turn on me, even with everything I'd found out. I was wrong."

Both of them were silent for a moment, digesting this. Then Billy looked at Buck sorrowfully. "There's no excuse for what happened. A serial killer on my watch. Those poor girls. The man responsible working on my force, coming to my house for dinner, taking my money and my good will, and I never once had the guts to take a good look at him, to ask myself who he really was. Well, I want you to know I own it. I let the town down, I let you down. There's no forgiving it, there's no fixing it. All I know to do is to spend the rest of eternity trying to make up for it. I guess maybe that's why I'm here."

Buck didn't know how to answer that. The silence grew

out between them, punctuated only by the soft beeping of the monitors.

At last Billy braced his hands on his knees in preparation for standing. "Well. I guess I'd better get going. You need your rest."

"Yeah," Buck said, and watched the other man walk toward the door. "Hey, Billy."

Billy looked back.

"Thanks for your help," Buck said.

Billy smiled. "Everything I told you, you already knew. Your subconscious just needed a little help putting it together."

"I know," Buck said. "Still... I'm going to miss you."

"Oh, I'll be around if you need me," Billy assured him. "I told you I would, and I keep my promises. See you, Buck."

Buck smiled and closed his eyes. "See you, Billy."

When Buck woke up, Jolene was sitting in the mustard-colored chair beside his bed. At first he thought he was dreaming again, and he murmured, "Hi, baby." But when she leaned over him to stroke his cheek, he realized that if he had dreamed her, he would have conjured a better version than the tired, pale-lipped, worried woman in the battered baseball cap who was swimming into focus now.

"Hi, yourself," she replied. "It's about time you woke up. Who have you been muttering to all night?"

He was going to tell her, but his throat was too dry. She handed him a plastic cup with a straw in it. "You're supposed to drink plenty of fluids," she said.

She found the button that raised the head of the bed and

he drank the water, after which he started to come more awake. His arm still hurt and his fingers were still stiff, but he felt considerably better than he had in the emergency room last night. He said, "What are you doing here? What time is it, anyway?"

She took the cup from him and returned it to the bedside table. "I drove down right after we talked yesterday, and got here just in time to find out you were in the hospital. Damn it, Buck Lawson, I can't leave you alone for a minute." But she said it with a tender smile, stroking his hair away from his forehead. "And what the hell happened to your wedding ring?"

Buck looked down at the discolored fingers that protruded from the bandaged arm that was strapped to his chest. "They had to cut it off in the emergency room," he remembered. "Next time get one that fits."

Jolene gave his cheek a playful tap and sat back, the tight lines in her face easing. "They're springing you from his place as soon as the doctor gets here. Apparently you're not as sick as you look. You missed breakfast, by the way. It was pretty good."

He rested his head against the pillow, looking at her in bemusement. "I don't get it," he said. "Where's Willis? And your mom?"

Jolene said, "They're driving down tomorrow. Mama wanted to leave everything organized for the movers when they get there Friday, but there's no way they were going to miss your 'inauguration' ceremony." She put "inauguration" in air quotes.

He only picked up on one word. "Movers?"

"Oh, please." She gave a dismissing wave of her hand. "Did you really think we were going to let you do this all by yourself? I already talked to Willis's principal about letting him finish out the year with home-schooling, not that there's that much to school—a lot of field days and drawing cat pictures. Not that much to pack, either. Mama's nice dining room set, the pretty chaise from her bedroom, kitchenware, linens, Willis's toys. And let's face it, Buck, the only thing you own that wouldn't stick out like a sore thumb in that fancy house you're living in is your grandma's hutch. Maybe that rug with the roses in the bedroom nobody ever uses."

"I like my chair," he protested. He was referring to the recliner that was so old it was threadbare in spots, and even he would have to admit, if forced, it wasn't worth moving.

"We'll get you another chair," Jo told him, and that was that. "Anyway, we already arranged for a truck and a couple of guys to come load everything we're keeping. We'll have to take a few weekends this summer to go back and clear out the junk, close up the houses."

He tried to concentrate, but he felt as though he was a couple of steps—at least—behind the conversation. "I don't get it. You did all this since Sunday?"

She gave another flick or her wrist. "Don't be ridiculous. Mama and I have been making lists for weeks."

He smiled, helpless and bemused. "You ladies," he said, "are amazing. Don't know how I ever managed without you."

"Neither do I," she replied frankly.

He frowned a little. "But what about your job?"

She replied, "I've been trying to tell you for two days, but I guess you had other things on your mind. I was offered an instructor's position at the Police Officers Standards and Training center in Albany. You remember, the interview I did last month. It's a two-hour drive, but the pay is good and I only work three days a week. Besides, I thought it might be good if Willis had at least one parent who didn't put her life on the line every day. I start the first week of June, and the sheriff is okay with me leaving early."

Buck smiled, both at the easy way in which she said "parent," and at the fact that she was here to stay. "Instructor, huh? I'm impressed. What are you teaching?"

The steadiness of her gaze dared him to laugh. "De-escalation and sensitivity training."

Buck tried his best to keep his lips from twitching as he reached for her hand. "Baby," he assured her, "you'll be great."

She jerked her hand away in annoyance, and just then there was a tap on the door. Sully looked in cautiously, and Buck gestured him inside, sitting up straighter.

"Sully," he said. "You okay?"

Sully looked tired and a little pale, but he was freshly shaved and dressed in uniform. "A couple of stitches," he assured Buck, coming into the room. "No big deal. He barely nicked me." He held up a shopping bag from Aikens Department Store. "I hear they're cutting you loose this morning. Lydia went out and got you some clean clothes. The ones you were wearing were wrecked."

Jolene stood to take the bag from him and Buck said, "Sully, have you met my wife, Jo?"

"He's the one who answered your phone last night when I called," Jolene pointed out with a quick, grateful glance at Sully. "Scared me half to death. I thought for sure you'd gone and gotten yourself killed."

"You know better than that," Buck said. "I promised Willis I was going to take him fishing, and I keep my promises. No way I was going to die."

She looked at him with eyes that were suddenly bright with tears, and then quickly away. She busied herself examining the contents of the bag. "They're the right sizes," she observed in surprise.

"Lydia's pretty good about things like that," Sully replied.

Buck said, "How's Peyton?"

"She was in pretty rough shape," Sully replied solemnly, "but she's a tough kid and I think she'll be okay. I heard they're air-lifting her to Atlanta this morning for surgery. Her folks are here. They wanted me to make sure to thank you."

Buck shook his head. "You're the one who found her. How'd you do it, anyway?"

Sully said, "It wasn't me; it was Frankie and Baker. Her parents brought a full-sized picture of her when they got here, not long after you'd left for the day. Baker noticed she was wearing one of those fitness trackers, and Frankie got her parents to check her phone to see if it was synchronized. Sure enough, the app showed right where the tracker was."

Buck said sharply, "Why didn't you notify me?"

Sully scratched his chin uncertainly. "Well, boss, in general, we don't update the chief of police on something like this until we check it out. Chain of command, you know."

Buck frowned. "We're about to get a new policy."

Sully said, "Right." He went on, "Of course, just because she had a tracker, that didn't mean she was still wearing it, and the GPS showed it so close to the marsh that I was afraid… well, we didn't want to get her parents' hopes up. So I went out there to check it out, and the door to the garage was unlocked." He fell silent, reliving, no doubt, the moments before Buck had arrived. "The minute she saw my uniform, she freaked," he went on. "I can't blame her. But all I could think about was getting her out of there. I'd seen Torrance's car in the barn and I knew he couldn't be far away. I guess I should've had a better plan."

They both were quiet for a moment. Jolene, who had seen her share of horrors, let them have their silence.

Then Sully said, "You know, boss, we're not going to be able to prove a lot of what Torrance told us yesterday. I mean, if the victims were disposed of in the marsh, there's not a lot of evidence to work with. But we did get a couple of breaks. Did you notice that game camera set up outside the garage? I'm guessing he had it there in case one of his victims tried to escape. But he must've forgot about it the day he shot Billy because it recorded everything. We found a bloody tarp in the barn, which we think he used to transport Billy's body to Lost Creek where we'd be sure to find it. Then he drove Billy's car over there and left it in plain sight. He would've known that a man like Billy couldn't just disappear without a massive manhunt, so he made sure he could frame a likely suspect for the murder. Frankie told me about the video showing him using Billy's key card to get into the evidence room and swipe Tucker's gun. One thing you've got to say about the SOB—he was smart. Almost got away with it, too."

"Yeah," said Buck. "Good work. I guess I'd better give the prosecutor's office a call."

"Tomorrow," put in Jolene.

Sully said, "When we searched Torrance's apartment, we found a wonky journal full of weird, twisted shit. Something about a marsh dragon. It's got entries going back eight years. A good forensic analyst might be able to do something with it, maybe somehow use the entries to identify the victims. He talks about his daddy in there, and his grandaddy, too. Like killing was the family business." He shook his head slowly. "Weird shit."

Buck winced as he struggled to sit up straighter in an effort to swing his legs out of bed. A warning look from

Jolene made him abandon the effort. "There are some things at the house you should see," he told Sully. "Maybe come by after lunch."

"Maybe tomorrow," said Jolene with another warning look. And then she looked uncertainly from Buck to Sully, and back again. "So this sicko, this Torrance... are you telling me he was the same one that's been assaulting women at traffic stops all this time?"

Buck shook his head against the pillow. "No. You were right about that. They were two different guys." He looked at Sully. "I've got some pretty damning evidence against Teller. Billy kept a notebook."

Sully nodded somberly. "Frankie filled me in on what she's found out so far. It doesn't look good for him. Do you want me to put him on suspension pending an investigation?"

"As of this time and date," Buck replied. "But it's going to be a very short investigation. Have him report to my office at noon tomorrow. I'm looking forward to sharing our findings with him."

Sully almost smiled. "You got it, Chief." Then he said, "Well, I'm going to get on in to work, get started on some of the paperwork. There were already a couple of news vans in front of the office when I came through town. The Atlanta stations will probably be down here by now. Do you want to approve the statement before we release it?"

"Yeah," said Buck. "Tell Lydia I'll be a couple of hours late this morning, but..."

"Tell Lydia," Jolene interrupted firmly, "the chief of police is taking a sick day. If you need anything, you can reach him at home. I'll be screening his calls."

Sully glanced at Buck in brief amusement, then turned to

Jolene. "It's good meeting you, Miz Lawson," he said. "And welcome to town."

"Thank you," she replied, extending her hand. "And it's Smith. Jolene Smith."

———

The doctor released him two hours later to bed rest and painkillers, recheck in three days. A nurse wheeled him out the emergency room exit, where they waited under a burgundy canopy for Jolene to bring the car around. The morning was thick and fetid-smelling, the sky heavy with deep gray, low-hanging clouds.

"Well, look at that," Buck remarked. "It looks like it might rain."

"Sixty percent chance," agreed the nurse cheerfully. "Maybe it will cool things off."

"I doubt it," replied Buck, sounding just like a native. "It'll probably just make things hotter and wetter."

She laughed and took his arm to help him up as Jolene parked the car at the curb. "Take care, Chief Lawson," said the nurse as she turned the wheelchair back toward the door. "And welcome to Mercy."

Jolene walked him to the passenger side of her car, wrinkling her nose in distaste as she sniffed the air. "Do you smell that? It's like sulfur. I've been noticing it since I got here. What *is* that smell?"

Buck chuckled and draped an arm around her shoulders. "Honey," he said, "that's nothing but the sweet, sweet smell of home."

CHAPTER THIRTY-FOUR

The installation of the new police chief was every bit as elegant and impressive as the mayor had promised. The city auditorium was packed. A robed choir performed. There were inspirational readings and speeches from city and county officials. Representatives from each shift, all in dress blues, formed an arrow across the stage and held a salute as Buck put his hand on the Bible and repeated for posterity the oath he had sworn in Miss Corinne's office a week earlier. Eloise, dressed in blue silk with a matching chiffon hat, sat on the front row with Willis and Jolene, dabbing at her eyes with a lace handkerchief the entire time, just as she had at the wedding. Willis sat straight and proud. Jolene held his hand. Flashbulbs strobed. Buck, in his dress uniform with four stars on the collar, posed for the official photograph that would hang on his office wall next to Billy's.

Afterwards there was a reception with hot hors d'oeuvres catered by a nearby restaurant, and champagne and lemonade served in plastic stemware. Buck stood in a reception line with his family and shook hands with what felt very much like every single citizen in the city of Mercy and all its surrounding areas. His injured arm was out of the sling but he still hadn't gotten all the feeling back in his hand. As the line wore on, his right hand grew almost as numb as his left.

"Have you met my wife, Jolene Smith?" he said over and over and over again. "My mother-in-law, Eloise, and my stepson, Wilson."

At this point, Willis, dressed in the blue suit he had worn to their wedding, would thrust out his hand and offer formally, "I'm pleased to meet you, sir. You can call me Willis." Or "It's a pleasure to meet you ma'am. Please call me Willis." And Buck would share a grin with Jo that was so filled with pride and contentment it threatened to split his face.

There had been, over the past few days, press conferences and interviews, with the questions becoming more clamorous as the increasingly bizarre details of the case came to light. *Dateline* wanted to do a special. Buck said no. The charges against Carl Tucker were dismissed. Sully assured Buck that Carl would be back in jail on drug charges within the month. Buck took care of some long-overdue personnel issues. And the moving truck came. Buck told Jolene that he was thinking about going back to the hospital, just to get some peace and quiet. She did not think that was funny.

Two pastors, three commissioners, the county sheriff, coroner, and fire chief moved through the line. Buck gave each of them, in turn, his undivided attention. Officer Baker introduced his wife, a plump, cheerful woman who immediately invited Jolene and Eloise to lunch the next week, and then to his children. The second grader studied Willis carefully for a long moment and said, "You want to come swim in my pool?"

Willis regarded the other boy for an equally thoughtful moment, then agreed, "Okay."

While the women worked out the details, Buck turned to his officer. "You did good work on the McGilroy case. Stop by my office tomorrow morning. I want to talk to you about taking the detective's exam."

Baker couldn't hide his surprise. "Detective?"

"You've got the qualifications," Buck said. "And it happens that there's an opening in that department."

Baker's lips tightened with a smile and he gave a short nod. "Yes, sir. And," he added, "welcome to Mercy, Chief."

The surprise of the day was when Lydia, with her arm threaded through Frankie's, came up to congratulate him. "Have you met my wife?" Buck said, by rote, and Lydia smiled.

"Have you met mine?" she replied, squeezing Frankie's arm.

Frankie, in makeup and a dress, with her unruly curls pinned back from her face and her nails done bright pink, looked almost pretty. She certainly looked more confident than she had since Buck had known her, which might have had something to do with the fact that Craig Teller was no longer employed by the police department. Buck looked from one to the other of the women and, while he couldn't hide his surprise, he didn't try to hide a smile of approval. "I'm glad," he said. "I was afraid Lydia would be married to somebody I didn't like. Frankie, too."

He opened his hand to Jolene. "Jo, this is the famous Lydia Browning, and my top detective Frankie Moreno, her wife."

When they were gone, Jolene murmured to him, "Boy, talk about nepotism. The two people on your staff you absolutely can't live without. If one of them gets mad at you..."

"Yeah," said Buck, trying to sound sanguine. "I guess I'd better make sure that doesn't happen."

The last in line to offer her congratulations was, of course, Miss Corinne. Buck made the introductions, and Corinne took both of Jolene's hands, holding them warmly. "Buck, *darling*, she is gorgeous!" she exclaimed. She gave Jolene's hands another little squeeze and repeated, "You are gorgeous!"

Jolene did look particularly gorgeous today in a cream-colored pantsuit and pearl teardrop earrings that glistened against her dark skin. Her hair was arranged in a braided coronet that set off her classic features and her wide dark eyes. Buck slipped his arm around her waist and said, "Miss New Jersey, 2007."

Jolene's pleasant expression didn't change, but he knew he'd pay for that later.

Corinne gave a little squeal and pressed her hands to her breast. "Miss Peach State, 19… well, you just never mind how long ago that was. Darling, we have so much in common! Welcome to Mercy, Jolene. I think you're going to like it here. We're so proud of the diversity of our little town."

Buck replied before Jolene could, "It might look even more diverse if you'd take down that Confederate statue in the park and put it in a museum where it belongs."

"Oh, Buck," Jolene put in smoothly, "that sounds like an awful lot of trouble, when all they really have to do is change the plaque to be more historically accurate. After all, Colonel Seth Aikens, a West Point graduate, actually fought on the Union side during the Civil War, didn't he, Miss Corinne?"

A quick half-dozen emotions flitted across Corinne's face—surprise, embarrassment, anger, defensiveness, indignation, and, finally, a sugary smile. "Do you know, sweetheart, I've been saying for years they need to tear down that eyesore and put up a statue of Hobo in its place. And I think you might be just the person to head up that committee."

Buck began, "Jo isn't much of a…"

But Jolene spoke over him. "I'd love to," she told the mayor. "And my mother will serve on the committee with me. Won't you, Mama?"

She expertly guided the rather bemused mayor down the line to her mother and then met Buck's stunned look defiantly. "What?" she demanded. "You think you're the only one who can change?" She added, "And on that note, I need a drink. Bring you something?"

Buck gave an uncertain shake of his head. "I'll be there in a minute."

Jolene took Willis's hand and they moved off in the direction of the serving tables.

Buck waited until there was a break in the conversation with Eloise to touch Corinne's arm lightly. "Miss Eloise, will you let me pull the mayor away for a minute? Jo and Willis went to get something to drink."

Eloise squeezed Corinne's hand warmly and assured her, "I'll be in touch."

Corinne turned to Buck, smiling. "Well now, Buck Lawson, the man of the hour. Your family is charming. I can see they're really going to stir things up in this town."

He replied pleasantly, "That's the plan."

"And you!" she went on, tapping his forearm flirtatiously. "Your press conference was covered on all three networks, the story even got thirty-five seconds on *World News Tonight*… and you haven't even been here a week. You must be feeling pretty good about yourself." Her expression sobered. "You did a good job, Buck. You found Billy's killer, freed an innocent man, and stopped a serial killer—and you did it all without once casting Mercy in a negative light."

Buck replied, "There's going to be some negative publicity, that can't be helped in a case like this. But not every detail of a police report has to be released to the press, and I don't see any reason to focus on the ugliest aspects of the case."

A slight measure of anxiety touched her eyes. "I heard the FBI will be taking over?"

"We turned over the evidence we have to the FBI," Buck told her, "and that's enough to keep them busy for a few years trying sift back through the cold cases. But if you're worried about agents swarming all over Mercy asking uncomfortable questions, I don't see that happening."

Relief softened her features. "I knew Billy picked the right man for the job," she said, beaming. "I knew it the first minute I laid eyes on you."

"I'm glad you feel that way, Miss Corinne," Buck said. "Because this seems like as good a time as any to bring up a couple of things. First off, I'm ordering body cameras for all shifts. That's not exactly a line item in my budget, so I'll need your support in funding."

Her brows came together reluctantly. "Well, Buck, I don't know. The police department is supposed to be self-supporting…"

"Secondly," he went on, "I hope the city's liability insurance is up to date, because Monday morning you're probably going to have eight to ten wrongful termination lawsuits land on your desk. I just fired every officer on the force who's ever been involved in taking money from citizens for any reason, or in making traffic stops for the purpose of inflating fines or meeting quotas, or in seeking out or manufacturing high-ticket violations just to receive one of your incentive bonuses."

She stared at him, all humor leaving her face. "But… you can't do that!"

He smiled. "Sure I can. The best thing about being the boss is you get to make the rules, remember? And my rules are, if you want to work for me, you walk a straight line."

"But—that's almost a third of the police force! You're leaving the people of Mercy unprotected. Memorial Day is coming up! You can't—"

"With what we're paying, I don't think we'll have any trouble hiring good officers to fill those positions," he told her. "And it just so happens I have a connection at the POST training center who can send me the best and the brightest recruits."

"Well," she said stiffly, "I'll certainly have to talk this over with the city attorney."

"Feel free," he replied easily, "but I already did. Ken Jefferies felt a whole lot better about the situation when I pointed out that if any of those officers who feel they've been wrongfully terminated want to take it to court, I will be more than happy to file criminal charges against them. Also, Ken and I agreed that it's in the best interest of the city to keep some of the things that have been going on in Mercy just between us, especially since I have such a large public platform now. And it would be a hell of a shame if word got out that a lowlife like Craig Teller—not to mention Jim Torrance—were both able to ply their trades because of a policy instituted by the mayor's office that rewarded police officers for intimidating citizens." He held her gaze firmly, but pleasantly. "After all, we all just want what's best for the city, don't we?"

Slowly the hard corners of a smile began to curve her lips

upward again, amusement tinged with admiration. "Buck Lawson," she said softly, "I do believe I might have underestimated you."

His gaze wandered casually around the room until it found Willis, standing near his grandmother like a little gentleman with a glass of lemonade in one hand and a cupcake in the other, engaged in an earnest conversation with a councilman. *Good Lord*, Buck thought, amused, *I'm raising a little politician*. He looked back to Corinne.

"A wise man once told me you don't always have to outsmart them, or out-fight them, or out-maneuver them. Sometimes you just have to outlast them. And you need to know I have an awful lot of lasting power, Miss Corinne."

She considered that for a moment, then gave a rueful shake of her head. "Buck, darling. Your stock may be high now, but that won't last forever. Why are you making your job so hard? Just go with the flow, as they say, and you'll be fine. Nobody ever expected you to come sweeping in here like some kind of superhero and fix the whole damn town. It's unfixable, sweetheart, and we're fine with that."

"Is it?" He looked at her, his expression thoughtful. "Well, we'll just see about that." Then he smiled, patted her hand, and went to join his family.

Somewhere in the crowd, he could hear Billy laughing.

ABOUT THE AUTHOR

Donna Ball is the author of over 100 books under a variety of pseudonyms. Though she has been published in virtually every genre, she is best known for her work in women's fiction, mystery and suspense. Her novels have been translated into multiple languages and published around the world.

She lives in the heart of the Blue Ridge Divide in a restored Victorian barn which was the inspiration for the bestselling *A Year on Ladybug Farm*. She spends her spare time hiking, painting, and enjoying canine sports with her three dogs.

Made in United States
Orlando, FL
04 April 2022